My sincere thanks and profound gratitude to Walter C. Young, M.D., Medical Director of the National Center for the treatment of Dissociative Disorders in Aurora, Colorado; Trish Keller Knode, A.T.R., L.P.C., art therapist; and Kay Adams, M.A., journal therapist, for the Center. Their guidance, assistance and encouragement have been infinitely invaluable in allowing me to tell this story.

Kudos and heartfelt thanks to my editor Michael V. Korda; his associate, senior editor Chuck Adams; my agent, Eugene H. Winick; Ina Winick, M.S.; and my publicist, Lisl Cade. And of course my terrific family and friends.

Bless you, my dears, one and all.

FOR MY NEWEST GRANDSON,
JUSTIN LOUIS CLARK,
WITH LOVE AND JOY.

Part
One

1

TEN MINUTES BEFORE it happened, four-year-old Laurie Kenyon was sitting cross-legged on the floor of the den rearranging the furniture in her dollhouse. She was tired of playing alone and wanted to go in the pool. From the dining room she could hear the voices of Mommy and the ladies who used to go to school with her in New York. They were talking and laughing while they ate lunch.

Mommy had told her that because Sarah, her big sister, was at a birthday party for other twelve-year-olds, Beth, who sometimes minded her at night, would come over to swim with Laurie. But the minute Beth arrived she started making phone calls.

Laurie pushed back the long blond hair that felt warm on her face. She had gone upstairs a long time ago and changed into her new pink bathing suit. Maybe if she reminded Beth again . . .

Beth was curled up on the couch, the phone stuck between her shoulder and ear. Laurie tugged on her arm. "I'm all ready."

Beth looked mad. "In a minute, honey," she said. "I'm having a very important discussion." Laurie heard her sigh into the phone. "I *hate* baby-sitting."

3

Laurie went to the window. A long car was slowly passing the house. Behind it was an open car filled with flowers, then a lot more cars with their lights on. Whenever she saw cars like that Laurie always used to say that a parade was coming, but Mommy said no, that they were funerals on the way to the cemetery. Even so, they made Laurie *think* of a parade, and she loved to run down the driveway and wave to the people in the cars. Sometimes they waved back.

Beth clicked down the receiver. Laurie was just about to ask her if they could go out and watch the rest of the cars go by when Beth picked up the phone again.

Beth was *mean,* Laurie told herself. She tiptoed out to the foyer and peeked into the dining room. Mommy and her friends were still talking and laughing. Mommy was saying, "Can you *believe* we graduated from the Villa thirty-two years ago?"

The lady next to her said, "Well, Marie, at least *you* can lie about it. You've got a four-year-old daughter. I've got a four-year-old *granddaughter!*"

"We still look pretty darn good," somebody else said, and they all laughed again.

They didn't even bother to look at Laurie. They were mean too. The pretty music box Mommy's friend had brought her was on the table. Laurie picked it up. It was only a few steps to the screen door. She opened it noiselessly, hurried across the porch and ran down the driveway to the road. There were still cars passing the house. She waved.

She watched until they were out of sight, then sighed, hoping that the company would go home soon. She wound up the music box and heard the tinkling sound of a piano and voices singing, "'Eastside, westside . . .'"

"Little girl."

Laurie hadn't noticed the car pull over and stop. A woman was driving. The man sitting next to her got out, picked Laurie up, and before she knew what was happening she was squeezed between them in the front seat. Laurie was too surprised to say anything. The man was smiling at her, but it wasn't a nice smile. The woman's hair was hanging around her face, and she didn't wear lipstick. The man had a beard, and his arms had a lot of curly hair. Laurie was pressed against him so hard she could feel it.

The car began to move. Laurie clutched the music box. Now the voices were singing: "'All around the town . . . Boys and girls together . . .'"

"Where are we going?" she asked. She remembered that she wasn't supposed to go out to the road alone. Mommy would be mad at her. She could feel tears in her eyes.

The woman looked so angry. The man said, "All around the town, little girl. All around the town."

2

SARAH HURRIED ALONG the side of the road, carefully carrying a piece of birthday cake on a paper plate. Laurie loved chocolate filling, and Sarah wanted to make it up to her for not playing with her while Mommy had company.

She was a bony long-legged twelve-year-old, with wide gray eyes, carrot red hair that frizzed in dampness, milk-white skin and a splash of freckles across her nose. She looked like neither of her parents—her mother was petite, blond and blue eyed; her father's gray hair had originally been dark brown.

It worried Sarah that John and Marie Kenyon were so much older than the other kids' parents. She was always afraid they might die before she grew up. Her mother had once explained to her, "We'd been married fifteen years and I'd given up hope of ever having a baby, but when I was thirty-seven I knew you were on the way. Like a gift. Then eight years later when Laurie was born— oh, Sarah, it was a miracle!"

When she was in the second grade, Sarah remembered asking Sister Catherine which was better, a gift or a miracle?

"A miracle is the greatest gift a human being can receive," Sister Catherine had said. That afternoon, when Sarah suddenly began to cry in class, she fibbed and said it was because her stomach was sick.

Even though she knew Laurie was the favorite, Sarah still loved her parents fiercely. When she was ten she had made a bargain with God. If He wouldn't let Daddy or Mommy die before she was grown, she would clean up the kitchen every night, help to take care of Laurie and never chew gum again. She was keeping her side of the bargain, and so far God was listening to her.

An unconscious smile touching her lips, she turned the corner of Twin Oaks Road and stared. Two police cars were in her driveway, their lights flashing. A lot of neighbors were clustered outside, even the brand-new people from two houses down, whom they hadn't even really met. They all looked scared and sad, holding their kids tightly by the hand.

Sarah began to run. Maybe Mommy or Daddy was sick. Richie Johnson was standing on the lawn. He was in her class at Mount Carmel. Sarah asked Richie why everyone was there.

He looked sorry for her. Laurie was missing, he told her. Old Mrs. Whelan had seen a man take her into a car, but hadn't realized Laurie was being kidnapped . . .

3

1974–1976
Bethlehem, Pennsylvania

THEY WOULDN'T take her home.

They drove a long time and took her to a dirty house, way out in the woods somewhere. They slapped her if she cried. The man kept picking her up and hugging her. Then he would carry her upstairs. She tried to make him stop, but he laughed at her. They called her Lee. Their names were Bic and Opal. After a while she found ways to slip away from them, in her mind. Sometimes she just floated on the ceiling and watched what was happening to the little girl with the long blond hair. Sometimes she felt sorry for the little girl. Other times she made fun of her. Sometimes when they let her sleep alone she dreamt of other people,

Mommy and Daddy and Sarah. But then she'd start to cry again and they'd hit her, so she made herself forget Mommy and Daddy and Sarah. *That's good,* a voice in her head told her. *Forget all about them.*

4

AT FIRST the police were at the house every day, and Laurie's picture was on the front page of the New Jersey and New York papers. Beyond tears, Sarah watched her mother and father on "Good Morning America," pleading with whoever took Laurie to bring her back.

Dozens of people phoned saying they'd seen Laurie, but none of the leads was useful. The police had hoped there'd be a demand for ransom, but there was none.

The summer dragged on. Sarah watched as her mother's face became haunted and bleak, as her father reached constantly for the nitroglycerin pills in his pocket. Every morning they went to the 7 A.M. mass and prayed for Laurie to be sent home. Frequently at night Sarah awoke to hear her mother's sobbing, her father's exhausted attempts to comfort her. "It was a miracle that Laurie was born. We'll count on another miracle to bring her back to us," she heard him say.

School started again. Sarah had always been a good student. Now she pored over the books, finding that she could blot out her own relentless sorrow by escaping into study. A natural athlete, she began taking golf and tennis lessons. Still she missed her little sister, with aching pain. She wondered if God was punishing her for the times she'd resented all the attention paid to Laurie. She hated herself for going to the birthday party that day and pushed aside the thought that Laurie was strictly forbidden to go out front alone. She promised that if God would send Laurie back to them she would always, *always* take care of her.

5

THE SUMMER PASSED. The wind began to blow through the cracks in the walls. Laurie was always cold. One day Opal came back with long-sleeved shirts and overalls and a winter jacket. It wasn't pretty like the one Laurie used to wear. When it got warm again they gave her some other clothes, shorts and shirts and sandals. Another winter went by. Laurie watched the leaves on the big old tree in front of the house begin to bud and open, and then all the branches were filled with them.

Bic had an old typewriter in the bedroom. It

made a loud clatter that Laurie could hear when she was cleaning up the kitchen or watching television. The clatter was a good sound. It meant that Bic wouldn't bother with her.

After a while, he'd come out of the bedroom holding a bunch of papers in his hand and start reading them aloud to Laurie and Opal. He always shouted and he always ended with the same words, "Hallelujah. Amen!" After he was finished, he and Opal would sing together. Practicing, they called it. Songs about God and going home.

Home. It was a word that her voices told Laurie not to think about anymore.

Laurie never saw anyone else. Only Bic and Opal. And when they went out, they locked her in the basement. It happened a lot. It was scary down there. The window was almost at the ceiling and had boards over it. The basement was filled with shadows, and sometimes they seemed to move around. Each time, Laurie tried to go to sleep right away on the mattress they left on the floor.

Bic and Opal almost never had company. If someone did come to the house, Laurie was put down in the basement with her leg chained to the pipe, so she couldn't go up the stairs and knock on the door. "And don't you dare call us," Bic warned her. "You'd get in big trouble, and, anyhow, we couldn't hear you."

After they'd been out they usually brought money home. Sometimes not much. Sometimes a lot. Quarters and dollar bills, mostly.

They let her go out in the backyard with them. They showed her how to weed the vegetable garden and gather the eggs from the chicken coop. There was a newborn baby chick they told her she could keep as her pet. She played with it whenever she went outside. Sometimes when they locked her in the basement and went away they let her keep it with her.

Until the bad day when Bic killed it.

Early one morning they began to pack—just their clothes and the television set and Bic's typewriter. Bic and Opal were laughing and singing, "Ha-lay-loo-ya."

"A fifteen-thousand-watt station in Ohio!" Bic shouted, "Bible Belt, here we come!"

They drove for two hours. Then from the backseat where she was scrunched against the battered old suitcases, Laurie heard Opal say, "Let's go into a diner and get a decent meal. Nobody will pay any attention to her. Why should they?"

Bic said, "You're right." Then he looked quickly over his shoulder at Laurie. "Opal will order a sandwich and milk for you. Don't you talk to anybody, you hear?"

They went to a place with a long counter and tables and chairs. Laurie was so hungry that she could almost taste the bacon she could smell frying. But there was something else. She could remember being in a place like this with the other people. A sob that she couldn't force back rose in her throat. Bic gave her a push to follow Opal, and she began to cry. Cry so hard she couldn't get her breath. She could see the lady at the cash register staring at her. Bic grabbed her and hustled her out to the parking lot, Opal beside him.

Bic threw her in the backseat of the car, and he and Opal rushed to get in front. As Opal slammed her foot on the gas pedal, he reached for her. She tried to duck when the hairy hand swung forward and back across her face. But after the first blow she didn't feel any pain. She just felt sorry for the little girl who was crying so hard.

6

June 1976
Ridgewood, New Jersey

SARAH SAT with her mother and father watching the program about missing children. The last segment was about Laurie. Pictures of her taken just before she disappeared. A computerized image that showed how she would probably look today, two years after she'd been kidnapped.

When the program ended, Marie Kenyon ran from the room screaming, "I want my baby. I want my baby."

Tears running down her face, Sarah listened to her father's agonized attempt to comfort her mother. "Maybe this program will be the instrument of a miracle," he said. He did not sound as if he believed it.

It was Sarah who answered the phone an hour later. Bill Conners, the police chief of Ridgewood, had always treated Sarah as an adult. "Your folks pretty upset after the program, honey?" he asked.

"Yes."

"I don't know whether to get their hopes up, but a call has come in that may be promising. A cashier in a diner in Harrisburg, Pennsylvania, is positive she saw Laurie this afternoon."

"This afternoon!" Sarah felt her breath stop.

"She'd been worried because the little girl suddenly became hysterical. But it was no tantrum. She was practically choking herself trying to stop crying. The Harrisburg police have Laurie's updated picture."

"Who was with her?"

"A man and woman. Hippie types. Unfortunately the description is pretty vague. The cashier's attention was on the kid, so she hardly got a glimpse of the couple."

He left it to Sarah to decide whether it was wise to tell her parents, to raise her parents' hopes. She made another bargain with God. "Let this be their miracle. Let the Harrisburg police find Laurie. I'll take care of her forever."

She hurried upstairs to offer her mother and father the new reason to hope.

7

THE CAR STARTED to have trouble a little while after they left the diner. Every time they slowed down in traffic the engine sputtered and died. The third time it happened and cars had to pull out from behind them, Opal said, "Bic, when we break down for good and a cop comes along, you'd better be careful. He might start asking questions about her." She jerked her head toward Laurie.

Bic told her to look for a gas station and pull off the road. When they found one, he made Laurie lie down on the floor and piled garbage bags filled with old clothes over her before they drove in.

The car needed a lot of work; it wouldn't be ready till the next day. There was a motel next to the gas station. The attendant said it was cheap and pretty comfortable.

They drove over to the motel. Bic went inside the office and came back with the key. They drove around to the room and rushed Laurie inside. Then, after Bic drove the car back to the gas station, they watched television for the rest of the afternoon. Bic brought in hamburgers for dinner. Laurie fell asleep just when the program came on about missing children. She woke up to hear Bic cursing. *Keep your eyes shut,* a voice warned her. *He's going to take it out on you.*

"The cashier got a good look at her," Opal was saying. "Suppose she's watching this. We'll have to get rid of her."

The next afternoon, Bic went to get the car by himself. When he came back he sat Laurie on the bed and held her arms against her. "What's my name?" he asked her.

"Bic."

He jerked his head at Opal. "What's her name?"

"Opal."

"I want you to forget that. I want you to forget us. Don't you ever talk about us. Do you understand, Lee?"

14

Laurie did not understand. *Say yes,* a voice whispered impatiently. *Nod your head and say yes.*

"Yes," she said softly and felt her head nodding.

"Remember the time I cut the head off the chicken?" Bic asked.

She shut her eyes. The chicken had flopped around the yard, blood spilling out from its neck. Then it had fallen on her feet. She had tried to scream as the blood sprayed over her, but no sound came out. She never went near the chickens after that. Sometimes she dreamed that the headless chicken was running after her.

"Remember?" Bic asked, tightening his grip on her arms.

"Yes."

"We have to go away. We're going to leave you where people will find you. If you ever tell anyone my name or Opal's name or the name we called you or where we lived or anything that we did together, I'm going to come with the chicken knife and cut your head off. Do you understand that?"

The knife. Long and sharp and streaked with blood from the chicken.

"Promise you won't tell anybody," Bic demanded.

"Promise, promise," she mumbled desperately.

They got in the car. Once more they made her lie on the floor. It was so hot. The garbage bags stuck to her skin.

When it was dark they stopped in front of a big building. Bic took her out of the car. "This is a school," he told her. "Tomorrow morning a lot of people will come, and other kids you can play with. Stay here and wait for them."

She shrank from his moist kiss, his fierce hug.

"I'm crazy about you," he said, "but remember, if you say one word about us . . ." He lifted his arm, closed his fist as though he was holding a knife and made a slashing motion on her neck.

"I promise," she sobbed, "I promise."

Opal handed her a bag with cookies and a Coke. She watched them drive off. She knew that if she didn't stay right here they'd come back to hurt her. It was so dark. She could hear animals scurrying in the woods nearby.

Laurie shrank against the door of the building and wrapped her arms around her body. She'd been hot all day and now she was cold and she was so scared. Maybe the headless chicken was running around out there. She began to tremble.

Look at the 'fraidy cat. She slipped away to be part of the jeering voice that was laughing at the small figure huddled at the entrance to the school.

8

POLICE CHIEF CONNERS phoned again in the morning. The lead looked promising, he said. A child who answered Laurie's description had been found when the caretaker arrived to open a school in a rural area near Pittsburgh. They were rushing Laurie's fingerprints there.

An hour later he phoned back. The prints were a perfect match. Laurie was coming home.

9

*J*OHN AND MARIE KENYON flew to Pittsburgh. Laurie had been taken to a hospital to be checked out. The next day on the noon edition of the TV news, Sarah watched as her mother and father left the hospital, Laurie between them. Sarah crouched in front of the set and gripped it with her hands. Laurie was taller. The waterfall of blond hair was shaggy. She was very thin. But it was more than that. Laurie had always been so friendly. Now even though she kept her head down, her eyes darted around as if she were looking for something she was afraid to find.

The reporters were bombarding them with questions. John Kenyon's voice was strained and tired as he said, "The doctors tell us Laurie is in good health, even though she is a touch underweight. Of course she's confused and frightened."

"Has she talked about the kidnappers?"

"She hasn't talked about anything. Please, we're so grateful for your interest and concern, but it would be a great kindness to allow our family to reunite quietly." Her father's voice was almost pleading.

"Is there any sign that she was molested?"

Sarah saw the shock on her mother's face. "Absolutely not!" she said. Her tone was appalled. "We believe that people who wanted a child took Laurie. We only hope they don't put another family through this nightmare."

Sarah needed to release the frantic energy that was churning inside her. She made Laurie's bed with the Cinderella sheets that Laurie loved. She arranged Laurie's favorite toys around her room, the twin dolls in their strollers, the dollhouse, the bear, her Peter Rabbit books. She folded Laurie's security blanket on the pillow.

Sarah bicycled to the store to buy cheese and pasta and chopped meat. Laurie loved lasagna. While Sarah was making it, she was constantly interrupted by phone calls. She managed to convince everyone to put off visiting for at least a few days.

They were due home at six o'clock. By five-thirty the lasagna was in the oven, the salad in the refrigerator, the table set for four again. Sarah went upstairs to change. She studied herself in the mirror. Would Laurie remember her? In the past two years she'd grown from five-four to five-seven. Her hair was short. It used to be shoulder-length. She used to be straight up and down. Now that she was fourteen her breasts had begun to fill out. She wore contact lenses instead of glasses.

That last night, before Laurie had been kidnapped, Sarah remembered that she had worn jeans and a long T-shirt to dinner. She still had the T-shirt in her closet. She put it on with jeans.

Crews with television cameras were in the driveway when the car pulled up. Groups of neighbors and friends waited in the background. Everyone began to cheer when the car door opened and John and Marie Kenyon led Laurie out.

Sarah ran to her little sister and dropped on her knees. "Laurie," she said softly. She stretched out her hands and watched as Laurie's hands fled to cover her face. She's afraid I'll hit her, Sarah thought.

It was she who picked Laurie up and took her inside the house as her parents once again spoke to the media.

Laurie did not show any sign that she remembered the house. She did not speak to them. At dinner she ate silently, her eyes looking down at the plate. When she had finished she got up, brought her plate to the sink and began to clear the table.

Marie stood up. "Darling, you don't have to—"

"Leave her alone, Mom," Sarah whispered. She helped Laurie clear, talking to her about what a big girl she was and how Laurie always used to help her with the dishes. Remember?

Afterwards they went into the den and Sarah turned on the television. Laurie pulled away trembling when Marie and John asked her to sit between them. "She's frightened," Sarah warned. "Pretend she isn't here."

Her mother's eyes filled with tears, but she managed to look absorbed in the program. Laurie sat cross-legged on the floor, choosing a spot where she could see but not be seen.

At nine o'clock when Marie suggested a nice warm bath and going to bed, Laurie panicked. She pressed her knees against her chest and buried her face in her hands. Sarah and her father exchanged glances.

"Poor little tyke," he said. "You don't have to go to bed now." Sarah saw in his eyes the same denial

19

she had seen in her mother's. "It's just everything is so strange for you, isn't it?"

Marie was trying to hide the fact that she was weeping. "She's afraid of us," she murmured.

No, Sarah thought. She's afraid to go to bed. Why?

They left the television on. At quarter of ten, Laurie stretched out on the floor and fell asleep. It was Sarah who carried her up, changed her, tucked her into bed, slipped the security blanket between her arms and under her chin.

John and Marie tiptoed in and sat on either side of the small white bed, absorbing the miracle that had been granted them. They did not notice when Sarah slipped from the room.

Laurie slept long and late. In the morning Sarah looked in on her, drinking in the blessed sight of the long hair spilling on the pillow, the small figure nestling the security blanket against her face. She repeated the promise she had made to God. "I will always take care of her."

Her mother and father were already up. Both looked exhausted but radiant with joy. "We kept going in to see if she was really there," Marie said. "Sarah, we were just saying we couldn't have made it through these two years without you."

Sarah helped her mother prepare Laurie's favorite breakfast, pancakes and bacon. Laurie pattered into the room a few minutes later, the nightgown that used to be ankle length now stopping at her calves, her security blanket trailing behind her.

She climbed on Marie's lap. "Mommy," she said, her tone injured. "Yesterday I wanted to go in the pool and Beth kept talking on the phone."

Part
Two

10

September 12, 1991
Ridgewood, New Jersey

DURING THE MASS, Sarah kept glancing sideways at Laurie. The sight of the two caskets at the steps of the sanctuary had clearly mesmerized her. She was staring at them, tearless now, seemingly unaware of the music, the prayers, the eulogy. Sarah had to put a hand under Laurie's elbow to remind her to stand or kneel.

At the end of the mass, as Monsignor Fisher blessed the coffins, Laurie whispered, "Mommy, Daddy, I'm sorry. I won't go out front alone again."

"Laurie," Sarah whispered.

Laurie looked at her with unseeing eyes, then turned and with a puzzled expression studied the crowded church. "So many people." Her voice sounded timid and young.

The closing hymn was "Amazing Grace."

With the rest of the congregation, a couple near the back of the church began to sing, softly at first, but he was used to leading the music. As always he got carried away, his pure baritone becoming louder, soaring above the others, swelling over the thinner voice of the soloist. People turned distracted, admiring.

" 'I once was lost but now am found . . .' "

Through the pain and grief, Laurie felt icy terror.

23

The voice. Ringing through her head, through her being.

I am lost, she wailed silently. *I am lost.*

They were moving the caskets.

The wheels of the bier holding her mother's casket squealed.

She heard the measured steps of the pallbearers.

Then the clattering of the typewriter.

"'. . . was blind but now I see.'"

"No! No!" Laurie shrieked as she crumpled into merciful darkness.

Several dozen of Laurie's classmates from Clinton College had attended the mass, along with a sprinkling of faculty. Allan Grant, Professor of English, was there and with shocked eyes watched Laurie collapse.

Grant was one of the most popular teachers at Clinton. Just turned forty, he had thick, somewhat unruly brown hair, liberally streaked with gray. Large dark brown eyes that expressed humor and intelligence were the best feature in his somewhat long face. His lanky body and casual dress completed an appearance that many young women undergraduates found irresistible.

Grant was genuinely interested in his students. Laurie had been in one of his classes every year since she entered Clinton. He knew her personal history and had been curious to see if there might be any observable aftereffects of her abduction. The only time he'd picked up anything had been in his creative writing class. Laurie was incapable of writing a personal memoir. On the other hand, her critiques of books, authors and plays were insightful and thought-provoking.

Three days ago she had been in his class when the

word came for her to go to the office immediately. The class was ending and, sensing trouble, he had accompanied her. As they hurried across the campus, she'd told him that her mother and father were driving down to switch cars with her. She'd forgotten to have her convertible inspected and had returned to college in her mother's sedan. "They're probably just running late," she'd said, obviously trying to reassure herself. "My mother says I'm too much of a worrier about them. But she hasn't been that well and Dad is almost seventy-two."

Somberly the dean told them that there had been a multivehicle accident on Route 78.

Allan Grant drove Laurie to the hospital. Her sister, Sarah, was already there, her cloud of dark red hair framing a face dominated by large gray eyes that were filled with grief. Grant had met Sarah at a number of college functions and been impressed with the young assistant prosecutor's protective attitude toward Laurie.

One look at her sister's face was enough to make Laurie realize that her parents were dead. Over and over she kept moaning "my fault, my fault," seeming not to hear Sarah's tearful insistence that she must not blame herself.

Distressed, Grant watched as an usher carried Laurie from the nave of the church, Sarah beside him. The organist began to play the recessional hymn. The pallbearers, led by the monsignor, started to walk slowly down the aisle. In the row in front of him, Grant saw a man making his way to the end of the pew. "Please excuse me. I'm a doctor," he was saying, his voice low but authoritative.

Some instinct made Allan Grant slip into the

aisle and follow him to the small room off the vestibule where Laurie had been taken. She was lying on two chairs that had been pushed together. Sarah, her face chalk white, was bending over her.

"Let me . . ." The doctor touched Sarah's arm.

Laurie stirred and moaned.

The doctor raised her eyelids, felt her pulse. "She's coming around but she must be taken home. She's in no condition to go to the cemetery."

"I know."

Allan saw how desperately Sarah was trying to keep her own composure. "Sarah," he said. She turned, seemingly aware of him for the first time. "Sarah, let me go back to the house with Laurie. She'll be okay with me."

"Oh, would you?" For an instant gratitude replaced the strain and grief in her expression. "Some of the neighbors are there preparing food, but Laurie trusts you so much. I'd be so relieved."

"'I once was lost but now am found . . .'"

A hand was coming at her holding the knife, the knife dripping with blood, slashing through the air. Her shirt and overalls were soaked with blood. She could feel the sticky warmth on her face. Something was flopping at her feet. The knife was coming . . .

Laurie opened her eyes. She was in bed in her own room. It was dark. What happened?

She remembered. The church. The caskets. The singing.

"Sarah!" she shrieked, "Sarah! Where are you?"

11

THEY WERE STAYING at the Wyndham Hotel on West Fifty-eighth Street in Manhattan. "Classy," he'd told her. "A lot of show business people go there. Right kind of place to start making connections."

He was silent on the drive from the funeral mass into New York. They were having lunch with the Reverend Rutland Garrison, pastor of the Church of the Airways, and the television program's executive producer. Garrison was ready to retire and in the process of choosing a successor. Every week a guest preacher was invited to co-host the program.

She watched as he discarded three different outfits before settling on a midnight blue suit, white shirt and bluish gray tie. "They want a preacher. They're gonna get a preacher. How do I look?"

"Perfect," she assured him. He did too. His hair was now silver even though he was only forty-five. He watched his weight carefully and had taught himself to stand very straight so that he always seemed to stand above people, even taller men. He'd practiced widening his eyes when he thundered a sermon until that had become his usual expression.

He vetoed her first choice of a red-and-white

27

checked dress. "Not classy enough for this meeting. It's a little too Betty Crocker."

That was their private joke when they wanted to impress the congregations who came to hear him preach. But there was nothing joking about him now. She held up a black linen sheath with a matching jacket. "How's this?"

He nodded silently. "That will do." He frowned. "And remember . . ."

"I never call you Bic in front of anyone," she protested coaxingly. "Haven't for years." He had a feverish glitter in his eyes. Opal knew and feared that look. It had been three years since the last time he was brought in by local police for questioning because some little girl with blond hair had complained to her mother about him. He'd always managed to scorn the complainant into stammering apologies, but even so it had happened too often in too many different towns. When he got that look it meant he was losing control again.

Lee was the only child he'd ever kept. From the minute he spotted her with her mother in the shopping center, he'd been obsessed by her. He followed their car that first day and after that cruised past their house hoping to get a glimpse of the child. He and Opal had been doing a two-week stint, playing the guitar and singing at some crummy nightclub on Route 17 in New Jersey and staying in a motel twenty minutes from the Kenyon home. It was going to be their last time singing in a nightclub. Bic had started gospel singing at revivals and then preaching in upstate New York. The owner of a radio station in Bethlehem, Pennsylvania, heard him and asked him to start a religious program on his small station.

It had been bad luck that he'd insisted on driving

past the house one last time on their way back to Pennsylvania. Lee was outside alone. He'd scooped her up, brought her with them, and for two years Opal lived in a state of perpetual fear and jealousy that she didn't dare let him see.

It had been fifteen years since they dumped her in the schoolyard, but Bic had never gotten over her. He kept her picture hidden in his wallet, and sometimes Opal would find him staring at it, running his fingers over it. In these last years, as he became more and more successful, he worried that someday FBI agents would come up to him and tell him he was under arrest for kidnapping and child molestation. "Look at that girl in California who got her daddy put in prison because she started going to a psychiatrist and remembering things best forgotten," he would sometimes say.

They had just arrived in New York when Bic read the item in the *Times* about the Kenyons' fatal accident. Over Opal's beseeching protests, they'd gone to the funeral mass. "Opal," he had told her, "we look as different as day and night from those two guitar-playing hippies Lee remembers."

It was true that they looked totally different. They'd begun to change their appearance the morning after they got rid of Lee. Bic shaved his beard off and got a short haircut. She'd dyed her hair ash blond and fastened it in a neat bun. They'd both bought sensible clothes at JC Penney, the kind of stuff that made them blend in with everyone else, gave them the middle-American look. "Just in case anyone in that diner got a good look at us," he'd said. That was when he'd warned her never to refer to him as Bic in front of anyone and said that from now on, in public he'd call her by her real name, Carla. "Lee heard our names over and over again in those two years," he'd said. "From now on I'm the Reverend Bobby Hawkins to everyone we meet."

Even so she'd felt the fear in him when they hurried up the steps of the church. At the end of the mass as the organist began to play the first notes of "Amazing Grace," he'd whispered, "That's our song, Lee's and mine." His voice soared over all the others. They were in the seats at the end of the pew. When the usher carried Lee's limp body past them, Opal had to grab his hand to keep him from reaching out and touching her.

"I'll ask you again. Are you ready?" His voice was sarcastic. He was standing at the door of the suite.

"Yes." Opal reached for her purse, then walked over to him. She had to calm him down. The tension in him was something that shot through the room. She put her hands on the sides of his face. "Bic, honey. You gotta relax," she said soothingly. "You want to make a good impression, don't you?"

It was as though he hadn't heard a word she'd said. He murmured, "I still have the power to scare that little girl half to death, don't I?" Then he began sobbing, hard, dry, racking sobs. "God, how I love her."

12

DR. PETER CARPENTER was the Ridgewood psychiatrist Sarah called ten days after the funeral. Sarah had met him occasionally, liked him, and her inquiries justified her own impressions. Her boss, Ed Ryan, the Bergen County prosecutor, was Carpenter's most emphatic supporter. "He's a straight shooter. I'd trust any one of my family with him, and you know that for me that's saying a lot. Too many of those birds are yo-yos."

She asked for an immediate appointment. "My sister blames herself for our parents' accident," she told Carpenter. Sarah realized as she spoke that she was avoiding the word "death." It was still so unreal to her. Gripping the phone, she said, "There was a recurrent nightmare she's had over the years. It hasn't happened in ages, but now she's having it regularly again."

Dr. Carpenter vividly remembered Laurie's kidnapping. When she was abandoned by her abductors and returned home, he had discussed with colleagues the ramifications of her total memory loss. He was keenly interested in seeing the girl now, but he told Sarah, "I think it would be wise if I talk to you before I see Laurie. I have a free hour this afternoon."

As his wife often teased, Carpenter could have been the model for the kindly family doctor. Steel gray hair, pink complexion, rimless glasses, benign expression, trim body, looking his age, which was fifty-two.

His office was deliberately cozy: pale green walls, tieback draperies in tones of green and white, a mahogany desk with a cluster of small flowering plants, a roomy wine-colored leather armchair opposite his swivel chair, a matching couch facing away from the windows.

When Sarah was ushered in by his secretary, Carpenter studied the attractive young woman in the simple blue suit. Her lean, athletic body moved with ease. She wore no makeup, and a smattering of freckles was visible across her nose. Charcoal brown brows and lashes accentuated the sadness in her luminous gray eyes. Her hair was pulled severely back from her face and held by a narrow blue band. Behind the band a cloud of dark red waves floated, ending just below her ears.

Sarah found it easy to answer Dr. Carpenter's questions. "Yes. Laurie was different when she came back. Even then I was certain she must have been sexually abused. But my mother insisted on telling everyone that she was sure loving people who wanted a child had taken her. Mother needed to believe that. Fifteen years ago people didn't talk about that kind of abuse. But Laurie was so frightened to go to bed. She loved my father but would never sit on his lap again. She didn't want him to touch her. She was afraid of men in general."

"Surely she was examined when she was found?"

"Yes, at the hospital in Pennsylvania."

"Those records may still exist. I wish you'd

arrange to send for them. What about that recurring dream?"

"She had it again last night. She was absolutely terrified. She calls it the knife dream. Ever since she came back to us, she's been afraid of sharp knives."

"How much personality change did you observe?"

"At first a great deal. Laurie was an outgoing sociable child before she was kidnapped. A little spoiled, I suppose, but very sweet. She had a play group and loved to visit back and forth with her friends. After she came back she would never stay overnight in anyone's house again. She always seemed a little distant with her peers.

"She chose to go to Clinton College because it's only an hour-and-a-half drive away and she came home many weekends."

Carpenter asked, "What about boyfriends?"

"As you'll see, she's a very beautiful young woman. She certainly got asked out plenty and in high school did go to the usual dances and games. She never seemed interested in anyone until Gregg Bennett, and that ended abruptly."

"Why?"

"We don't know. Gregg doesn't know. They went together all last year. He attends Clinton College as well and would often come home weekends with her. We liked him tremendously, and Laurie seemed so happy with him. They're both good athletes, especially fine golfers. Then one day last spring it was over. No explanations. Just over. She won't talk about it, won't talk to Gregg. He came to see us. He has no idea what caused the break. He's in England this semester, and I don't know that he's even heard about my parents."

"I'd like to see Laurie tomorrow at eleven."

The next morning Sarah drove Laurie to the appointment and promised to return in exactly fifty minutes. "I'll bring in some stuff for dinner," she told her. "We've got to perk up that appetite of yours."

Laurie nodded and followed Carpenter into his private office. With something like panic in her face, she refused to recline on the couch, choosing to sit across the desk from him. She waited silently, her expression sad and withdrawn.

Obvious profound depression, Carpenter thought. "I'd like to help you, Laurie."

"Can you bring back my mother and father?"

"I wish I could. Laurie, your parents are dead because a bus malfunctioned."

"They're dead because I didn't have my car inspected."

"You forgot."

"I didn't forget. I decided to break the appointment at the gas station. I said I'd go to the free inspection center at the Motor Vehicle Agency. That one I forgot, but I deliberately broke the first appointment. It's my fault."

"Why did you break the first appointment?" He watched closely as Laurie Kenyon considered the question.

"There was a reason but I don't know what it was."

"How much does it cost to have the car inspected at the gas station?"

"Twenty dollars."

"And it's free at the Motor Vehicle Agency. Isn't that a good enough reason?"

She seemed to be immersed in her own thoughts. Carpenter wondered if she had heard him. Then she whispered, "No," and shook her head.

"Then why do you think you broke the first appointment?"

Now he was sure she had not heard him. She was in a different place. He tried another tack. "Laurie, Sarah tells me that you've been having bad dreams again, or rather the same bad dream you *used* to have has come back."

Inside her mind, Laurie heard a loud wail. She pulled her legs against her chest and buried her head. The wailing wasn't just inside her. It was coming from her chest and throat and mouth.

13

THE MEETING with Preacher Rutland Garrison and the television producers was sobering.

They had eaten lunch in the private dining room of Worldwide Cable, the company that syndicated Garrison's program to an international audience. Over coffee, he made himself very clear. "I began the 'Church of the Airways' when ten-inch black-and-white TVs were luxuries," he said. "Over the years this ministry has given comfort, hope and faith to millions of people. It has raised a great deal of money for worthwhile charities. I intend to see that the right person continues my work after me."

Bic and Opal had nodded, their faces set in expressions of deference, respect and piety. The following Sunday they were introduced on the "Church of the Airways." Bic spoke for forty minutes.

He told of his wasted youth, his vain desire to be a rock star, of the voice the good Lord had given him and how he had abused it with vile secular songs. He spoke of the miracle of his conversion. Yea, verily, he understood the road to Damascus. He had traveled it in the footsteps of Paul. The Lord didn't say, "Saul, Saul, why persecuteth thou Me?" No, the question hurt even more. At least Saul thought he was acting in the name of the Lord when he tried to blot out Christianity. As he, Bobby, stood in that crowded dirty nightclub, singing those filthy lyrics, a voice filled his heart and soul, a voice that was so powerful and yet so sad, so angry and yet so forgiving. The voice asked, "Bobby, Bobby, why do you blaspheme me?"

Here he began to cry.

At the end of the sermon, Preacher Rutland Garrison put a fatherly arm around him. Bobby beckoned to Carla to join him. She came onto the set, her eyes moist, her lips quivering. He introduced her to the Worldwide audience.

They led the closing hymn together. "'Bringing in the sheaves . . .'"

After the program the switchboard came alive with calls praising the Reverend Bobby Hawkins. He was invited to return in two weeks.

On the drive back to Georgia, Bic was silent for hours. Then he said, "Lee's at the college in Clinton, New Jersey. Maybe she'll go back. Maybe she won't. The Lord is warning me it's time to remind her of what will happen if she talks about us."

Bic was going to be chosen as Rutland Garrison's

successor. Opal could sense it. Garrison had been taken in the same as all the others. But if Lee started remembering . . . "What are you going to do about her, Bic?"

"I got ideas, Opal. Ideas that came to me full blown while I was praying."

14

ON HER SECOND VISIT to Dr. Carpenter, Laurie told him that she was returning to college the next Monday. "It's better for me, better for Sarah," she said calmly. "She's so worried about me that she hasn't gone back to work, and work will be the best thing for her. And I'll have to study like crazy to make up for losing nearly three weeks."

Carpenter was not sure what he was seeing. There was something different about Laurie Kenyon, a brisk matter-of-fact attitude that was at total variance with the crushed, heartbroken girl he had seen a week earlier.

That day she had worn a gold cashmere jacket, beautifully cut black slacks, a gold, black and white silk blouse. Her hair had been loose around her shoulders. Today she had on jeans and a baggy sweater. Her hair was pulled back and held by a clip. She seemed totally composed.

"Have you had any more nightmares, Laurie?"

She shrugged. "I'm positively embarrassed remembering the way I carried on last week. Look, a lot of people have bad dreams and they don't go mewing around about them. Right?"

"Wrong," he said quietly. "Laurie, since you feel so much stronger, why don't you stretch out on the couch and relax and let's talk?" Carefully he watched her reaction.

It was the same as last week. Absolute panic in her eyes. This time the panic was followed by a defiant expression that was almost a sneer. "There's no need to stretch out. I'm perfectly capable of talking sitting up. Not that there's much to talk about. Two things went wrong in my life. In both cases I'm to blame. I admit it."

"You blame yourself for being kidnapped when you were four?"

"Of course. I was forbidden to go out front alone. I mean really forbidden. My mother was so afraid that I'd forget and run into the road. There was a teenager who lived down the block, and he had a lead foot on the accelerator. The only time that I remember my mother really scolding me was when she caught me on the front lawn, alone, throwing a ball in the air. And you know I'm responsible for my parents' death."

It was not the time to explore that. "Laurie, I want to help you. Sarah told me that your parents believed that you were better off not to have psychological counseling after your abduction. That probably is part of the reason you're resisting talking to me now. Why don't you just close your eyes and rest and try to learn to feel comfortable with me? In other sessions we may be able to work together."

"You're so sure there will be other sessions?"

"I hope so. Will there be?"

"Only to please Sarah. I'll be coming home weekends, so they'll have to be on Saturdays."

"That can be arranged. You're coming home every weekend?"

"Yes."

"Is that because you want to be with Sarah?"

The question seemed to excite her. The matter-of-fact attitude disappeared. Laurie crossed her legs, lifted her chin, reached her hand back and opened the clip that held her hair in a ponytail.

Carpenter watched as the shining blond mass fell around her face. A secretive smile played on her lips. "His wife comes home weekends," she said. "There's no use hanging around the college then."

15

LAURIE OPENED the door of her car. "Starting to feel like fall," she said.

The first leaves were falling from the trees. Last night the heat had gone on automatically. "Yes, it does," Sarah said. "Now look, if it's too much for you . . ."

"It won't be. You put all the creeps in prison, and I'll make up all the classes I missed and keep my cum laude. I still may even have a shot at magna. You left me in the dust with your summa. See you

Friday night." She started to give Sarah a quick hug, then clung to her. "Sarah, don't you ever let me switch cars with you."

Sarah smoothed Laurie's hair. "Hey, I thought we'd agreed that Mom and Dad would get real upset about that kind of thinking. After you see Dr. Carpenter on Saturday, let's go for a round of golf."

Laurie attempted a smile. "Winner buys dinner."

"That's because you know you'll beat me."

Sarah waved vigorously until the car was no longer in sight, then turned back to the house. It was so quiet, so empty. The prevailing wisdom was to make no dramatic changes after a family death, but her instinct told her that she should start hunting immediately for another place, perhaps a condo, and put the house on the market. Maybe she'd phone Dr. Carpenter and ask him about that.

She was already dressed for work. She picked up her briefcase and shoulder bag, which were on the table in the foyer. The delicate eighteenth-century table, inlaid with marble, and the mirror above it were antiques that had belonged to her grandmother. Where would they and all the other lovely pieces, all the first-edition volumes of classics that lined John Kenyon's library fit in a two-bedroom condo? Sarah pushed the thought away.

Instinctively she glanced in the mirror and was shocked at what she saw. Her complexion was dead white. There were deep circles under her eyes. Her face had always been thin, but now her cheeks were hollowed out. Her lips were ashen. She remembered her mother saying that last morning, "Sarah, why not wear a little makeup? Shadow would bring out your eyes . . ."

She dropped her shoulder bag and briefcase back on the table and went upstairs. From the vanity in her bathroom she took her seldom-used cosmetic case. The image of her mother in her shell-pink dressing gown, so naturally pretty, so endearingly maternal, telling her to put on eyeshadow brought at last the scalding tears she had forced back for Laurie's sake.

It was so good to get to her airless office with its chipped-paint walls, stacks of files, ringing telephone. Her coworkers in the prosecutor's office had come to the funeral home en masse. Her closest friends had been at the funeral, had phoned and stopped at the house these past few weeks.

Today they all seemed to understand that she wanted to get back to a semblance of normality. "Good to have you back." A quick hug. Then the welcome "Sarah, let me know when you have a minute . . ."

Lunch was a cheese on rye and black coffee from the courthouse cafeteria. By three o'clock Sarah had the satisfying feeling that she'd made a dent in responding to the urgent messages from plaintiffs, witnesses and attorneys.

At four o'clock, unable to wait any longer, she called Laurie's room at college. The phone was picked up immediately. "Hello."

"Laurie, it's me. How's it going?"

"So-so. I went to three classes, then cut the last one. I just felt so tired."

"No wonder. You haven't had a decent night's sleep. What are you doing tonight?"

"Going to bed. Got to clear out my brain."

"Okay. I'm going to work late. Be home around eight. Why don't I give you a call?"

"I'd like that."

Sarah stayed at the office until seven-fifteen, stopped at a diner and bought a hamburger to go. At eight-thirty she phoned Laurie.

The ringing at the other end continued. Maybe she's showering, maybe she's had some kind of reaction. Sarah held the receiver as the staccato sound buzzed and buzzed in her ear. Finally an impatient voice answered. "Laurie Kenyon's line."

"Is Laurie there?"

"No, and please, if the phone isn't answered in five or six rings, give me a break. I'm right across the hall and I've got a test to prepare for."

"I'm sorry. It's just that Laurie was planning to go to bed early."

"Well, she changed her plans. She went out a few minutes ago."

"Did she seem to be all right? I'm her sister and I'm a bit concerned."

"Oh, I didn't realize. I'm so sorry about what happened to your mother and father. I think Laurie was okay. She was all dressed up, like for a date."

Sarah called again at ten, at eleven, at twelve, at one. The last time, a sleepy Laurie answered. "I'm fine, Sarah. I went to bed right after dinner and have been asleep since then."

"Laurie, I rang so long the girl across the hall came over and picked up your phone. She told me you went out."

"Sarah, she's wrong. I swear to God I was right here." Laurie sounded frightened. "Why would I lie?"

I don't know, Sarah thought.

"Well, as long as you're okay. Get back to sleep," she said and replaced the receiver slowly.

16

DR. CARPENTER could sense the difference in Laurie's posture as she leaned back in the roomy leather chair. He did not suggest that she lie on the couch. The last thing he wanted was to have her lose this tentative trust in him that he sensed she was developing. He asked her how the week at college had been.

"Okay, I guess. People were awfully nice to me. I have so much catching up to do that I'm burning the midnight oil." She hesitated then stopped.

Carpenter waited then said mildly, "What is it, Laurie?"

"Last night when I got home, Sarah asked me if I'd heard from Gregg Bennett."

"Gregg Bennett?"

"I used to go out with him. My mother and father and Sarah liked him a lot."

"Do you like him?"

"I did, until . . ."

Again he waited.

Her eyes widened. "He wouldn't let go of me."

"You mean he was forcing himself on you?"

"No. He kissed me. And that was all right. I liked it. But then he pressed my arms with his hands."

"And that frightened you."

"I knew what was going to happen."

"What was going to happen?"

She was looking off into the distance. "We don't want to talk about that."

For ten minutes she was silent, then said sadly, "I could tell that Sarah didn't believe I hadn't been out the other night. She was worried."

Sarah had called him about that. "Maybe you were out," Dr. Carpenter suggested. "It would be good for you to be with friends."

"No. I don't care about dating now. I'm too busy."

"Any dreams?"

"The knife dream."

Two weeks ago she had become hysterical when she was asked about it. Today her voice was almost indifferent. "I have to get used to it. I'm going to keep having it until the knife catches up with me. It will, you know."

"Laurie, in therapy we call acting out an emotionally disturbing memory *abreaction*. I'd like you to abreact for me now. Show me what you see in the dream. I think you dread going to sleep because you're afraid you'll have the dream. Nobody can do without sleep. You don't have to talk. Just show me what is happening in the dream."

Laurie got up slowly, then raised her hand. Her mouth twisted into a cunning thin-lipped smile. She started walking around the desk toward him, her steps deliberate. Her hand jerked up and down as she swung an imaginary blade. Just before she reached him she stopped. Her posture changed. She stood, riveted to the spot, staring. Her hand tried to wipe away something from her face and hair. She looked down and jumped back terrified.

She collapsed on the floor, her hands over her

face, then crouched against the wall, shivering and making hurting sounds like a wounded animal.

Ten minutes passed. Laurie quieted, dropped her hands and got up slowly.

"That's the knife dream," she said.

"Are you in the dream, Laurie?"

"Yes."

"Who are you, the one who has the knife or the one who is afraid?"

"Everybody. And in the end we all die together."

"Laurie, I'd like to talk to a psychiatrist I know who's had a great deal of experience with people who have suffered childhood trauma. Will you sign a release to let me discuss your case with him?"

"If you like. What difference can it make to me?"

17

AT SEVEN-THIRTY Monday morning, Dr. Justin Donnelly walked rapidly up Fifth Avenue from his Central Park South apartment to Lehman Hospital on Ninety-sixth Street. He constantly competed with himself to cover the two-mile distance a minute or two faster each day. But short of actually jogging, he could not better his twenty-minute record.

He was a big man who always looked as if he'd be at home in cowboy boots and a ten-gallon hat, not an inaccurate image. Donnelly had been raised on a sheep station in Australia. His curly black hair had a permanently tousled look. His black mustache was luxuriant, and when he smiled, it accentuated his strong white teeth. His intense blue eyes were framed by dark lashes and brows that women envied. Early in his psychiatric training he had decided to specialize in multiple personality disorders. A persuasive ground-breaker, Donnelly fought to establish a clinic for MPD in New South Wales. It quickly became a model facility. His papers, published in prominent medical journals, soon brought him international recognition. At thirty-five he was invited to set up a multiple personality disorder center at Lehman.

After two years in Manhattan, Justin considered himself a dyed-in-the-wool New Yorker. On his walks to and from the office he affectionately drank in the newly familiar sights: the horses and carriages arriving at the park, the glimpse of the zoo at Sixty-fifth Street, the doormen at the swank Fifth Avenue apartment buildings. Most of them greeted him by name. Now as he strode past, several remarked about the fine October weather.

It was going to be a busy day. Justin usually tried to keep the ten-to-eleven time slot free for staff consultations. This morning he'd made an exception. An urgent phone call Saturday from a New Jersey psychiatrist had piqued his interest. Dr. Peter Carpenter wanted to consult with him immediately about a patient who he suspected was an MPD and potentially suicidal. Justin had agreed to a ten o'clock meeting today.

He reached Ninety-sixth and Fifth in twenty-five

minutes and consoled himself that the heavy pedestrian traffic had slowed his progress. The main entrance to the hospital was on Fifth Avenue. The MPD clinic was entered by a discreet private door on Ninety-sixth. Justin was almost invariably the first one there. His office was a small suite at the end of the corridor. The outer room, painted a soft ivory and simply furnished with his desk and swivel chair, two armchairs for visitors, bookcases and a row of files, was enlivened by colorful prints of sailboats in Sydney Harbor. The inner room was where he treated patients. It was equipped with a sophisticated video camera and tape recorder.

His first patient was a forty-year-old woman from Ohio who had been in treatment for six years and was diagnosed as schizophrenic. It was only when an alert psychologist began to believe that the voices the woman kept hearing were those of alter personalities that she had come to him. She was making good progress.

Dr. Carpenter arrived promptly at ten. Courteously grateful to Justin for seeing him on such short notice, he immediately began to talk about Laurie.

Donnelly listened, took notes, interjected questions. Carpenter concluded, "I'm not an expert on MPD, but if ever there were signs of it, I've been seeing them. There's been a marked change in her voice and manner during her last two visits. She definitely is unaware of at least one specific incident when she left her room and was out for hours. I'm sure she's not lying when she claims to have been asleep at that time. She has a recurring nightmare of a knife slashing at her. Yet during

47

abreaction at one point she was acting out holding the knife and doing the slashing. Then she switched to trying to avoid it. I've made a copy of her file."

Donnelly read down the pages swiftly, stopping to circle or check when something jumped out at him. The case fascinated him. A beloved child kidnapped at the age of four and abandoned by the kidnappers at age six, with total memory loss of the intervening two years! A recurring nightmare! A sister's perception that since her reunion with the family, Laurie had responded to stress with child-like anxiety. Tragic parental death for which Laurie blamed herself.

When he laid the file down, he said, "The records from the hospital in Pittsburgh where she was examined indicated probable sexual abuse over a long period of time and counseling was strongly recommended. I gather there was none."

"There was total denial on the part of the parents," Dr. Carpenter answered, "and therefore no therapy whatsoever."

"Typical of the pretend-it-didn't-happen thinking of fifteen years ago, plus the Kenyons were significantly older parents," Donnelly observed. "It would be a good idea if we could persuade Laurie to come here for evaluation, and I'd say the sooner the better."

"I have a feeling that will be very difficult. Sarah had to beg her to come to me."

"If she resists, I'd like to see the sister. She should watch for signs of aberrant behavior and of course she must not take any talk of suicide lightly."

The two psychiatrists walked to the door together. In the reception room a dark-haired teenaged girl was staring moodily out the window. Her arms were covered with bandages.

In a low voice, Donnelly said, "You have to take it seriously. The patients who have experienced trauma in their childhood are at high risk for self-harm."

18

THAT EVENING when Sarah got home from work the mail was neatly stacked on the foyer table. After the funeral, Sophie, their longtime daily housekeeper, had proposed cutting down to two days a week. "You don't need me more than that anymore, Sarah, and I'm not getting any younger."

Monday was one of the days she came in. That was why the mail was sorted, the house smelled faintly of furniture polish, the draperies were drawn and the soft light of lamps and sconces gave a welcoming glow to the downstairs rooms.

This was the hardest part of the day for Sarah, coming into an empty house. Before the accident, if she was expected home, her mother and father would be waiting to have their predinner cocktail with her.

Sarah bit her lip and pushed aside the memory. The letter on top of the pile was from England. She ripped open the envelope, certain it was from Gregg Bennett. She read the letter quickly then again, slowly. Gregg had just learned about the accident. His expression of sympathy was profoundly moving. He wrote about his affection for John and Marie Kenyon, about the wonderful visits to their home, how rough it must be for her and Laurie now.

The final paragraph was disturbing: "Sarah, I tried to phone Laurie, and she sounded so despondent when she answered. Then she screamed something like, 'I won't, I won't,' and hung up on me. I'm terribly worried about her. She's so fragile. I know you're taking good care of her, but be very careful. I'll be back at Clinton in January and would like to see you. My love to you, and kiss that girl for me, please. Gregg."

Her hands trembling, Sarah carried the mail into the library. Tomorrow she'd call Dr. Carpenter and read this to him. She knew he had given Laurie antidepressants, but was she taking them? The answering machine was blinking. Dr. Carpenter had called and left his home number.

When she reached him, she told him about Gregg's letter then listened, shocked and frightened, to his careful explanation of why he had seen Dr. Justin Donnelly in New York and why it was imperative that Sarah see him as soon as possible. He gave her the number of Donnelly's service. Her voice low and strained, she had to repeat her phone number twice to the operator.

Sophie had roasted a chicken, prepared a salad. Sarah's throat closed as she picked at the food. She had just made coffee when Dr. Donnelly returned her call. His day was full, but he could see her at six tomorrow evening. She hung up, reread Gregg's letter and, with a frantic sense of urgency, dialed Laurie. There was no answer. She tried every half hour until finally at eleven o'clock she heard the receiver being picked up. Laurie's "Hello" was cheerful enough. They chatted for a few minutes, then Laurie said, "How's this for a pain? After dinner I propped myself up on the bed to research this damn paper and fell asleep. Now I've got to burn the midnight oil."

19

AT ELEVEN O'CLOCK on Monday evening, Professor Allan Grant stretched out on his bed and switched on the night table lamp. The long bedroom window was partially open, but the room was not cool enough for his taste. Karen, his wife, used to teasingly tell him that in a previous incarnation he must have been a polar bear. Karen hated a cold bedroom. Not that she was around much to joke about it anymore, he thought as he threw back the blanket and swung his feet onto the carpet.

For the last three years, Karen had been working at a travel agency in the Madison Arms Hotel in Manhattan. At first she'd stayed overnight in New York only occasionally. Then more and more often she'd phone in late afternoon. "Sweetie, we're so busy, and I've got stacks of paperwork. Can you fend for yourself?"

He'd fended for himself for thirty-four years

before he'd met her six years ago on a tour of Italy. Getting back in the habit wasn't that hard. Karen now had an apartment in the hotel and usually stayed there most of the week. She did come home weekends.

Grant padded across the room and cranked the window wide open. The curtains billowed in, followed by an eminently satisfying blast of chilly air. He hurried toward the bed but hesitated and turned in the direction of the hallway. It was no use. He was not sleepy. Another bizarre letter had come in his office mail today. Who the hell was Leona? He had no students by that name, had never had.

The house was a comfortable-size ranch model. Allan had bought it before he and Karen were married. For a time she'd seemed interested in decorating it and replacing shabby or dull furniture, but now it was beginning to look as it had in his bachelor days.

Scratching his head and yanking up pajama bottoms, which always seemed to settle around his hips, Grant walked down the hallway past the guest bedrooms, across the center hall, past the kitchen, living and dining rooms, and into the den. He turned on the overhead lights. After rummaging successfully for the key to the top drawer of his desk, he opened it, got out the letters and began to reread them.

The first one had come two weeks ago: "Darling Allan, I'm reliving now the glorious hours we spent together last night. It's hard to believe that we haven't always been madly in love, but maybe it's because no other time counts for us, does it? Do you know how hard it is for me not to shout from the rooftops that I'm crazy about you? I know you feel the same way. We have to hide what we are to each other. I understand that. Just keep on loving me and wanting me the way you do now. Leona."

All the letters were in the same vein. One arrived every other day, each talking about wild love scenes with him in his office or this house.

He'd had enough informal workshops here that any number of students knew the layout. Some of the letters referred to the shabby brown leather chair in the den. But never once had he had a student alone in the house. He wasn't that much of a fool.

Grant studied the letters carefully. They were obviously typed on an old machine. The *o* and the *w* were broken. He'd gone through his student files, but no one used a machine like that. He also did not recognize the scrawled signature.

Once again he agonized about whether to show them to Karen and to the administration. It would be hard to predict how Karen would react. He didn't want to upset her. Neither did he want her to decide to give up her job and stay home. Maybe he would have wanted that a few years ago, but not now. He had a big decision to make.

The administration. He'd bring the Dean of Student Affairs in on this the minute he found out who was sending them. The trouble was he simply didn't have a clue, and if anyone believed they contained an iota of truth, he could kiss his future at this college goodbye.

He read the letters once more, searching for a writing style, phrases or expressions that might bring one of his students to mind. Nothing. Finally he replaced them in the drawer, locked it, stretched and realized that he was dead tired. And chilly. It was one thing to sleep in a cold room under warm blankets, another to be in the path of a direct draft when you're sitting there in cotton pajamas. Where the heck was the draft coming from?

Karen always closed the draperies when she was home but he never bothered. He realized that the sliding glass door from the den to the patio was open a few inches. The door was heavy and slow to move on the track. He probably hadn't closed it completely the last time he went out. The lock was a pain in the neck too. Half the time it didn't catch. He walked over, shoved the door closed, snapped the lock and without bothering to see if it had caught, turned out the light and went back to bed.

He hunched under the covers in the now satisfyingly cold bedroom, closed his eyes and promptly fell asleep. In his wildest dreams he could not have imagined that half an hour ago a slender figure with long blond hair had been curled up in his brown leather chair and had only slipped away at the sound of his approaching footsteps.

20

*F*IFTY-EIGHT-YEAR-OLD private investigator Daniel O'Toole was known in New Jersey as Danny the Spouse Hunter. Under his hard-drinking, hail-fellow-well-met exterior, he was a remarkably thorough worker and quietly discreet in compiling information.

Danny was used to people using false names when they hired him to check on possibly erring husbands or wives. It didn't bother him. As long as he received his retainer and follow-up bills were paid promptly, his clients could call themselves anything they pleased.

Even so it was a bit surprising when a woman identifying herself as Jane Graves phoned his Hackensack office Tuesday morning, hinting at a possible insurance claim and engaging him to investigate the activities of the Kenyon sisters. Was the older sister working at her job? Was the younger sister back in college, completing her studies? Did she come home often? How were they reacting to the death of their parents? Were there any signs of breakdown? Very important, was either young woman seeing a psychiatrist?

Danny sensed something fishy. He had met Sarah Kenyon a few times in court. The accident that killed the parents had been caused by a speeding chartered bus with failed brakes. It was entirely possible that there was a suit pending against the bus company, but insurance companies usually had their own investigators. Still a job was a job, and because of the recession the divorce business was lousy. Breaking up was really hard to do when money was tight.

Taking a gamble, Danny doubled his usual retainer and was told the check would be in the mail immediately. He was instructed to send his reports and further bills to a private post office box in New York.

Smiling broadly, Danny replaced the receiver.

21

SARAH DROVE into New York after work on Tuesday evening. She was on time for the six o'clock appointment with Dr. Justin Donnelly, but when she entered his reception area he was hurrying out of his office.

With a quick apology he explained that he had an emergency and asked her to wait. She had an impression of height and breadth, dark hair and keen blue eyes—then he was gone.

The receptionist had obviously gone home. The phones were quiet. After ten minutes of scanning a news magazine and registering nothing, Sarah put it down and sat quietly absorbed in her own thoughts.

It was after seven o'clock when Dr. Donnelly returned. "I'm very sorry," he said simply as he brought her into his office.

Sarah smiled faintly, trying to ignore her hunger pangs and the unmistakable beginning of a headache. It had been a long time since noon when she'd gulped a ham on rye and coffee.

The doctor indicated the chair across from his desk. She sat there, aware that he was studying her, and got to the point immediately.

"Dr. Donnelly, I had my secretary go to the library and copy material on multiple personality disorder. I'd only known about it vaguely, but what I read today frightens me."

He waited.

"If what I understand is accurate, a primary cause is childhood trauma, particularly sexual abuse over a prolonged period. Isn't that right?"

"Yes."

"Laurie certainly had the trauma of being kidnapped and held captive away from home for two years when she was a small child. The doctors who examined her when she was found believe she was abused."

"Is it okay if I call you Sarah?" he asked.

"Of course."

"All right then, Sarah. If Laurie has become a multiple personality, it probably started back at the time of her abduction. Assuming she was abused, she must have been so frightened, so terrified, that one small human being couldn't absorb everything that was happening. At that point, there was a shattering. Psychologically Laurie, the child as you knew her, withdrew from the pain and fear and alter personalities came to help her. The memory of those years is locked away in them. It would seem that the other personalities have not been apparent until now. From what I understand, after Laurie came home at age six she gradually returned to pretty much her old self except for a recurring nightmare. Now, in the death of your parents, she's experienced another terrible trauma, and Dr. Carpenter has seen distinct personality changes in her during her recent sessions with him. The reason he came to me so quickly is that he's afraid she might be suicidal."

"He didn't tell me that." Sarah felt her mouth go

dry. "Laurie's been depressed, of course, but . . . Oh God, surely you don't think that's possible?" She bit her lip to keep it from quivering.

"Sarah, can you persuade Laurie to see me?"

She shook her head. "It's a job to make her see Dr. Carpenter. My parents were wonderful human beings but they had no use for psychiatry. Mother used to quote one of her college teachers. According to him there are three types of people: the ones who go for therapy when they're under stress; the ones who talk out their troubles with a friend or a cabdriver or bartender; the ones who hug their problems to themselves. The teacher claimed that the rate of recovery is exactly the same in all three types. Laurie grew up listening to that."

Justin Donnelly smiled. "I'm not sure that opinion isn't shared by quite a lot of people."

"I know Laurie needs professional help," Sarah said. "The problem is she doesn't want to open up to Dr. Carpenter. It's as though she's afraid of what he might find out about her."

"Then at least for now it's important to work around her. I've reread her file and made some notes."

At eight o'clock, observing Sarah's drawn, tired face, Dr. Donnelly said, "I think we'd better stop here. Sarah, listen for any reference to suicide, no matter how offhand it might seem, and report it to Dr. Carpenter and me. I'm going to be perfectly honest. I'd like to stay involved in Laurie's case. My work is research into multiple personality disorder and it's not often we catch a patient at the beginning of the emergence of alter personalities. I'll be discussing Laurie with Dr. Carpenter after her next several sessions with him. Unless there's a radical change, I have a hunch that we'll get more information from you than from Laurie. Be very observant."

Sarah hesitated then asked, "Doctor, isn't it a fact that until Laurie unlocks those lost years, she'll never really be well?"

"Think of it this way, Sarah. My mother broke her nail down to the quick once and an infection developed. A few days later the whole finger was swollen and throbbing. She kept doctoring it herself because she was afraid to have it lanced. When she finally went to the emergency room she had a red streak up her arm and was on the verge of blood poisoning. You see, she had ignored the warning signs because she didn't want the immediate pain of treatment."

"And Laurie is exhibiting warning signs of psychological infection?"

"Yes."

They walked together through the long corridor to the front door. The security guard let them out. There was no wind but the October evening had an unmistakable bite in the air. Sarah started to say good night.

"Is your car nearby?" Donnelly asked.

"Miracle of miracles, I found a parking spot right down the block."

He walked her to it. "Keep in touch."

What a nice guy, Sarah thought as she drove away. She tried to analyze her own feelings. If anything she was more worried now about Laurie than she had been before she saw Dr. Donnelly, but at least now she had a sense of solid help available to her.

She drove across Ninety-sixth Street past Madison and Park avenues, heading for the FDR Drive. At Lexington Avenue she impulsively turned right and headed downtown. She was famished, and Nicola's was only a dozen blocks away.

Ten minutes later she was being ushered to a small table. "Gee, it's great to see you again, Sarah," Lou, Nicola's longtime waiter, told her.

The restaurant was always cheery, and the delectable sight of steaming pasta being carried from the kitchen lifted Sarah's spirits. "I know what I want, Lou."

"Asparagus vinaigrette, linguine with white clam sauce, Pellegrino, a glass of wine," he rattled off.

"You've got it."

She reached into the bread basket for a warm crusty roll. Ten minutes later, just after the asparagus was served, the small table to her left was taken. She heard a familiar voice say, "Perfect, Lou. Thanks. I'm starving."

Sarah glanced up quickly and found herself looking into the surprised then obviously pleased face of Dr. Justin Donnelly.

22

SEVENTY-EIGHT-YEAR-OLD Rutland Garrison had known from the time he was a boy that he was called to the ministry. In 1947 he had been inspired to recognize the potential reach of television and persuaded the Dumont station in

New York to allocate time on Sunday mornings for a "Church of the Airways" religious hour. He had been preaching the Lord's word ever since.

Now his heart was quite simply wearing out and his doctor had warned him to retire immediately. "You've done enough in your lifetime for a dozen men, Reverend Garrison," he'd said. "You've built a Bible college, a hospital, nursing homes, retirement communities. Now be good to yourself."

Garrison knew more than anyone how vast sums could be diverted from worthy causes to greedy pockets. He did not intend that his ministry fall into the hands of anyone of that ilk.

He also knew that by its very nature a television ministry needed a man in the pulpit who could not only inspire and lead his flock but also preach a rousing good sermon.

"We must choose a man with showmanship but not a showman," Garrison cautioned the members of the Church of the Airways Council. Nevertheless in late October, after Reverend Bobby Hawkins's third appearance as guest preacher, the council voted to invite him to accept the pulpit.

Garrison had the power of veto over council decisions. "I am not sure of that man," he told the members angrily. "There's something about him that troubles me. There's no need to rush into a commitment."

"He has a messianic quality," one of them protested.

"The Messiah Himself was the one who warned us to beware of false prophets." Rutland Garrison saw from the tolerant but somewhat irritated expressions on the faces of the men around him that they all believed his objections were based solely on his unwillingness to retire. He got up. "Do what you want," he said wearily. "I'm going home."

That night Reverend Rutland Garrison died in his sleep.

23

BIC HAD BEEN edgy since the last time he'd preached in New York. "That old man has it in for me, Opal," he told her. "Jealous because of all the calls and letters they're getting about me. I called one of those council members to see why I haven't heard from them again and that's the reason."

"Maybe it's better if we stay here in Georgia, Bic," Opal suggested. She turned away from his scornful glance. She was at the dining room table, surrounded by stacks of envelopes.

"How were the donations this week?"

"Very good." Every Thursday on his local program and when he spoke at meetings, Bic made appeals for different overseas charities. Opal and he were the only ones allowed to touch the donations.

"They're not good compared to what the 'Church of the Airways' takes in whenever I speak."

On October 28 a call came from New York. When Bic hung up the phone he stared at Opal, his face and eyes luminescent. "Garrison died last night. I'm invited to become the pastor of the Church of the Airways. They want us to move permanently to New York as soon as possible. They want us to stay at the Wyndham until we select a residence."

Opal started to run to him, then stopped. The look on his face warned her to leave him alone. He went into his study and closed the door. A few minutes later she heard the faint sounds of music and knew that once again he had taken out Lee's music box. She tiptoed over to the door and listened as high-pitched voices sang, "All around the town . . . Boys and girls together . . ."

24

*I*T WAS so hard to keep Sarah from realizing how afraid she was. Laurie stopped telling Sarah and Dr. Carpenter when she had the knife dream. There was no use talking about it. Nobody, not even Sarah, could understand that the knife was getting closer and closer.

Dr. Carpenter wanted to help her, but she had to be so careful. Sometimes the hour with him went by so swiftly, and Laurie knew she had told him things she didn't remember talking about.

She was always so tired. Even though almost every night she stayed in her room and studied, she was always struggling to keep up with assignments. Sometimes she'd find them finished on her desk and not remember having done them.

She was getting so many loud thoughts that pounded in her head like people shouting in an echo chamber. One of the voices told her she was a wimp and stupid and caused trouble for everyone and to shut her mouth around Dr. Carpenter. Other times a little kid kept crying inside Laurie's mind. Sometimes the child cried very softly, sometimes she sobbed and wailed. Another voice, lower and sultry, talked like a porno queen.

Weekends were so hard. The house was so big, so quiet. She never wanted to be alone in it. She was glad Sarah had listed it with a real estate agency.

The only time Laurie felt like herself was when she and Sarah played golf at the club and had brunch or dinner with friends. Those days made her think of playing golf with Gregg. She missed him in an aching, hurting way but was so afraid of him now, the fear blotted out all the love. She dreaded the thought that he'd be coming back to Clinton in January.

25

JUSTIN DONNELLY had already gathered from his meeting with Dr. Carpenter that Sarah Kenyon was a remarkably strong young woman, but he had not been prepared for the impact she had on him when he met her. That first evening in his office she'd sat across the desk from him, lovely and poised, only the pain in her eyes hinting at the grief and anxiety she was experiencing. Her quietly expensive dark blue tweed suit had made him remember that wearing subdued colors was once considered an appropriate gesture for someone in mourning.

He'd been impressed that her immediate response to the possibility of her sister suffering from multiple personality disorder had been to gather information about it even before she saw him. He'd admired her intelligent understanding of Laurie's psychological vulnerability.

When he'd left Sarah at her car, it had been on the tip of Justin's tongue to suggest dinner. Then he'd walked into Nicola's and found her there. She'd looked pleased to see him, and it felt easy and natural to suggest that he join her and free up the last small table for the couple who came in just behind him.

It was Sarah who had set the tone of the conversation. Smiling, she passed him the basket of rolls. "I imagine you had the same kind of lunch on the run I did," she'd told him. "I'm starting to work on a murder case and I've been talking to witnesses all day."

She'd talked about her job as an assistant prosecutor, then skillfully turned the conversation to him. She knew he was Australian. Over osso buco Justin told her about his family and growing up on a sheep station. "My paternal great-grandfather came over from Britain in chains. Of course for generations that wasn't mentioned. Now it's a matter of pride to have an ancestor who was a guest of the Crown in the penal colony. My maternal grandmother was born in England, and the family moved to Australia when she was three months old. All her life Granny kept sighing how she missed England. She was there twice in eighty years. That's the other kind of Aussie mind-set."

It was only as they sipped cappuccino that the talk turned to his decision to specialize in the treatment of multiple personality disorder patients.

After that evening, Justin spoke to Dr. Carpenter and Sarah at least once a week. Dr. Carpenter reported that Laurie was increasingly uncooperative. "She's dissembling," he told Justin. "On the surface she agrees that she should not feel responsible for her parents' death, but I don't believe her. She talks about them as though it's a safe subject. Tender memories only. When she becomes emotional she talks and cries like a small child. She continues to refuse to take the MMPI or Rorschach tests."

Sarah reported that she saw no indication of suicidal depression. "Laurie hates going to Dr. Carpenter on Saturdays," she told him. "Says it's a waste of money and it's perfectly normal to be very sad when your parents die. She does brighten up when we go to the club. A couple of her midterm marks were pretty bad, so she told me to call her by eight o'clock if I want to talk to her in the evening. After that she wants to be able to study without interruption. I think she doesn't want me checking up on her."

Dr. Justin Donnelly did not tell Sarah that both he and Dr. Carpenter sensed that in Laurie's behavior they were witnessing a calm before the storm.

Instead he continued to urge her to keep a careful watch on Laurie. Whenever he hung up he realized he was starting to look forward to Sarah's calls in a highly unprofessional way.

26

IN THE OFFICE, the murder case Sarah was prosecuting was a particularly vicious one in which a twenty-seven-year-old woman, Maureen Mays, had been strangled by a nineteen-year-old youth who forced his way into her car in the parking lot of the railroad station.

It was a welcome change to plunge into final preparation as the trial date drew near. With intense concentration, she pored over the statements of the witnesses who had seen the defendant lurking in the station. If only they had done something about it, Sarah thought. They all had the feeling that he was up to no good. She knew that the physical evidence of the victim's desperate attempt to save herself from her attacker would make a strong impression on the jury.

The trial began December second, no longer open and shut, as a hearty, likable sixty-year-old defense attorney, Conner Marcus, attempted to tear apart Sarah's case. Under his skillful questioning, witnesses admitted that it had been dark in the parking area, that they did not know if the defendant had opened the door to the car or if Mays had opened it to allow him in.

But when it was Sarah's turn on redirect examination, all of the witnesses firmly declared that when James Parker came on to Maureen Mays in the train station, she had clearly rebuffed him.

The combination of the viciousness of the crime and the showmanship of Marcus caused the media to descend in droves. Spectators' benches filled. Courtroom junkies placed bets on the outcome.

Sarah was in the rhythm that in the past five years had become second nature to her. She ate, drank and slept the matter of State v. James Parker. Laurie began going back to college on Saturdays after she saw Dr. Carpenter. "You're busy and it's good for me to get involved too," she told Sarah.

"How's it going with Dr. Carpenter?"

"I'm starting to blame the bus driver for the accident."

"That's good news." On her next weekly call to Dr. Donnelly, Sarah said, "I only wish I could believe her."

Thanksgiving was spent with cousins in Connecticut. It wasn't as bad as Sarah had feared. At Christmas she and Laurie flew to Florida and went on a five-day Caribbean cruise. Swimming in the outside pool on the Lido deck made Christmas with all its attendant memories seem far away. Still Sarah found herself longing for the holiday court recess to be over so that she could get back to the trial.

Laurie spent much of the cruise in the cabin, reading. She had signed on for Allan Grant's class in Victorian women writers and wanted to do some advance study. She had brought along their mother's old portable typewriter, supposedly to make notes. But Sarah knew she was also writing letters on it, letters she would rip from the machine and cover if Sarah entered the cabin. Had Laurie become interested in someone? Sarah wondered. Why be so secretive about it?

She's twenty-one, Sarah told herself sternly. Mind your own business.

27

ON CHRISTMAS EVE, Professor Allan Grant had an unpleasant scene with his wife, Karen. He'd forgotten to hide the key to his desk drawer and she'd found the letters. Karen demanded to know why he'd kept them from her; why he had not turned them over to the administration if, as he claimed, they were all ridiculous fabrications.

Patiently and then not so patiently, he explained. "Karen, I saw no reason to upset you. As far as the administration is concerned, I can't even be sure that a student is sending them, although I certainly suspect it. What is the dean going to do except just what you're doing right now, wonder how much truth there is in them?"

The week between Christmas and New Year's Day the letters stopped coming. "More proof that they're probably from a student," he told Karen. "Now I *wish* I'd get one. A postmark would be a big help."

Karen wanted him to spend New Year's Eve in New York. They'd been invited to a party at the Rainbow Room.

"You know I hate big parties," he told her. "The Larkins invited us to their place." Walter Larkin was the Dean of Student Affairs.

On New Year's Eve it snowed heavily. Karen called from her office. "Darling, turn the radio on. The trains and buses are all delayed. What do you think I should do?"

Allan knew what he was supposed to answer. "Don't get stuck in Penn Station or on the highway in a bus. Why don't you stay in town?"

"Are you sure you don't mind?"

He didn't mind.

Allan Grant had entered marriage with the definite idea that it was a lifetime commitment. His father had walked out on his mother when Allan was a baby and he'd vowed he'd never do that to any woman.

Karen was obviously very happy with their arrangement. She liked living in New York during the week and spending weekends with him. At first it had worked pretty well. Allan Grant was used to living alone and enjoyed his own company. But now he was experiencing growing dissatisfaction. Karen was one of the prettiest women he'd ever seen. She wore clothes like a fashion model. Unlike him, she had a good business sense, which was why she handled all their finances. But her physical attraction for him had long since died. Her amusing hardheaded common sense had become predictable.

What did they really have in common? Allan asked himself yet again as he dressed to go to the dean's home. Then he put the nagging question aside. Tonight he'd just enjoy the evening with good friends. He knew everyone who would be there and they were all attractive, interesting people.

Especially Vera West, the newest member of the faculty.

28

IN EARLY JANUARY, the campus of Clinton College had been a crystal palace. A heavy storm inspired students to create imaginative snow sculptures. The below-freezing temperature preserved them in pristine beauty, until the arrival of an unseasonably warm rain. .

Now the remaining snow clung to soggy brown grass. The remnants of the sculptures seemed grotesque in their half-melted state. The frivolous postexam euphoria was over and business as usual began in the classrooms.

Laurie walked quickly across the campus to Professor Allan Grant's office. Her hands were clenched in the pockets of the ski jacket she was wearing over jeans and a sweater. Her tawny blond hair was pulled back and clipped in a ponytail. In preparation for the conference she had started to dab on eyeshadow and lipliner, then scrubbed them off.

Don't try to kid yourself. You're ugly.

The loud thoughts were coming more and more often. Laurie quickened her steps as though somehow she might be able to outrun them. *Laurie, everything is your fault. What happened when you were little is your fault.*

Laurie hoped she hadn't done badly in the first test on Victorian authors. She'd always gotten good marks till this year, but now it was like being on a roller coaster. Sometimes she'd get an A or B+ on a paper. Other times the material was so unfamiliar that she knew she must not have been paying attention in class. Later she'd find notes she didn't remember taking.

Then she saw him. Gregg. He was walking across the driveway between two dormitories. When he'd gotten back from England last week he'd called her. She'd shouted at him to leave her alone and slammed down the phone.

He hadn't spotted her yet. She ran the remaining distance to the building.

Mercifully the corridor was empty. She leaned her head against the wall for an instant, grateful for the coolness.

'Fraidy cat.

I'm not a 'fraidy cat, she thought defiantly. Straightening her shoulders, she managed a casual smile for the student emerging from Allan Grant's office.

She knocked on the partly open door. A pleasant warmth and a sense of brightness permeated her at his welcoming, "Come on in, Laurie." He was always so kind to her.

Grant's tiny office was painted a sunny yellow.

72

Crammed bookshelves lined the wall to the right of the window. A long table held reference books and student papers. The top of his desk was tidy, holding only a phone, a plant and a fishbowl in which a solitary goldfish swam aimlessly.

Grant motioned toward the chair opposite his desk. "Sit down, Laurie." He was wearing a dark blue sweater over a white turtleneck shirt. Laurie had the fleeting thought that the effect was almost clerical.

He was holding her last paper in his hand, the one she'd written on Emily Dickinson. "You didn't like it?" she asked apprehensively.

"I thought it was terrific. It's just I don't see why you changed your mind about old Em."

He liked it. Laurie smiled in relief. But what did he mean about changing her mind?

"Last term when you wrote about Emily Dickinson, you made a strong case for her life as a recluse, saying that her genius could only be fully expressed by removing herself from contact with the many. Now your thesis is that she was a neurotic filled with fear, that her poetry would have reached greater heights if she hadn't suppressed her emotions. You conclude, 'A lusty affair with her mentor and idol, Charles Wadsworth, would have done her a lot of good.'"

Grant smiled. "I've sometimes wondered the same thing, but what made you change your mind?"

What indeed? Laurie found an answer. "Maybe my mind works like yours. Maybe I started to wonder what would have happened if she had found a physical outlet for her emotions instead of being afraid of them."

73

Grant nodded. "Okay. These couple of sentences in the margin . . . You wrote them?"

It didn't even look like her writing, but the blue cover had her name on it. She nodded.

There was something about Professor Grant that was different. The expression on his face was thoughtful, even troubled. Was he just trying to be nice to her? Maybe the paper was lousy after all.

The goldfish was swimming slowly, indifferently. "What happened to the others?" she asked.

"Some joker overfed them. They all died. Laurie, there is something I want to talk to you about . . ."

"I'd rather die from overeating than being smashed in a car, wouldn't you? At least you don't bleed. Oh, I'm sorry. What did you want to talk about?"

Allan Grant shook his head. "Nothing that won't keep. It isn't getting much better, is it?"

She knew what he meant.

"Sometimes I can honestly agree with the doctor that if there was any fault, it was with the bus with faulty brakes that was going much too fast. Other times, no."

The loud voice in her head shouted: *You robbed your mother and father of the rest of their lives just as you robbed them of two years when you waved at that funeral procession.*

She didn't want to cry in front of Professor Grant. He'd been so nice, but people got sick of always having to bolster you up. She stood up. "I . . . I have to go. Is there anything else?"

With troubled eyes, Allan Grant watched Laurie leave. It was too soon to be sure, but the term paper he was holding had given him the first solid clue as to the identity of the mysterious letter writer who signed herself "Leona."

There was a sensual theme in the paper that was totally unlike Laurie's usual style but similar to the tone of the letters. It seemed to him that he recognized some unusually extravagant phrases as well. That wasn't proof, but at least it gave him a place to start looking.

Laurie Kenyon was the last person he'd have dreamt could be the writer of those letters. Her attitude toward him had been consistently that of a respectful student toward a teacher whom she admired and liked.

As Grant reached for his jacket, he decided he would say nothing to either Karen or the administration about his suspicions. Some of those letters were downright salacious. It would be embarrassing for any innocent person to be questioned about them, particularly a kid living through the kind of tragedy Laurie was. He turned out the light and started home.

From behind a row of evergreens, Leona watched him go, her nails digging into her palms.

Last night she had hidden outside his house again. As usual he'd left the draperies open, and she'd watched him for three hours. He'd heated a pizza around nine and brought it and a beer to his den. He'd stretched out in that old leather chair, kicked off his shoes and rested his feet on the ottoman.

He was reading a biography of George Bernard Shaw. It was so endearing the way Allan would run his hand through his hair unconsciously. He did it in class occasionally as well. When he finished the beer he looked at the empty glass, shrugged, then went into the kitchen and came back with a fresh one.

75

At eleven he watched the news then turned out the light and left the den. She knew he was going to bed. He always left the window open, but the bedroom draperies were drawn. Most nights she simply went away after he turned out the light, but one night she'd pulled at the handle of the sliding glass door and discovered that the lock didn't catch. Now some nights she went inside and curled up in his chair and pretended that in a minute he'd call her. "Hey, darling, come to bed. I'm lonesome."

Once or twice she'd waited till she was sure he was asleep and tiptoed in to look at him. Last night she was cold and very tired and went home after he turned out the den light.

Cold and very tired.
Cold.
Laurie rubbed her hands together. It had gotten so dark all of a sudden. She hadn't noticed how dark it was when she left Professor Grant's office a minute ago.

29

"*R*IDGEWOOD *IS ONE* of the finest towns in New Jersey," Betsy Lyons explained to the quietly dressed woman who was going over pictures of real estate properties with her. "Of course it is in the upscale price bracket, but even so, with market conditions as they are, there are some excellent buys around."

Opal nodded thoughtfully. It was the third time she had visited Lyons Realty. Her story was that her husband was being transferred to New York and she was doing preliminary househunting in New Jersey, Connecticut and Westchester.

"Let her get to trust you," Bic had instructed. "All these real estate agents are taught to keep an eye on prospective buyers so they don't get light-fingered when they're being shown around houses. Right off, tell whoever sees you that you're looking in different locations, then, after a visit or two, that you like New Jersey best. First time you go in, say you didn't want to go as high as Ridgewood prices. Then drop hints that you think it's a nice town and you really could afford it. Finally get her to show you Lee's house on one of the Fridays we come out. Distract her and then . . ."

It was early Friday afternoon. The plan was in motion. Opal had won Betsy Lyons's confidence. It was time to see the Kenyon place. The housekeeper was in on Monday and Friday mornings. She would be gone by now. The older sister was busy in court, involved in a highly publicized trial. Opal would be alone inside Lee's home with someone who would be off guard.

Betsy Lyons was an attractive woman in her early sixties. She loved her job and was good at it. She frequently bragged that she could spot a phony a mile away. "Listen, I don't waste my time," she would tell new agents. "Time is money. Don't think because people obviously can't afford the houses they want to see that you should automatically steer them away. Daddy might be sitting in the background with a bundle of cash he made in his 7-Eleven. On the other hand, don't assume because people look as though they can pay steep prices that they're really serious. Some of the wives just want to get inside pricey houses to see the decorating. *And never take your eyes off any of them.*"

The thing that Betsy Lyons liked about Carla Hawkins was that she was so on the level. Straight off, she'd put her cards on the table. She was looking in other locations. She didn't gush at every house she saw. Neither did she point out what was wrong with it. Some people did that whether or not they had any plans to buy. "The baths are too small." Sure, honey. You're used to a Jacuzzi in the bedroom.

Mrs. Hawkins asked intelligent questions about the houses that sparked mild interest in her. There was obviously money there. A good real estate agent learned to spot expensive clothes. The bottom line was that Betsy Lyons had a feeling that this could turn into a big sale.

"This is a particularly charming place," she said, pointing to the picture of an all-brick ranch house. "Nine rooms, only four years old, in mint condition, a fortune in landscaping and on a cul-de-sac."

Opal pretended interest, poring over the specifics listed under the picture. "That would be interesting," she said slowly, "but let's keep looking. Oh, what's this?" She had finally come to the page with the picture of the Kenyon home.

"Now if you want a really beautiful, roomy, comfortable house, this is a buy," Lyons said enthusiastically. "Over an acre of property, a swimming pool, four large bedrooms, each with its own bath; a living room, dining room, breakfast room, den and library on the main floor. Eight thousand square feet, crown molding, wainscoting, parquet floors, butler's pantry."

"Let's see both of these this morning," Opal suggested. "That's about as much as I'm up to with this ankle."

Bic had fastened an Ace bandage on her left ankle. "You tell that agent you sprained it," he told her. "Then when you say you must have dropped a glove up in one of the bedrooms she won't mind leaving you in the kitchen."

"I'll check about the ranch," Lyons said. "They have young children and want us to call ahead. I can go in the Kenyon place any weekday without notice."

They stopped at the ranch house first. Opal remembered to ask all the right questions. Finally they were on their way to the Kenyon home. Mentally she reviewed Bic's instructions.

"Rotten weather, isn't it," Lyons said as she drove through the quiet streets of Ridgewood. "But it's nice to think that spring is on the way. The Kenyon property is alive with flowering trees in the spring. Dogwood. Cherry blossoms. Mrs. Kenyon loved gardening and there are three blooms a year. Whoever gets this place will be lucky."

"Why is it being sold?" It seemed to Opal that it would be unnatural not to ask the question. She hated driving down this road. It reminded her of those two years. She remembered how her heart pounded when they turned at the pink corner house. That house was painted white now.

Lyons knew there was no use trying to hide the

truth. Problem was, some people steered clear of a hard-luck house. Better to say it right out than let them nose around and find out for themselves was her motto. "There are just two sisters living here now," she said. "The parents were killed in an automobile accident last September. A bus slammed into them on Route 78." Skillfully she attempted to make Opal concentrate on the fact that the accident had taken place on Route 78 and not in the house.

They were turning into the driveway. Bic had told Opal to be sure to notice everything. He was real curious about the kind of place where Lee lived. They got out of the car, and Lyons fished for the key to the lock.

"This is the central foyer," she said as she opened the door. "See what I mean about a well-kept place? Isn't this beautiful?"

Be quiet, Opal wanted to tell her as they walked around the first floor. The living room was to the left. Archway. Big windows. Upholstery predominantly blue. Dark polished floor with a large Oriental and a contrasting small rug in front of the fireplace. Opal felt a nervous impulse to laugh. They had taken Lee from this place to that dumpy farm. Wonder she didn't crack up on the spot.

In the library, portraits lined the walls. "Those are the Kenyons," Betsy Lyons pointed out. "Handsome couple, weren't they? And those are watercolors of the girls when they were little. From the time Laurie was born, Sarah was always such a little mother to her. I don't know if, being in Georgia, you would have known about it but . . ."

As she heard the story of the disappearance seventeen years earlier, Opal felt her heart begin to race. On an end table there was a picture of Lee with an older girl. Lee was wearing the pink bathing suit she'd had on when they picked her up. With the cluster of framed photos in this room, it was crazy that her eye fell on that one. Bic was right. There was a reason why God had sent them here to be on guard against Lee now.

She chose to fake a sneeze, pull her handkerchief from her coat pocket and drop a glove in Lee's bedroom. Even if Betsy Lyons hadn't told her, it was easy to figure which one was Lee's. The sister's room was loaded with law books over the desk.

Opal followed Lyons down the stairs, then asked to see the kitchen again. "I love this kitchen," she sighed. "This house is a dream." At least that was honest, she thought with some amusement. "Now I'd really better be going. My ankle is telling me to stop walking." She sat on one of the tall stools in front of the island counter.

"Of course." Betsy Lyons could smell a potential sale warming up.

Opal reached in her coat pocket for her gloves, then frowned. "I know I had both of them when we came in." She fished in the other pocket, brought out her handkerchief. "Oh, I know. I bet when I sneezed, I pulled out my glove with the hankie. That was in the bedroom with the blue carpet." She began to slide from the stool.

"You wait right there," Betsy Lyons ordered. "I'll run up and look for it."

"Oh, would you?"

Opal waited until a faint padding on the staircase assured her that Lyons was on her way to the second floor. Then she jumped from the stool and raced to the row of blue-handled knives attached to the wall next to the stove. She grabbed the largest one, a long carving knife, and dropped it in her oversize shoulder bag.

She was back on the stool, slightly bent over, her hand rubbing her ankle, when Betsy Lyons returned to the kitchen, a triumphant smile on her face, the missing glove clutched in her fingers.

30

THE FIRST PART of the week had passed in a blur. Sarah worked through Thursday night, poring over her closing statement.

She read intently, clipping, inserting, preparing three-by-five cards with the highlights of the points she wanted to hammer at the jury. The morning light began to filter into the bedroom. At seven-fifteen, Sarah read her closing paragraph. "Ladies and gentlemen, Mr. Marcus is a skilled and experienced defense attorney. He hammered away at each of the witnesses who had been in the station that night. Admittedly it was not broad daylight but neither was it so dark they could not see James Parker's face. Every one of them had seen him approach and be rebuffed by Maureen Mays in the railroad station. Every one of them told you, without hesitation, that James Parker is the person who got into Maureen's car that night. . . .

"I would say, ladies and gentlemen, the evidence

has shown to you beyond any reasonable doubt that James Parker murdered this fine young woman and forever robbed her husband, mother, father and siblings of her love and support.

"There is nothing any of us can do to bring her back, but what you, the jury, can do is to bring her murderer to justice."

She had covered all the points. The solid mass of evidence was undeniable. Still Conner Marcus was the best criminal attorney she'd ever been up against. And juries were unpredictable.

Sarah got up and stretched. The adrenaline that always pulsed through her body during a trial would reach fever pitch when she began her final arguments. She was counting on that.

She went into the bathroom and turned on the shower. It was a temptation to linger under the cascade of hot water. Her shoulders especially seemed to be tied up in knots. Instead she turned off the hot water and twisted the cold-water tap completely to the right. Grimacing, she endured the icy blast.

She toweled dry quickly, pulled on a long, thick terry-cloth robe, stuck her feet in slippers and ran downstairs to make coffee. While she waited for it to seep through the coffee maker, she did stretching exercises and looked around the kitchen. Betsy Lyons, the real estate agent, seemed to think that she had a hot prospect for the house. Sarah realized she was still ambivalent about selling it. She had told Lyons she absolutely would not lower the price.

The coffee was ready. She dug out her favorite mug, the one her squad of detectives gave her when she was the assistant prosecutor in charge of the sex-crimes unit. It was inscribed "For Sarah, who made sex so interesting." Her mother had not been amused.

She carried the coffee upstairs and sipped while she dabbed on a touch of lipstick, blusher and eyeshadow. That had become a morning ritual, a loving tribute to her mother. Mom, if you don't mind I'll look tailored today, she thought. But she knew Marie would have approved of the blue-and-gray tweed suit.

Her hair. A cloud of curls . . . no, a mass of frizz. Impatiently she brushed it. "The sun will come out tomorrow . . ." she sang softly. All I need is a red dress with a white collar and a dopey-looking dog.

She checked her briefcase. All her notes for the closing argument were there. This is it, she thought. She was almost at the bottom of the stairs when she heard the kitchen door open. "It's me, Sarah," Sophie called. Footsteps padded across the kitchen. "I have to go to the dentist, so I thought I'd come a bit early. Oh, you look nice."

"Thanks. You didn't have to come so early. After ten years, don't you think you should just take some time off when you need it?" They smiled at each other.

The prospect of the house being sold distressed Sophie, and she'd said as much.

"Unless, of course, you girls get an apartment near here so I can look after you," she'd told Sarah.

This morning she looked troubled. "Sarah, you know the good set of knives next to the stove?"

Sarah was buttoning her coat. "Yes."

"Did you take one of them out for anything?"

"No."

"I just noticed the biggest carving knife is missing. It's the queerest thing."

"Oh, it's got to be around somewhere."

"Well, I can't tell you where."

Sarah felt suddenly uneasy. "When was the last time you saw it?"

"I'm not sure. I missed it on Monday and began looking around. It isn't in the kitchen, I'll tell you that. How long it's been gone, I have no idea." Sophie hesitated. "I don't suppose Laurie would have had any use for it at school?"

Sophie knew about the knife dream. "I hardly think so." Sarah swallowed over the sudden constriction in her throat. "Got to run." As she opened the door, she said, "If, by any chance, you come across that knife, leave a message for me at the office, will you? Just a simple 'I found it.' Okay?"

She saw the compassion in Sophie's face. She thinks Laurie took it, Sarah thought. My God!

Frantically she ran to the phone and dialed Laurie's number. A sleepy voice. Laurie had picked up on the first ring.

"Sarah? Sure. I'm fine. In fact I got a couple of my marks back. They're good. Let's celebrate somehow."

Relieved, Sarah hung up and rushed outside to the garage. A four-car garage with only her car in it. Laurie always left hers in the driveway. The other empty spaces were a constant reminder of the accident.

As she pulled out, she decided that for the moment Laurie sounded okay. Tonight she'd call Dr. Carpenter and Dr. Donnelly and tell them about the knife. But now she had to put it out of her mind. It wasn't fair to Maureen Mays or her family to do less than her best in court today. But why in the name of God would Laurie take the carving knife?

31

"*SARAH'S JURY* is still out," Laurie told Dr. Carpenter as she sat across from him in his office. "I envy her. She's so committed to what she does, to being a prosecutor, that she can block out everything she doesn't want to think about."

Carpenter waited. The temperature had changed. Laurie was different. It was the first time he had seen her express hostility toward Sarah. There was pent-up anger flashing in her eyes. Something had happened between her and Sarah. "I've been reading about that case," he said mildly.

"I'll bet you have. Sarah the prosecutor. But she's not as subtle as she thinks she is."

Again he waited. "I no sooner got home last night than she came in. All apologies. Sorry she hadn't been home to welcome me. Big sister. I said, 'Look, Sarah, at some point even I have to take care of myself. I'm twenty-one, not four.'"

"Four?"

"That's the age I was when she should have stayed home from her damn party. I wouldn't have been kidnapped if she'd stayed home."

"You've always blamed yourself for being kidnapped, Laurie."

"Oh, me too. But big sister had a hand in it. I bet she hates me."

Dr. Carpenter had intended as one of his goals to wean Laurie away from dependence on her sister, but this was something new. It was like being with a totally different patient. "Why would she hate you?"

"She has no time for a life of her own. You should have *her* as a patient. Boy, that would be something to hear! All her life being big sister. I read her old diary this morning. She's been keeping one since she was a little kid. She wrote a lot about me being kidnapped and then coming back and that she thought I was different. I guess I really chilled her out." There was satisfaction in Laurie's tone.

"Do you make it a habit to go through Sarah's diaries?"

The look Laurie gave him was pure pity. "You're the one who wants to know what everyone is thinking. What makes you better?"

It was the way she was sitting, the belligerent posture, knees pressed together, hands grasping the arms of the chair, head thrust forward, features rigid. Where was the soft, troubled young face, the hesitant Jackie Onassis voice?

"That's a good question, but I don't have any one-sentence answer to it. Why are you annoyed at Sarah?"

"The knife. Sarah thinks I sneaked a carving knife out of the kitchen."

"Why would she think that?"

"Only because it's missing. I sure as hell didn't take it. Sophie, our housekeeper, started the whole thing. I mean I don't mind admitting that a lot of things fall in my camp, but not this one, Doc."

"Did Sarah accuse you or just ask you about the knife? There's a big difference, you know."

"Buddy, I know an accusation when I hear one."

"I had the feeling that you were afraid of knives. Was I wrong, Laurie?"

"I wish you'd call me Kate."

"Kate? Any reason?"

"Kate sounds better than Laurie—more mature. Anyhow, my middle name is Katherine."

"That could be very positive. Putting away of childish things. Is that the way you feel now, that you're putting away childish things?"

"No. I just don't want to be afraid of knives."

"I was under the strong impression that you were desperately afraid of them."

"Oh no. Not me. Laurie is afraid of everything. A knife is her 'worst-case scenario.' You know, Doctor, there are some people who bring grief and pain to the rest of the universe. Our gal Laurie, for example."

Dr. Peter Carpenter realized that he now knew that Kate was the name of one of Laurie Kenyon's alter personalities.

32

*O*N SATURDAY MORNING they parked near Dr. Carpenter's office. Bic had deliberately rented the same color late-model Buick that Laurie drove. Only the interior was a different shade of leather. "If anyone happens to question my opening this door, I'll point to the other car," he explained, then answered her unspoken question. "We have observed that Lee never locks her car. Her tote bag filled with textbooks is always on the floor of the front seat. I'll just slip in that knife right at the bottom. Doesn't matter when she finds it. The point is that she's sure to come across it soon. Just a little reminder for her of what happens if she starts thinking on us with her head doctor. And now do what you must do, Opal."

Lee always left Dr. Carpenter's office at exactly five of twelve. At six of twelve Opal casually opened the door of the private entrance to his upstairs office. A narrow foyer with a flight of stairs led to his suite. She glanced around as though she'd made a mistake and meant to use the main door of the professional building at the corner of Ridgewood Avenue. There was no one on the stairs. Quickly she unwrapped the small package she was holding, dropped its contents in the center of the foyer and left. Bic was already in the rented car.

"A blind person couldn't miss it," Opal told him.

"Nobody was paying any attention to you," he assured her. "Now we'll just wait here a minute and see what happens."

Laurie stamped down the stairs. She was going directly back to college. Who the hell needed to be sitting having her head taken apart? Who needed to be fussed over by long-suffering Sarah? That was something else. It was time she concentrated on those trust funds and knew exactly how much money she was worth. Plenty. And when the house sold, she didn't want any talk of other people investing it for her. She was sick of having to deal with the wimp who said "Yes, Sarah; no, Sarah; whatever you say, Sarah."

She was at the bottom of the stairs. Her boot touched something soft, something squishy. She looked down.

The lifeless eye of a chicken stared up at her. Straggly feathers clung to its skull. The severed neck was crusted with dried blood.

Outside, Bic and Opal heard the first screams. Bic smiled. "Sound familiar?" He turned the key in the ignition, then whispered, "But now I should be comforting her."

33

THE JURY was filing in when Sarah's secretary hurried into the courtroom. Word had spread that a verdict had been reached, and there was a scramble for seats. Sarah's heart pounded as the judge asked, "Mr. Foreman, has the jury agreed upon a verdict?"

"Yes we have, your Honor."

This is it, Sarah thought as she stood at the prosecution table, facing the bench. She felt a tug on her arm and turned to see her secretary, Janet. "Not now," she said firmly, surprised that Janet would interrupt when a verdict was being rendered.

"Sarah, I'm sorry. A Dr. Carpenter has taken your sister to the emergency room of Hackensack Medical Center. She's in shock."

Sarah gripped the pen she was holding until her

knuckles turned white. The judge was looking at her, clearly annoyed. She whispered, "Tell him I'll be there in a few minutes."

"On the charge of murder what is your verdict, guilty or not guilty?"

"Guilty, your Honor."

A cry of "not fair!" went up from the family and friends of James Parker. The judge rapped his gavel, warned against further outbursts, ascertained that the verdict was unanimous and began to poll the jury.

Bail was revoked for James Parker. A sentencing date was set and he was led away in handcuffs. Court was adjourned. Sarah had no time to relish her victory. Janet was in the corridor holding her coat and shoulder bag. "Now you can go right to your car."

Dr. Carpenter was waiting for her in the emergency room. Briefly he explained what had happened. "Laurie had just left my office. As she approached the outside door on the ground floor, she began to scream. By the time we reached her, she had fainted. She was in deep shock but she's coming around now."

"What caused it?" The concerned kindness of the doctor brought hot tears to the back of Sarah's eyes. There was something about Carpenter that reminded her of her father. She longed for him to be with her now.

"Apparently she stepped on the head of a dead chicken, became hysterical then went into shock."

"The head of a chicken! In the lobby of your office!"

"Yes. I have a deeply disturbed patient who is involved in a cult and this is the sort of thing he would do. Does Laurie have an inordinate fear of chickens or mice or any animals?"

"No. Except she never eats chicken. She loathes the taste of it."

A nurse came out of the curtained-off area. "You can go in."

Laurie was lying quietly. Her eyes were closed. Sarah touched her hand. "Laurie."

Slowly she opened her eyes. It seemed to be an effort, and Sarah realized that she must be heavily sedated. Her voice was weak but crystal clear as she said, "Sarah, I'll kill myself before I see that doctor again."

34

ALLAN WAS in the kitchen eating a sandwich.

"Sweetie, I'm sorry I didn't get down last night, but it was really important to prepare my pitch for the Wharton account." Karen threw her arms around his neck.

He pecked at her cheek and stepped back from her embrace. "That's okay. Want some lunch?"

"You should have waited. I'd have taken care of that."

"You could have been another hour."

"You never care about food." Karen Grant

poured Chianti from the decanter and handed a glass to Allan. She clinked her glass against his. "Cheers, darling."

"Cheers," he said unsmilingly.

"Hey, Professor, something's wrong."

"What's wrong is that as of about an hour ago, I became certain that Laurie Kenyon is the mysterious Leona, the one writing those letters."

Karen gasped. "You're absolutely sure?"

"Yes, I was grading papers. The one she turned in had a note attached that her computer went on the blink and she had to finish it on the old portable typewriter she keeps as a backup. There's no question it's the same one the letters were written on—including the one that came yesterday." He reached in his pocket and handed it to Karen.

It read: "Allan, my dearest, I'll never forget tonight. I love to watch you sleep. I love to see the way you turn and scrunch up when you're getting more comfortable, the way you pull up the covers. Why do you let the room get so cold? I shut the window a little. Did you notice, darling? I'll bet not. In some ways you could be the prototype for the absentminded professor. But only in some ways. Don't ever permit me to be absent from your mind. Always remember. If your wife doesn't want you enough to be with you all the time, I do. My love to you. Leona."

Karen reread the letter slowly. "Good Lord, Allan, do you think that girl actually came in here?"

"I don't think so. She certainly fantasizes all those trysts in my office. She's fantasizing this too."

"I'm not sure about that. Come on."

He followed her into the bedroom. Karen stood

in front of the long window. She reached for the crank and turned it. The window opened outward noiselessly. She easily stepped over the low sill onto the ground then turned to him. Her hair blew in her face as a draft of cold air sent the curtain whirling. "Easy to get in, easy to get out," she said as she stepped back into the room. "Allan, maybe she is fantasizing, but she could have been here. You sleep like a dead man. From now on you can't leave that window open so wide."

"This has gone far enough. I'm damned if I'll change my sleeping habits. I've got to talk to Sarah Kenyon. I'm terribly sorry for Laurie, but Sarah has got to get her whatever help she needs."

He reached Sarah's answering machine and left a brief message: "It really is very important that I talk to you."

At two-thirty Sarah returned the call. Karen listened as Allan's voice changed from cool to solicitous. "Sarah, what's the matter? Laurie? Has anything happened to her?" He waited. "Oh God, that's lousy. Sarah, don't cry. I know how tough this has been for you. She'll be okay. Give it some time. No, I just wanted to see how you thought she was doing. Sure. Talk to you soon. 'Bye."

He replaced the receiver and turned to Karen. "Laurie's in the hospital. She had some sort of shock reaction on her way out of the shrink's office. I guess she's okay now, but they wanted her to stay overnight. Her sister is about at the end of her rope."

"Will Laurie come back to school?"

"She's determined to be here on Monday for classes." He shrugged helplessly. "Karen, I couldn't lay these letters on Sarah Kenyon now."

"You will turn them over to the office?"

"Of course. I'm sure Dean Larkin will have one of the psychologists speak to Laurie. I know she goes to a psychiatrist in Ridgewood, but maybe she needs counseling here as well. The poor kid."

35

LAURIE WAS propped up in bed reading the Bergen *Record* when Sarah arrived at the hospital late Sunday morning. Her greeting to Sarah was cheerful. "Hi. You brought the clothes. Terrific. I'll get dressed and let's go to the club for brunch."

It was what she had said she wanted to do when she'd phoned an hour earlier. "Are you sure it won't be too much for you?" Sarah asked anxiously. "You were pretty sick yesterday."

"It may be too much for *you*. Oh, Sarah, why don't you move and not leave a forwarding address? Honest to God, I'm such a damn nuisance to you." Her smile was both apologetic and rueful as Sarah bent down and hugged her.

Sarah had come in not knowing what to expect. But this was the real Laurie, sorry if she put anyone out, ready to have fun. "You look better than you have in ages," she said sincerely.

"They gave me something, and I slept like a rock."

"It's a mild sleeping pill. Dr. Carpenter has ordered that and an antidepressant for you."

Laurie stiffened. "Sarah, I wouldn't let him give me any pills, and he's been trying. You know I hate those things. But I will do *this:* I'll start the pills. But no more therapy, ever."

"You *will* have to check with Dr. Carpenter about any reaction to the medication."

"Over the phone. That I don't mind."

"And Laurie, you know Dr. Carpenter consulted with a psychiatrist, Dr. Donnelly, in New York about you. If you won't see him, will you allow me to talk to him?"

"Oh, Sarah, I wish you wouldn't, but okay, if it makes you happy." Laurie jumped out of bed. "Let's get out of this place."

In the club friends invited them to join their table. Laurie ate well and was in good spirits. Looking at her, Sarah found it hard to believe that only yesterday she herself had been near despair. She winced thinking of how she had been crying on the phone with that nice Professor Grant.

When they left the club, Sarah did not drive directly home. Instead she went in the opposite direction.

Laurie raised an eyebrow. "Where?"

"About ten minutes from the house. Glen Rock. They're about to open up some condominiums that are supposed to be great. I thought we'd take a look."

"Sarah, maybe we should just rent for a while. I mean, suppose you decide to go with a law firm in New York? You've had offers. Anyplace we live should be tied to you, not me. If I do give a shot at pro golf I'll be following the sun."

"I'm not going with a private firm. Laurie, when I sit with the families of these victims and I see their grief and anger, I know that I can't work on the other side looking for one damn loophole in the law to set them free. I can sleep a lot better prosecuting murderers than defending them."

There was a model with three levels that they both liked. "Nice layout," Sarah commented. "Dearly as I love the house, those up-to-date bathrooms are something else." She told the agent who was showing them around, "We seem to have serious interest in our home. When we know we have a sale we'll be back."

She linked her arm companionably with Laurie's as they walked to the car. It was a clear, cold day and the light wind had a bite. Even so there was a sense that spring was only six weeks away. "Nice grounds," Sarah commented. "And just think. We wouldn't have to worry about having them tended. Happy thought, isn't it?"

"Dad loved puttering outside and Mom was happiest on her knees in the garden. Wonder how we both missed it?" Laurie's tone was affectionate and amused.

Was she beginning to be able to talk about their parents without instantly being reduced to raw pain and self-recrimination? Please God, Sarah thought prayerfully. They reached the parking lot. It was busy with prospective buyers coming and going. Word of mouth about the new section of the Fox Hedge condos had been excellent. Laurie spoke hurriedly. "Sarah, let me say just one thing. When we get home, I don't want to talk about yesterday. The house has gotten to be a place where you study me with such a worried expression, where you ask questions that are not as casual as they seem. From now on, don't grill me about how I sleep, what I eat, do I date, that kind of thing. Let *me* tell you what I want to talk about. You do the same with me. Okay?"

"Okay," Sarah said matter-of-factly. You *have* been treating her like a little kid who has to tell Mommy everything, she told herself. Maybe it's a good sign that she's starting to resent it. But what happened yesterday?

It was as though Laurie could read her mind. "Sarah, I don't know what made me faint yesterday. I do know that it's a terrible ordeal to have Dr. Carpenter keep after me with leading questions that are nothing but traps. It's like trying to lock all the doors and windows when an intruder is breaking in."

"He's not an intruder. He's a healer. But you're not ready for him. Agreed on everything."

"Good."

Sarah drove past the security guards at the gate, noticing how all arriving cars were stopped and checked. Laurie had obviously taken that in as well. She said, "Sarah, let's put a deposit on that corner unit. I'd love to live here. With that gate and those guards, we'd be safe. I want to feel safe. And that's what scares me so much. I never do."

They were on the road. The car began to pick up momentum. Sarah had to ask the question that was torturing her. "Is that why you took the knife? Was it necessary for you to have it in order to feel safe? Laurie, I can understand that. Just as long as you don't let yourself get so depressed that you'd . . . hurt yourself. I'm so sorry to ask, but that's what scares me."

Laurie sighed. "Sarah, I have no intention of committing suicide. I know that's what you're getting at. I do wish you could believe me. On my oath, I did *not* take that knife!"

That night, back at college, in order to repack her tote bag Laurie dumped its contents on her bed. Textbooks, spiral pads, and loose-leaf binders tumbled out. The very last object was the one that had been concealed at the bottom of the deep carryall. It was the missing carving knife from the set on the kitchen wall.

Laurie backed away from the bed. "No! No! No!" She sank to her knees and buried her face in her hands. "I didn't take it Sarewuh," she sobbed. "Daddy said I mustn't play with knives."

A jeering voice crashed through her mind. *Oh, shut up, kid. You know why you have it. Why not take the hint and stick it in your throat. God, I need a cigarette.*

36

*G*REGG BENNETT told himself that he didn't give a damn. Being honest, what he really meant was that he *shouldn't* give a damn. There were plenty of attractive women on this campus. He'd be meeting plenty more in California. He'd have his degree in June and be on his way to Stanford to study for his MBA.

At twenty-five Gregg was and felt considerably older than his fellow students. He still looked back in bewilderment at the nineteen-year-old dope who had quit college after his freshman year to become an entrepreneur. Not that the experience had hurt. Even getting his ears pinned back had been a long-range blessing. If nothing else he found out exactly how much he didn't know. He'd also learned that international finance was the career for him.

He'd been back from England a month and the January blahs had by now caught up with him. At least he'd been able to get in some skiing at Camelback over the weekend. The powder snow had made the runs great.

Gregg lived in a studio apartment over the garage of a private home two miles from the campus. It was a nice setup that suited him well. He had no desire to share a place with three or four other guys and end up with constant partying. This place was clean and airy; the pullout couch was comfortable for both sitting and sleeping; he could prepare simple meals in the kitchenette.

When he first arrived at Clinton, he'd noticed Laurie around the campus. Who wouldn't? But they'd never been in a class together. Then, a year and a half ago they'd sat next to each other in the auditorium at a showing of *Cinema Paradiso*. The picture had been terrific. As the lights went on, she turned to him and asked, "Wasn't that wonderful?"

That was the beginning. If a girl that attractive gave him the signal that she wanted him to come on to her, Gregg was more than willing to make the next move. But there was something about Laurie that held him back. He'd known instinctively that he'd get nowhere if he tried anything too quickly; as a result, their relationship had developed more as a friendship. She was so darn sweet. Not sugar sweet —she could be bitingly funny and she could be strong-willed. On their third date he told her that it was obvious she'd been a spoiled kid. They'd gone golfing and the starter had overbooked. They had to wait an extra hour for tee-off time. She'd been sore.

"I bet you never had to wait. I bet Mommy and Daddy called you their little princess," he had told her. She'd laughed and said, actually they had. Over dinner that night she told him about having been abducted. "The last thing I remember was standing in front of my house in a pink bathing suit and someone picking me up. The next thing, I woke up in my own bed. The only problem is that was two years later."

"I'm sorry I said you were spoiled," he'd told her. "You deserved to be."

She'd laughed. "I was spoiled before and after. You hit the nail on the head."

Gregg knew that to Laurie he was a trusted friend. It wasn't that simple for him. You don't spend a lot of time with a girl who looks like Laurie, he thought, with that marvelous ripple of blond hair, those midnight blue eyes and perfect features, without wanting to spend all the time you'll ever have with her. But then when she started inviting him home some weekends, he'd been sure she had begun to fall in love too.

Then suddenly it came to an end one Sunday morning last May. He remembered it clearly. He had slept late, and Laurie took it into her head to stop by after church with bagels and cream cheese and smoked salmon. She rapped on the door, then when he didn't hear, yelled, "I know you're in there."

He grabbed a robe, opened the door and just looked at her. She was wearing a linen dress and sandals and looking cool and fresh as the morning itself. She came in, put on the coffee, set out the bagels and told him not to bother making up the bed. She was driving home and could only stay a few minutes. After she left, he could sack out all day if he wanted.

When she was leaving, she put her arms around his neck and kissed him lightly, telling him he needed a shave. "But I still like your looks," she'd teased. "Nice nose, strong chin, cute cowlick." She'd kissed him again, then turned to go. That was when it had happened. Impulsively Gregg followed her to the door, put his hands on her arms, swooped her up and hugged her. She went crazy. Sobbing. Kicking her legs to push him away. He dropped her, angrily asked her what the hell was the matter. Did she think he was Jack the Ripper? She ran out of the apartment and never even spoke to him again except to tell him to leave her alone.

He would have liked to do just that. The only problem was that over last summer, working an internship in New York, and during the fall term, studying at the Banking Institute in London, he'd never gotten her out of his mind. Now that he was back, she was still adamant about refusing to see him.

On Monday evening Gregg wandered over to the cafeteria at the student center. He knew Laurie sometimes dropped by there. He deliberately joined a group that included some of the people from her residence. "It makes sense," one of them was saying at the other end of the table. "Laurie goes out about nine o'clock a lot of weeknights. His wife stays in New York during the week. I tried kidding Laurie about it, but she just ignored me. Obviously she was meeting someone but she sure wasn't talking about it."

Gregg's ears pricked up. Casually he moved his chair to hear better.

"Anyhow, Margy works afternoons in the administration office. She picks up a lot of dirt and knew something was up when Sexy Allan came in looking worried."

"I don't think Grant is sexy. I think he's just a very nice guy." The objection came from a dark-haired student with an air of common sense about her.

The gossiper waved aside the objection. *"You* may not think he's sexy, but a lot of people do. Anyhow, Laurie certainly does. I hear she's been sending him a bunch of love letters and signing them 'Leona.' He turned the letters over to the administration and claims that everything in them is fantasy. Maybe he's afraid if she's writing to him about their little romance she might be blabbing to other people too. I guess he's making a preemptive strike before anything gets back to his wife."

"What did she write?"

"What *didn't* she write? According to the letters, they were making out in his office, his house, you name it."

"No kidding!"

"Well, his wife's away a lot. These things happen. Remember how at her parents' funeral, he went racing down the aisle after her when she fainted?"

Gregg Bennett did not bother to pick up the chair that he knocked over as he strode from the cafeteria.

37

*W*HEN LAURIE CHECKED her mailbox on Tuesday, she found a note asking her to phone the Dean of Student Affairs for an appointment at her earliest convenience. What's that about? she wondered. When she made the call, the dean's secretary asked if she was free to come in at three o'clock that day.

At the end of the ski season last year, she'd bought a blue-and-white ski jacket on sale. It had hung in her closet unused this winter. Why not, she thought as she reached for it. Perfect for this weather, it's pretty and I might as well get some use out of it. She matched it with blue jeans and a white turtleneck sweater.

At the last minute she twisted her hair into a chignon. Might as well look like the sophisticated senior about to leave the halls of learning for the great world outside. Maybe when she was out of the college atmosphere and among working adults she'd lose this crazy feeling of being a scared kid.

It was another cold, clear day, the kind that made her take deep breaths and throw back her shoulders.. It was such a relief to know that Saturday morning she wouldn't be sitting in that damn office with Dr. Carpenter trying to look kindly but always probing, always digging.

She waved to a group of students from her residence then wondered if they were looking at her in a funny kind of way. Don't be silly, she told herself.

The knife. How had it gotten to the bottom of her tote bag? She certainly hadn't put it there. But would Sarah believe her? "Look, Sarah, the stupid thing was stuck between my books. Here it is. Problem solved."

And Sarah would reasonably ask, "How did it get in your bag?" Then she'd probably suggest talking to Dr. Carpenter again.

The knife was in the back of the closet now, hidden in the sleeve of an old jacket. The elastic cuff would keep it from falling. Should she simply throw it away, let the mystery go unsolved? But Dad valued that set of knives and always said they could cut anything clean as a whistle. Laurie hated the thought of something being cut clean as a whistle.

As she walked across the campus to the administration building she mulled over the best way to place the knife back in the house. Hide it in a kitchen cupboard? But Sarah had said that Sophie had looked everywhere in the kitchen for it.

An idea came to her that seemed simple and foolproof: Sophie was always looking for things to polish. Sometimes she'd take the knives down and do them when she was going over the silver flatware. That was it, Laurie thought! I'll sneak the knife into the silver chest in the dining room, way to the back so it won't be seen easily. Even if Sophie had looked there, she might think she'd missed it. The point was Sarah would know that was at least a good possibility.

The solution brought relief until inside her head a derisive voice shouted, *Very clever, Laurie, but how do you explain the knife to yourself? Do you think it jumped into your bag?* The mocking laugh made her curl her fingers into fists.

"Shut up!" she whispered fiercely. "Go away and leave me alone."

Dean Larkin was not alone. Dr. Iovino, the Director of the Counseling Center, was with him. Laurie stiffened when she saw him. A voice in her mind shouted, *Be careful. Another shrink. What are they trying to pull now?*

Dean Larkin invited her to sit down, asked her how she was feeling, how her classes were going, reminded her that everyone was aware of the terrible tragedy in her family and that he wanted her always to understand that the entire faculty had the deepest concern for her well-being.

Then he said he'd excuse himself. Dr. Iovino wanted to have a little talk with her.

The dean closed the door behind him. Dr. Iovino smiled and said, "Don't look scared, Laurie. I just wanted to talk to you about Professor Grant. What do you think of him?"

That was easy. "I think he's wonderful," Laurie said. "He's a great teacher and he's been a good friend."

"A good friend."

"Of course."

"Laurie, it's not uncommon for students to develop a certain attachment to a faculty member. In a case like yours, where you especially needed compassion and kindness, it would be unusual if in loneliness and grief you didn't misinterpret that kind of relationship. Fantasize about it. What you daydreamed it *might* be, became in your mind what it *is*. That's very understandable."

"What are you *talking* about?" Laurie realized that she sounded like her mother the time she became annoyed at a waiter who had suggested he'd like to phone Laurie for a date.

The psychologist handed her a stack of letters. "Laurie, did you write these letters?"

She skimmed them, her eyes widening. "These are signed by someone named Leona. What in the world gave you the idea I wrote them?"

"Laurie, you have a typewriter, don't you?"

"I write my assignments on a computer."

"But you do *have* a typewriter?"

"Yes, I do. My mother's old portable."

"Do you keep it here?"

"Yes. As a backup. Every once in a while, the computer has gone down when I had an assignment due."

"You turned in this term paper last week?"

She glanced at it. "Yes, I did."

"Notice that the *o* and *w* are broken wherever they appear on these pages. Now check that against the broken *o* and *w* that regularly appear in the letters to Professor Grant. They were typed on the same machine."

Laurie stared at Dr. Iovino. His face became superimposed with the face of Dr. Carpenter. *Inquisitors! Bastards!*

Dr. Iovino, heavyset, his manner one of all-is-well-don't-worry, said, "Laurie, comparing the signature 'Leona' with the written addenda to your term paper shows a great similarity in the handwriting."

The voice shouted: *He's not only a shrink. He's a handwriting expert now.*

Laurie stood up. "Dr. Iovino, as a matter of fact, I've let a number of people use that typewriter. I feel this conversation is nothing short of insulting. I am shocked that Professor Grant leapt to the conclusion that I wrote this trash. I'm shocked that you would send for me to discuss it. My sister is a prosecutor. I've seen her in court. She would make mincemeat of the kind of 'evidence' that you purport connects me with these disgusting outpourings."

She picked up the letters and threw them across the desk. "I expect a written apology, and if this has leaked out just as everything that happens in this office seems to leak out, I demand a public apology and retraction of this stupid accusation. As for Professor Grant, I considered him a good friend, an understanding friend at this very difficult time in my life. Clearly I was wrong. Clearly the students who call him 'Sexy Allan' and gossip about his flirtatious attitude are right. I intend to tell him that myself, immediately." She turned and walked rapidly from the room.

She was due in Allan Grant's class at 3:45. It was now 3:30. With any luck she'd catch him in the hallway. It was too late to go to his office.

She was waiting when he strode down the corridor. His cheery greetings to other students as he made his way to the classroom ended when he spotted her. "Hi, Laurie." He sounded nervous.

"Professor Grant, where did you get the preposterous idea that I wrote those letters to you?"

"Laurie, I know what a tough time you've been having and . . ."

"And you thought you'd make it easier by telling Dean Larkin that I was fantasizing sleeping with you? Are you crazy?"

"Laurie, don't be upset. Look, we're getting an audience. Why don't you see me in my office after class?"

"So we can strip for each other and I can see your gorgeous body and satisfy my lust for it?" Laurie did not care that people were stopping and listening to their exchange. "You are disgusting. You are going to regret this." She spat out the words. "As God is my witness, you are going to regret this."

She broke through the crowd of stunned students and ran back to the dorm. She locked the door, fell on the bed and listened to the voices that were now shouting at her.

One said, *Well at least you stood up for yourself for a change.*

The other screamed, *How could Allan have betrayed me? He was warned not to show those letters to anyone. You bet he's going to regret it. It's a good thing you have the knife. Kiss-and-Tell will never have to worry about hearing from us again.*

38

BIC AND OPAL flew to Georgia directly after the Sunday program. That night there was a farewell banquet for them.

On Tuesday morning they started driving to New York. In the trunk were Bic's typewriter, their luggage and a can of gasoline carefully wrapped in towels. No other personal possessions would be forwarded. "When we pick a house, we'll get ourselves a state-of-the-art entertainment center," Bic decreed. Till then they would live in the suite at the Wyndham.

As they drove, Bic explained his reasoning to Opal. "That case I told you, where a grown-up woman remembered something her daddy did and Daddy's in prison now. She had vivid memories of what happened in her house and in the van. Now suppose the Lord tests us by allowing Lee to start remembering little bits of our life with her. Suppose she talks about the farmhouse, the way the rooms are laid out, the short steps to the upstairs? Suppose somehow they find it and start going back to see who rented it those years? That house is visible proof that she was under our protection. Other than that, well, Lee's a troubled woman. No one ever saw her with us 'cept that cashier who couldn't describe us. So we got to get rid of the house. The Lord has dictated that."

It was dark when they drove through Bethlehem and arrived in Elmville. Even so they were able to see that little had changed in the fifteen years since they'd left. The shabby diner off the highway, the one gas station, the row of frame houses whose porch lights revealed peeling paint and sagging steps.

Bic avoided Main Street and drove a circuitous route the five miles to the farm. As they neared it, he turned off the headlights. "Don't want anyone to happen to get a look at this car," he said. "Not likely of course. There's never anyone on this road."

"Suppose a cop comes along?" Opal was worried. "Suppose he asks why you don't have lights on?"

Bic sighed. "Opal, you have no faith. The Lord is caring for us. Besides, the only places this road leads to are swamps and the farm." But when they reached the farmhouse, he did drive the car behind a clump of trees.

There was no sign of life. "Curious?" Bic asked. "Want to take a peek?"

"I just want to get out of here."

"Come with me, Opal." It was a command.

Opal felt herself sliding on the ice-crusted ground and reached for Bic's arm.

There was no sign that anyone was living in the house. It was totally dark. Windowpanes were broken. Bic turned the door handle. The door was locked, but when he pressed his shoulder against it, it squeaked open.

Bic set down the gasoline can and took a pencil-thin flashlight from his pocket. He directed the beam of light around the room. "Looks pretty much the same," he observed. "They sure didn't refurnish. That's the very rocking chair where I used to sit with Lee on my lap. Sweet, sweet child."

"Bic, I want to get out of here. It's cold and this place always gave me the creeps. That whole two years I was always so worried someone would come along and see her."

"No one did. And now if this place exists in her memory that's the only place it will exist. Opal, I'm going to sprinkle this gasoline around. Then we'll go outside and you can light the match."

They were in the car and moving rapidly away

when the first flames shot above the tree line. Ten minutes later they were back on the highway. They had not encountered another car in their half-hour visit to Elmville.

39

ON MONDAY Sarah had been interviewed by *The New York Times* and the Bergen *Record* about the Parker conviction. "I realize that he has a right to argue that the victim was the enticer, but in this case, it makes my blood boil."

"Are you sorry you didn't ask for the death penalty?"

"If I'd thought I could have made it stick, I would have asked for it. Parker stalked Mays. He cornered her. He killed her. Tell me that isn't cold-blooded, premeditated murder."

In the office, her boss, the Bergen County prosecutor, led the congratulations. "Conner Marcus is one of the two or three best criminal defense attorneys in this country, Sarah. You did a hell of a job. You could make yourself a bundle if you wanted to switch to the other side of the courtroom."

"Defend them? No way!"

Tuesday morning the phone rang as Sarah settled at her desk. Betsy Lyons, the real estate agent, was bubbling with news. There was another potential buyer seriously interested in the house. Problem was the woman was pregnant and anxious to get settled before the new baby arrived. How soon would the house be available if they decided to buy?

"As fast as they want it," Sarah said. Making that commitment felt as if she were taking a weight off her shoulders. Furniture or anything else she and Laurie decided to keep could be stored.

Tom Byers, a thirty-year-old attorney who was making a name for himself in the patent infringement field, poked his head in. "Sarah, congratulations. Can I buy you a drink tonight?"

"Sure." She liked Tom a lot. It would be fun to have a drink with him. But he'd never be special, she thought, as Justin Donnelly's face popped into her mind.

It was seven-thirty when she unlocked the front door of the house. Tom had suggested going on to dinner, but she'd taken a rain check. The unwinding process that always followed an intense trial had been taking place all afternoon, and as she told Tom, "My bones are starting to ache."

She changed immediately to pajamas and a matching robe, stuck her feet in slippers and looked in the refrigerator. Bless Sophie, she thought. There was a small pot roast already cooked. Vegetables, potatoes and gravy were in individual plastic-wrapped dishes waiting to be heated.

She was just about to carry the dinner tray into the den when Allan Grant phoned. Sarah's cheerful greeting died on her lips as she heard him say, "Sarah, I started to tell you this the other day. I know now that it wasn't fair not to warn both you and Laurie before I went to the administration."

"Warn about what?"

As she listened, Sarah felt her knees go weak. Holding the receiver with one hand, she pulled out a kitchen chair and sat down. The typewriter. The letters Laurie had been writing on the cruise and the way she'd been so secretive about them. When Allan told her about his confrontation with Laurie, Sarah closed her eyes and wished she could close her ears instead. Allan concluded, "Sarah, she needs help, a lot of help. I know she's seeing a psychiatrist, but . . ."

Sarah did not tell Allan Grant that Laurie had refused to continue seeing Dr. Carpenter. "I . . . I can't tell you how sorry I am, Professor Grant," she said. "You've been so kind to Laurie, and this is very difficult for you. I'll call her. I'll somehow find whatever help she needs." Her voice broke. "Goodbye. Thank you."

There was no way she could put off talking to Laurie, but what was the best approach to take? She dialed Justin Donnelly's home number. There was no answer.

She reached Dr. Carpenter. His questions were brief. "Laurie adamantly denies writing the letters? I see. No, she's not lying. She's blocking. Sarah, call her, reassure her of your support, suggest she come home. I don't think it's wise for her to be around Professor Grant. We've got to get her in to see Dr. Donnelly. I knew that at the Saturday session."

The dinner was forgotten. Sarah dialed Laurie's room. There was no answer. She tried every half hour until midnight. Finally she phoned Susan Grimes, the student who roomed across the hall from Laurie.

Susan's sleepy voice became instantly alert when

Sarah identified herself. Yes, she knew what had happened. Of course she'd look in on Laurie.

While she waited, Sarah realized she was praying. Don't let her have done anything to herself. Please God, not that. She heard the sound of the receiver being picked up.

"I looked in. Laurie's fast asleep. I can tell; she's breathing evenly. Do you want me to wake her up?"

Relief flooded through Sarah. "I'll bet she took a sleeping pill. No, don't disturb her and please forgive me for bothering you."

Exhausted, Sarah went up to bed and fell asleep instantly, secure in the knowledge that at least she didn't have to worry about Laurie anymore tonight. She'd call her first thing in the morning.

40

THAT REALLY PUTS the icing on a perfect day, Allan Grant thought as he replaced the receiver after his call to Sarah. She'd sounded heartsick. Why wouldn't she? Her mother and father dead five months, her kid sister well into a nervous breakdown.

Allan went into the kitchen. One corner of the largest cabinet held the liquor supply. Except for a beer or two at night, he was not a solitary drinker, but now he poured a generous amount of vodka in a tumbler and reached for the ice cubes. He hadn't bothered much with lunch, and the vodka burned his throat and stomach. He'd better get something to eat.

There were only leftovers in the refrigerator. Grimacing, he dismissed them as potential dinner material, opened the freezer and reached for a frozen pizza.

While it heated, Allan sipped the drink and continued to debate with himself how badly he had botched the business with Laurie Kenyon. Both Dean Larkin and Dr. Iovino had been impressed by Laurie's adamant denials. As the dean pointed out, "Allan, Miss Kenyon is quite right when she says that it's a typewriter anyone in her residence might have used, and that a similarity in handwriting style is hardly proof that she is the author of those letters."

So now they feel that I've started something that may embarrass the college, Allan thought. Great. How do I deal with her in class until the end of the term? Is there any chance at all that I'm wrong?

As he took the pizza from the oven, he said aloud, "There's no chance that I'm wrong. Laurie wrote those letters."

Karen phoned at eight. "Darling, I've been thinking about you. How did it go?"

"Not well, I'm afraid." They talked for twenty minutes. When they finally hung up, Allan felt a lot better.

At ten-thirty the phone rang again. "I'm really okay," he said. "But, God—it's so good to finally have it out on the table. I'm going to take a sleeping pill now and go to bed. See you tomorrow." He added, "I love you."

He put the radio on the SLEEP button, tuned the dial to CBS and promptly fell asleep.

Allan Grant never heard the soft footsteps, never sensed the figure bending over him, never woke up as the knife slid through the flesh over his heart. A moment later, the sound of the flapping curtains muffled the choking gasps that escaped him as he died.

41

IT WAS the knife dream again, but this time it was different. The knife wasn't coming at her. She was holding it and moving it up and down, up and down. Laurie sat bolt upright in bed, clamping her hand over her mouth to keep from shrieking. Her hand felt sticky. Why? She looked down. Why was she still wearing jeans and her jacket? Why were they so stained?

Her left hand was touching something hard. She closed her fingers around it and a quick stab of pain raced through her hand. Warm, wet blood trickled from her palm.

She threw back the bedclothes. The carving knife was half-hidden under the pillow. Smears of dried blood covered the sheets. What had happened? When did she cut herself? Had she been bleeding that much? Not from that cut. Why had she taken the knife from the closet? Was she still dreaming? Was this part of the dream?

Don't waste a minute, a voice shouted. *Wash your hands. Wash the knife. Hide it in the closet. Do as I tell you. Hurry up. Take off your watch. The band is filthy. The bracelet in your pocket. Wash that too.*

Wash the knife. Blindly she ran into the bathroom, turned on the taps in the tub, held the knife under the gushing water.

Put it in the closet. She raced back into the bedroom. *Throw your watch in the drawer. Get those clothes off. Strip the bed. Throw everything in the tub.*

Laurie stumbled into the bathroom, flipped the handle to the shower setting and dropped the bedding into the tub. As she stripped, she flung her clothes into the water. She stared as it turned red.

She stepped into the tub. The sheets billowed around her feet. Frantically she scrubbed the stickiness from her hands and face. The cut on her palm continued to bleed even when she wrapped a washcloth around it. For long minutes she stood, eyes closed, the water cascading over her hair and face and body, shivering even as the bathroom filled with steam.

Finally she stepped out, wrapped her hair in a towel, pulled on her long terry-cloth robe and plugged the drain. She washed her clothes and the bedding until the water ran clear.

She bundled everything into a laundry bag, dressed and went down to the dryer in the basement. She waited while the dryer spun and whirled. When it clicked off, she folded the sheets and her clothing neatly and brought them back to her room.

Now remake the bed and get out of here. Be at your first class and stay calm. You're really in a mess this time. The phone's ringing. Don't answer it. It's probably Sarah.

On the walk across the campus, she met several other students, one of whom rushed to assure her that she had a real sexual harassment case, a kind of reverse one, but she ought to press it against Professor Grant. What a nerve he had to accuse her that way.

She nodded in an absent way, wondering who the little kid was who kept crying so hard, a muffled kind of crying like her head was buried in a pillow. The image came to her of a small child with long blond hair lying on a bed in a cold room. Yes, she was the one who was crying.

Laurie did not notice when the other students left her to go to their own classes. She was unaware of the stares as they glanced back at her. She did not hear one of them say, "She is really weird."

Automatically she entered the building, took the elevator to the third floor. She started down the corridor. As she passed the classroom where Allan Grant was scheduled to teach, she poked her head in the doorway. A dozen students were gathered in a circle waiting for him. "You're wasting your time," she told them. "Sexy Allan is dead as a doornail."

Part Three

42

WHEN SARAH COULD not reach Laurie in her room Wednesday morning, she called Susan Grimes again. "Please leave a note on Laurie's door to call me at the office. It's very important."

At eleven o'clock Laurie phoned from the police station.

Total numbness took over Sarah's emotions. She took precious minutes to phone Dr. Carpenter, told him what had happened, and asked him to contact Dr. Donnelly. Then she grabbed her coat and purse and rushed to the car. The hour-and-a-half-long drive to Clinton was hell.

Laurie's halting, stunned voice saying, "Sarah, Professor Grant has been found murdered. They think I did it. They arrested me and brought me to the police station. They said I could make one call."

Her only question to Laurie, "How did he die?" She'd known the answer before Laurie told her. Allan Grant had been stabbed. Oh God, merciful God, why?

Sarah arrived at the police station and was told that Laurie was being interrogated. Sarah demanded to see her.

The desk lieutenant knew Sarah was an assistant

prosecutor. He looked at her sympathetically. "Miss Kenyon, you know that the only one allowed in while she's being questioned is her lawyer."

"I'm her lawyer," Sarah said.

"You can't—"

"As of this minute, I've quit my job. You can listen while I call in my resignation."

The interrogation room was small. A video camera was filming Laurie, who was seated on a rickety wooden chair, staring into the lens. Two detectives were with her. When she saw Sarah, Laurie rushed into her arms. "Sarah, this is crazy. I'm so sorry about Professor Grant. He was so good to me. I was so angry yesterday because of those letters that he thought I'd written. Sarah, tell them to find whoever wrote them. That's the crazy person who must have killed him." She began to sob.

Sarah pressed Laurie's head against her shoulder, instinctively rocking her, vaguely realizing it was the way their mother used to comfort them when they were little.

"Sit down, Laurie," the younger detective said firmly. "She's signed a Miranda warning," he told Sarah.

Sarah eased Laurie back onto the chair. "I'm staying right here with you. I don't want you to answer any more questions now."

Laurie buried her face in her hands. Her hair fell forward.

"Miss Kenyon, may I speak with you? I'm Frank Reeves." Sarah realized that the older detective looked familiar. He had testified in one of her trials. He drew her to the side. "I'm afraid it's an open-and-shut case. She threatened Professor Grant yesterday. This morning, before his body was discovered, she announced to a roomful of students that he was dead. There was a knife that is almost certainly the murder weapon hidden in her room. She tried to wash her clothing and bedding, but there are faint bloodstains on them. The lab report will clinch it."

"Sare-wuh."

Sarah spun around. It was Laurie but it wasn't Laurie in the chair. Her expression was different, childlike. The voice was that of a three-year-old. *Sare-wuh.* That's how the toddler Laurie used to pronounce her name. "Sare-wuh, I want my teddy."

Sarah held Laurie's hand as she was arraigned on the complaint. The judge set bail at one hundred fifty thousand dollars. She promised Laurie, "I'll have you out of here in a few hours." Beyond pain, she watched a handcuffed, uncomprehending Laurie led away.

Gregg Bennett came into the courthouse as she was filling out forms for the bondsman. "Sarah."

She glanced up. He looked as shocked and heartsick as she felt. She had not seen him for months; Laurie had once seemed so happy with this nice young man.

"Sarah, Laurie would never willfully hurt anyone. Something must have snapped in her."

"I know. Insanity will be her defense. Insanity at the time of the killing." As she said the words, Sarah thought of all the defense attorneys whom she had defeated in court who had tried that strategy. It seldom worked. The best it usually did was to create enough doubt to keep the accused from the death sentence.

She realized that Gregg had put his hand on her

125

shoulder. "You look as though you could use some coffee," he told her. "Still take it black?"

"Yes."

He returned carrying two steaming Styrofoam cups as she completed the last page of the application; then he waited with her while it was processed. He's such a nice guy, Sarah thought. Why didn't Laurie fall in love with him? Why a married man? Had she chosen Allan Grant as a father substitute? As the shock wore off, she thought of Professor Grant, of how he'd rushed to be with Laurie when she fainted. Was there any chance he had led her on in subtle ways? Led her on, at a time when she was emotionally bereft? Sarah realized that possible defenses were forming in her mind.

At quarter-past six, Laurie was freed on bond. She came out of the jail accompanied by a uniformed matron. When she saw them, her knees began to buckle. Gregg rushed to catch her. Laurie moaned as he grabbed her. Then she began to shriek, "Sarah, Sarah, don't let him hurt me."

43

At eleven o'clock Wednesday morning the phone rang in the Global Travel Agency in the Madison Arms Hotel on East Seventy-sixth Street in Manhattan.

Karen Grant was on her way out the door. She

hesitated, then called over her shoulder, "If it's for me say I'll be back in ten minutes. I have to get this settled before I do anything else."

Connie Santini, the office secretary, picked up the receiver. "Global Travel Agency, good morning," she said, then listened. "Karen just stepped out. She'll be back in a few minutes." Connie's tone was brisk.

Anne Webster, owner of the agency, was standing at the file cabinet. She turned. The twenty-two-year-old Santini was a good secretary but sounded too abrupt on the telephone for Anne's taste. "Always get a name immediately," Anne would preach. "If it's a business call, always ask if someone else can help."

"Yes, I'm sure she'll be back right away," Connie was saying. "Is something wrong?"

Anne hurried over to Karen's desk, picked up the extension and nodded to Connie to hang up. "This is Anne Webster. May I help you?"

Any number of times in her sixty-nine years Anne had received bad news over the phone about a relative or friend. When this caller identified himself as Dean Larkin of Clinton College, she knew with icy certainty that something was wrong with Allan Grant. "I'm Karen's employer and friend," she told the dean. "Karen is right across the lobby in the jeweler's. I can get her for you."

She listened as Larkin hesitantly said, "Perhaps it would be wise if I tell you. I'd drive in but I'm so afraid Karen might hear about it on the radio or a reporter might phone her before I can get there . . ."

A horrified Anne Webster then heard the terrible news of Allan Grant's murder. "I'll take care of it," she said. Tears were welling in her eyes as she hung up the receiver and told the secretary what had happened. "One of Allan's students has been writing love letters to him. He turned them over to the administration. Yesterday the student made a terrible scene and threatened him. This morning when Allan was late for class, this student told everyone he was dead. They found him in bed, stabbed through the heart. Oh, poor Karen."

"She's coming," Connie said. Through the glass wall that separated the travel agency from the lobby, they could see Karen approaching. Her step was springy. A smile was playing on her lips. Her dark hair was swirling around her collar. Her Nippon suit, red with pearl buttons, enhanced her model-size figure. Obviously the errand had been a success.

Webster bit her lip nervously. How should she begin to break the news? Say there'd been an accident and wait until they were in Clinton to say more? Oh God, she prayed, give me the strength I'll need.

The door was opening. "They apologized," Karen said triumphantly. "Admitted it was their fault." Then her smile faded. "Anne, what's wrong?"

"Allan is dead." Webster could not believe she had blurted out those words.

"Allan? Dead?" Karen Grant's tone was questioning, uncomprehending. Then she repeated, "Allan. Dead."

Webster and Santini saw her complexion fade to an ashen pallor and rushed to her. Each taking an arm, they eased her into a chair. "How?" Karen asked, her voice a monotone. "The car? The brakes have been getting soft. I warned him. He's not good at taking care of things like that."

"Oh, Karen." Anne Webster put her arms around the trembling shoulders of the younger woman.

It was Connie Santini who gave what details they knew, who called the garage and told them to have Karen's car brought around immediately, who collected coats and gloves and purses. She offered to go with them and drive. It was Karen who vetoed the suggestion. The office needed to be covered.

Karen insisted on driving. "You don't know the roads, Anne." On the way down, she was tearless. She talked about Allan as though he were still alive. "He's the nicest guy in the whole world . . . He's so good . . . He's the smartest man I've ever known . . . I remember . . ."

Webster was grateful that the traffic was light. It was as though Karen were on automatic pilot. They were passing Newark Airport, going onto Route 78.

"I met Allan on a trip," Karen said. "I was leading a group to Italy. He joined it at the last minute. That was six years ago. It was over the holidays, and his mother had died that year. He told me that he realized he had no place to go for Christmas and he didn't want to stay around the college. By the time we got back to Newark Airport we were engaged. I called him my Mr. Chips."

It was a few minutes past noon when they arrived in Clinton. Karen began to sob as she saw the cordoned area around her home. "Up till this minute I thought it was a bad dream," she whispered.

A policeman stopped them at the driveway, then quickly stepped aside to let the car pass through. Cameras flashed as they got out of the car. Anne put a comforting arm around Karen as they hurried the few steps to the front door.

The house was filled with police. They were in

the living room, the kitchen, the hallway that led to the bedrooms. Karen started down the hallway. "I want to see my husband," she said.

A gray-haired man stopped her, led her into the living room. "I'm Detective Reeves," he said. "I'm very sorry, Mrs. Grant. We've taken him away. You can see him later."

Karen began to tremble. "That girl who killed him. Where is she?"

"She's under arrest."

"Why did she do this to my husband? He was so kind to her."

"She claims she's innocent, Mrs. Grant, but we found a knife that may be the murder weapon in her room."

At last the dam broke. Anne Webster had known that it would. Karen Grant let out a strangled cry that was half laugh, half sob, and became hysterical.

44

*B*IC TURNED ON the noon news as they were eating lunch in his office in the television studio on West Sixty-first Street. The breaking story was headlined: FATAL ATTRACTION MURDER AT CLINTON COLLEGE.

Opal gasped and Bic turned white as the picture of the child, Laurie, flashed on the screen. "As a four-year-old, Laurie Kenyon was the victim of an abduction. Today, at twenty-one, Kenyon is accused of stabbing to death a popular professor to whom she is alleged to have written dozens of love letters. Allan Grant was found in bed . . ."

A picture of a house flashed on the screen. The area around it was roped off. There was a shot of an open window. "It is believed that Laurie Kenyon entered and left Allan Grant's bedroom by this window." Squad cars lined the streets.

A student, her eyes popping with excitement, was interviewed. "Laurie was yelling at Professor Grant about having sex with him. I think he was trying to break off with her and she went crazy."

When the segment was over, Bic said, "Turn that off, Opal."

She obeyed.

"She gave herself to another man," Bic said. "She was creeping into his bed at night."

Opal didn't know what to do or say. Bic was trembling. His face was sweaty. He took off his jacket and rolled up his sleeves, then held out his arms. The lush curly hair on them was now steel gray. "Remember how scared she'd be when I held my arms out to her?" he asked. "But Lee knew I loved her. She's haunted me all these years. You've witnessed that, Opal. And while I suffered these last months, seeing her, being near enough to touch her, worrying that she'd talk about me to that doctor, threaten all I've worked for, she was writing filth to someone else."

His eyes were enormously wide, brilliantly bright, firing darts of lightning. Opal gave him the answer that was expected of her. "Lee should be punished, Bic."

"She will be. If the eye offends, pluck it out. If the

131

hand offends, cut it off. Lee is clearly under Satan's influence. It is my duty to send her to the healing forgiveness of the Lord by compelling her to turn the blade upon herself."

45

S*ARAH DROVE UP* the Garden State Parkway, Laurie beside her, sleeping. The matron had promised to call Dr. Carpenter and tell him they were on the way home. Gregg had thrust Laurie into Sarah's arms, protesting, "Laurie, Laurie, I'd never hurt you. I love you." Then, shaking his head, he'd said to Sarah, "I don't understand."

"I'll call you," Sarah told him hurriedly. She knew his phone number was in Laurie's address book. Last year Laurie had called Gregg regularly.

When she reached Ridgewood and turned into their street, she was dismayed to see three vans parked in front of the house. A crowd of reporters with cameras and microphones were clustered there, blocking the driveway. Sarah leaned on the horn. They let her pass but ran beside the car until it stopped at the porch steps. Laurie stirred, opened her eyes, looked around. "Sarah, why are these people here?"

To Sarah's relief, the front door opened. Dr.

Carpenter and Sophie rushed down the steps. Carpenter pushed his way through the reporters, opened the passenger door and put his arm around Laurie. Cameras flashed and questions were shouted at Laurie as he and Sophie half carried her up the steps into the house.

Sarah knew she had to make a statement. She got out of the car and waited as the microphones were thrust at her. Forcing herself to appear calm and confident, she listened to the questions: "Is this a fatal attraction murder? . . . Will you plea bargain? . . . Is it true you quit your job to defend Laurie? . . . Do you believe she's guilty?"

Sarah chose to answer the last query. "My sister is legally and morally innocent of any crime and we will prove that in court." She turned and pushed her way through the inquisitors.

Sophie was holding open the door. Laurie was lying on the couch in the den, Dr. Carpenter beside her. "I've given her a strong sedative," he whispered to Sarah. "Get her upstairs and into bed immediately. I've left a message for Dr. Donnelly. He's expected back from Australia today."

It was like dressing a doll, Sarah thought as she and Sophie pulled the sweater over Laurie's head and slipped the nightgown in its place. Laurie did not open her eyes nor seem to be aware of them. "I'll get another blanket," Sophie said quietly. "Her hands and feet are ice cold."

The first mewing sound came as Sarah was turning on the nightlight. It was a heartbroken weeping that Laurie was trying to muffle in the pillow.

"She's crying in her sleep," Sophie said. "The poor child."

That was it. If she were not looking at Laurie, Sarah would have thought the sound was coming from a frightened child. "Ask Dr. Carpenter to come up."

Her instinct was to put her arms around Laurie and comfort her, but she forced herself to wait until the doctor was in the room. He stood beside her in the dim light and studied Laurie. Then, as the sobs faded and Laurie's grip on the pillow relaxed, she began to whisper. They bent over to hear. "I want my daddy. I want my mommy. I want Sare-wuh. I want to go home."

46

THOMASINA PERKINS LIVED in a small four-room row house in Harrisburg, Pennsylvania. Now seventy-two, she was a cheerful presence whose one fault was that she loved to talk about the most exciting event of her life—her involvement in the Laurie Kenyon case. She had been the cashier who had called the police when Laurie became hysterical in the diner.

Her greatest regret was that she hadn't gotten a good look at the couple and couldn't remember what name the woman had called the man when they rushed Laurie out of the diner. Sometimes Thomasina would dream about them, especially the man, but he never had a face, just longish hair, a beard and powerful arms with a heavy growth of curly hair.

Thomasina heard about Laurie Kenyon's arrest on the six o'clock television news. That poor family, she thought sadly. All that trouble. The Kenyons had been so grateful to her. She had appeared with them on "Good Morning America" after Laurie returned home. That day John Kenyon had quietly given her a check for five thousand dollars.

Thomasina had hoped that the Kenyons would keep in touch with her. For a while she wrote regularly to them, long newsy letters describing how everyone who came into the diner wanted to hear about the case and how they'd get tears in their eyes when Thomasina described how frightened Laurie looked and how pitifully she had been crying.

Then one day she received a letter from John Kenyon. He thanked her again for her kindness but said maybe it would be better if she didn't write to them anymore. The letters upset his wife so much. They were all trying to put the memory of that terrible time behind them.

Thomasina had been intensely disappointed. She wanted so much to be invited to visit them and to be able to tell new stories about Laurie. But even though she continued to send Christmas cards every year, they never responded again.

Then she'd sent a sympathy note to Sarah and Laurie when she read about the accident in September and received a lovely note from Sarah saying her mother and father always felt that Thomasina was God's way of answering their prayers and thanking her for the fifteen happy years their family had enjoyed since Laurie's return. Thomasina framed the note and made sure any visitors became aware of it.

Thomasina loved to watch television, especially on Sunday morning. She was deeply religious, and the "Church of the Airways" was her favorite program. She'd been devoted to Reverend Rutland Garrison and was heartbroken when he died.

Reverend Bobby Hawkins was so different. Thomasina wasn't sure about him. He gave her a funny feeling. However, there was something mesmerizing about watching him and Carla together. She couldn't take her eyes off them. And he certainly was a powerful preacher.

Now Thomasina fervently wished that it was Sunday morning so that when Reverend Bobby told everyone to put their hands on the television and ask for a personal miracle, she could ask that Laurie's arrest would turn out to be a mistake. But it was Wednesday, not Sunday, and she'd have to wait the whole rest of the week.

At nine o'clock the phone rang. It was the producer of the local television show "Good Morning, Harrisburg." He apologized for the late call and asked if Thomasina would consider being on the program in the morning to talk about Laurie.

Thomasina was thrilled. "I was looking over the files of the Kenyon case, Miss Perkins," the producer said. "Boy, what a pity you couldn't remember the name of that guy who was with Laurie in the diner."

"I know," Thomasina acknowledged. "It's like it still rattles somewhere in my brain, but he's probably either dead or living in South America by now anyhow. What good would it do?"

"It would do a lot of good," the producer said.

"Your testimony is the only eyewitness proof that Laurie may have been abused by her abductors. They'll need a lot more evidence than that to create sympathy for her in court. We'll talk about it tomorrow on the program."

When she put down the phone, Thomasina sprang up and rushed into the bedroom. She reached for her best blue silk dress with the matching jacket and examined it carefully. No stains, thank heaven. She laid out her good corset, her Sunday oxfords, the pair of Alicia Pantihose from JC Penney she'd been saving for a special occasion. Since she'd stopped working she hadn't bothered putting pin curls in her hair at night, but now she carefully set every one of the thinning strands.

Just as she was about to get into bed, Reverend Bobby's advice to pray for a miracle flashed into her mind.

Thomasina's niece had given her lavender stationery for Christmas. She got it out and searched for the new Bic pen she'd bought at the supermarket. Settling at the dinette table she wrote a long letter to Reverend Bobby Hawkins telling him all about her involvement with Laurie Kenyon. She explained that years ago she had refused to undergo hypnosis to help her remember the name the woman had called the man. She'd always believed that to go under hypnosis meant that you were putting your soul in the power of another, and that it would be displeasing to God. What did Reverend Bobby think? She'd be guided by him. Please write soon.

She wrote a second letter to Sarah, explaining what she was doing.

As an afterthought, she enclosed an offering of two dollars in Reverend Bobby Hawkins's envelope.

47

$D_{R.}$ *JUSTIN DONNELLY* had gone home to Australia for Christmas vacation, with plans to stay a month. It was summer there and for those four weeks he visited his family, saw his friends, caught up with his old colleagues and reveled in the chance to unwind.

He also spent a great deal of time with Pamela Crabtree. Two years ago, when he'd left for the United States, they'd been close to making a commitment but agreed neither was ready. Pamela had her own career as a neurologist and was developing a considerable reputation in Sydney.

Over the holiday season they dined together, sailed together, went to the theater together. But as much as he'd always looked forward to being with Pamela, as much as he admired her and enjoyed her company, Justin sensed a vague feeling of dissatisfaction. Perhaps there were more than professional conflicts holding them back.

Justin's gnawing sense of unease gradually centered on the realization that he was thinking more and more of Sarah Kenyon. He'd only seen her that one time in October, yet he missed their weekly conversations. He wished he hadn't been so reluctant to suggest that they have dinner together again.

Shortly before he returned to New York, Pamela and he talked it through and agreed that whatever had been between them was over. With a vast sense of relief, Justin Donnelly boarded the plane to New York, arriving exhausted from the long trip at noon on Wednesday. When he got to the apartment he fell into bed and slept until ten o'clock, then checked his messages.

Five minutes later he was on the phone to Sarah. The sound of her voice, tired and strained, tore at his gut. Dismayed, he listened as she told him what had happened. "You must get Laurie in to see me," he told her. "Tomorrow I've got to sort out things in the clinic. Friday morning at ten?"

"She won't want to come."

"She has to."

"I know." There was a pause, then Sarah said, "I'm so glad you're back, Dr. Donnelly."

So am I, Justin thought as he replaced the receiver. He knew Sarah had not yet fully absorbed the ordeal she was facing. Laurie had committed murder in one of her altered states, and that might put the persona who was Laurie Kenyon already beyond his help.

48

*B*RENDON MOODY returned to Teaneck, New Jersey, late Wednesday night from a week of fishing with his buddies in Florida. His wife, Betty, was waiting up for him. She told him about Laurie Kenyon's arrest.

Laurie Kenyon! Brendon had been a detective with the Bergen County prosecutor's office seventeen years ago when four-year-old Laurie disappeared. Until his retirement, he'd been on the homicide squad there and knew Sarah very well. Shaking his head, he turned on the eleven o'clock news. The campus murder was the main story. The segment included shots of Allan Grant's home, Grant's widow being escorted into the house, Laurie and Sarah emerging from the police station, Sarah making a statement in front of the Kenyons' Ridgewood house.

With growing dismay, Brendon watched and listened. When the report was over, he snapped off the set. "That's a tough one," he said.

Thirty years ago, when Brendon was courting Betty, her father had said derisively, "That little bantam thinks he's the cock of the walk." There was an element of truth in the remark. Betty always felt that when Brendon was upset or angry, a certain electricity went through him. His chin went up; his thinning gray hair became tousled; his cheeks became flushed; his eyes behind rimless glasses seemed magnified.

At sixty Brendon had lost none of the feisty energy that had made him the top investigator in the prosecutor's office. In three days they were supposed to visit Betty's sister in Charleston. Knowing that she was giving him carte blanche to beg off from the trip, she said, "Isn't there something you can do?" Brendon was now a licensed private investigator, taking only cases that interested him.

Brendon's smile was both grim and relieved. "You bet there is. Sarah needs to have someone down on that campus gathering and sifting every possible tidbit of information she can get. This looks like an open-and-shut case. Bets, you've heard me say it a thousand times and I'll say it again. When you go in with that attitude the only thing you can hope for is a few years off the sentence. You gotta go in believing your client is as innocent as the babe in the manger. That's how you find extenuating circumstances. Sarah Kenyon is a hell of a nice woman and a hell of a good lawyer. I always predicted she'd have a gavel in her hand someday. But she needs help now. Real help. Tomorrow I go see her and sign on."

"If she'll have you," Betty suggested mildly.

"She'll have me. And Bets, you know how you hate the cold. Why don't you go down to Charleston and visit Jane on your own?"

Betty untied her robe and got into bed. "I might just as well. From now on, knowing you, you'll be eating, sleeping and dreaming this case."

49

"CARLA, describe Lee's bedroom in detail to me."

Opal was holding the coffeepot, about to pour coffee for Bic. She paused then carefully tilted the spigot over his cup. "Why?"

"I have many times warned you not to question my requests." The voice was gentle, but Opal shivered.

"I'm sorry. You just surprised me." She looked across the table, trying to smile. "You look so handsome in that velvet jacket, Bobby. Now let's see. Like I told you, her room and her sister's room are on the right side of the staircase. The real estate agent said that the Kenyons turned smaller rooms into baths, so the four bedrooms each have a bath. Lee's room has a double bed with a velvet headboard, a dresser, desk, a standing bookcase, night tables and a slipper chair. It's very feminine, blue-and-white flowered pattern on the spread and headboard and draperies. Two nice-sized closets, cross ventilation, pale blue carpet."

She could tell he was not yet satisfied and narrowed her eyes in concentration. "Oh yes, there are family pictures on her desk and a telephone on the night table."

"Is there a picture of Lee as a child in the pink bathing suit she was wearing when she joined us?"

"I think so."

"You think so?"

"I'm sure there is."

"You're forgetting something, Carla. Last time we discussed this, you told me that there was a stack of family albums on the bottom shelf of the bookcase and it looked as though Lee might have been going through them or perhaps was rearranging them. There appeared to be a great many loose pictures of Lee and her sister as young children."

"Yes. That's right." Opal sipped her coffee nervously. A few minutes ago she'd been telling herself that everything would be all right. She'd been reveling in the luxury of the pretty sitting room of their hotel suite, enjoying the feel of her new brushed-velvet Dior robe. She looked up and her gaze met Bic's stare. His eyes were flashing, messianic. With a sinking heart she knew he was going to demand something dangerous of her.

50

AT QUARTER of twelve on Thursday Laurie awakened from her sedated sleep. She opened her eyes and looked around the familiar room. A bewildering cacophony of thoughts shouted through her mind. Somewhere a child was crying. Two women in her head were screaming at each other. One of them was yelling, *I was mad at him but I loved him and I didn't want that to happen.*

The other was saying, *I told you to stay home that night. You fool. Look what you've done to her.*

I didn't tell everybody that he was dead. You're the fool.

Laurie pressed both hands to her ears. Oh God, had she dreamt it all? Was Allan Grant really dead? Could anyone believe that she had hurt him? The police station. That cell. Those cameras taking her picture. It hadn't happened to her, had it? Where was Sarah? She got out of bed and ran to the door. "Sarah! Sarah!"

"She'll be back soon." It was Sophie's familiar

voice, reassuring, soothing. Sophie was coming up the stairs. "How do you feel?"

Relief flowed through Laurie. The voices in her head stopped quarreling. "Oh, Sophie. I'm glad you're here. Where's Sarah?"

"She had to go to her office. She'll be back in a couple of hours. I have a nice lunch all fixed for you, consommé and tuna salad just the way you like it."

"Just the consommé, Sophie. I'll be down in ten minutes."

She went into the bathroom and turned on the shower. Yesterday she had washed sheets and clothes while she showered. What a strange thing to do. She adjusted the shower head until the hot water was a needle-sharp waterfall massaging the knotted muscles in her neck and shoulders. The groggy headache brought on by the sedatives began to clear and the enormity of what had happened started to sink in. Allan Grant, that lovely, warm human being had been murdered with the missing knife.

Sarah asked me if I had taken the knife, Laurie thought as she turned off the taps and stepped from the shower. She wrapped one of the giant bath towels around her body. Then I found the knife in my tote bag. Somebody must have taken it from my room, the same person who wrote those disgusting letters.

She wondered why she didn't feel more emotion for Allan Grant. He had been so kind to her. When she opened the closet door, trying to decide what to wear, she thought she understood. The shelves of sweaters. Mother had been with her when she bought most of them.

Mother, whose joy was to give and give. Daddy's

mock dismay when they arrived home with the packages. "I'm subsidizing the entire retail business."

Laurie wiped tears from her eyes as she dressed in jeans and a pullover. After you've lost two people like them, you haven't much grief left for anyone else.

She stood in front of the mirror, brushing her hair. It really needed a trim. But she couldn't make an appointment today. People would be staring at her, whispering about her. But I didn't do anything, she protested to her reflection in the mirror. Again a sharp, focused memory of Mother. How many times had she said, "Oh, Laurie, you look so like me when I was your age."

But Mother had never had that anxious, frightened look in her eyes. Mother's lips always curved in a smile. Mother made people happy. She didn't cause trouble and pain for everyone.

Hey, why should you take all the blame, a voice sneered. *Karen Grant didn't want Allan. She kept making excuses to stay in New York. He was lonesome. He had pizza for dinner half the time. He needed me. It was just that he didn't know it yet. I hate Karen. I wish she was dead.*

Laurie went over to the desk.

Minutes later, Sophie knocked and called in a worried voice, "Laurie, lunch is ready. Are you all right?"

"Will you please leave me alone? The damn consommé won't evaporate will it?" Irritated, she finished folding the letter she'd just written and inserted it in an envelope.

The mailman came around twelve-thirty. She watched from the window until he started up the walk, then hurried downstairs and opened the door as he reached the porch.

"I'll take it and here's one for you."

As Laurie closed the door, Sophie rushed from the kitchen. "Laurie, Sarah doesn't want you to go out."

"I'm not going out, silly. I just picked up the mail." Laurie put her hand on Sophie's arm. "Sophie, you'll stay with me until Sarah comes back, won't you? I don't want to be alone here."

51

EARLY WEDNESDAY evening a pale but composed Karen Grant drove back to New York with her partner, Anne Webster. "I'm better off in the city," she said. "I couldn't bear to stay in the house."

Webster offered to stay overnight, but Karen refused. "You look more exhausted than I am. I'm going to take a sleeping pill and go right to bed."

She slept long and deeply. It was nearly eleven when she awakened on Thursday morning. The three top floors of the hotel were residential apartments. In the three years she'd had her apartment, Karen had gradually added touches of her own: Oriental scatter rugs in tones of cardinal red, ivory and blue that transformed the bland off-white hotel carpeting; antique lamps; silk pillows; Lalique figurines; original paintings by promising new artists.

The effect was charming and luxurious and personal. Yet Karen loved the amenities of hotel living, especially the room service and maid service. She also loved the closet full of designer clothes, the Charles Jourdan and Ferragamo shoes, the Hermès scarves, the Gucci handbags. It was such a satisfying feeling to know that the uniformed desk clerks were always watching to see what she'd be wearing when she stepped off the elevator.

She got up and went into the bathroom. The thick terry-cloth robe that enveloped her from neck to toe was on the hook there. She pulled the belt tightly around her waist and studied herself in the mirror. Eyes still swollen a bit. Seeing Allan on that slab in the morgue had been awful. In one rush she'd thought of all the marvelous times they'd had together, of the way she used to thrill to the sound of his footsteps coming down the hall. The tears had been genuine. There would be more weeping when she looked at his face for the last time. Which reminded her, she'd have to make the necessary arrangements. Not now, however; now she wanted breakfast.

On the telephone, she pressed 4 for room service. Lilly was taking orders. "I'm so sorry, Mrs. Grant," she said. "We're all just shocked."

"Thank you." Karen ordered her usual: fresh juice, fruit compote, coffee, hard roll. "Oh, and send all the morning papers."

"Of course."

She was sipping the first cup of coffee when there was a discreet knock on the door. She flew to open it. Edwin was there, his handsome patrician features set in an expression of solicitous concern. "Oh, my dear," he sighed.

His arms closed around her, and Karen laid her face against the soft cashmere jacket she had given him for Christmas. Then she clasped her hands around his neck, careful not to dishevel his precisely combed dark blond hair.

52

JUSTIN DONNELLY met Laurie on Friday morning. He had seen newspaper pictures of her but still was not prepared for her striking good looks. Breathtaking blue eyes, shoulder-length golden blond hair that made him think of an illustration of a princess in a fairy tale. She was dressed simply in dark blue slacks, a white high-necked silk blouse and a blue-and-white jacket. There was an innate elegance despite the palpable fear he could sense emanating from her.

Sarah was sitting near her sister, but a little in back of her. Laurie had refused to come into the office alone. "I promised Sarah I'd talk to you, but I cannot do it without her."

Perhaps it was Sarah's reassuring presence, but even so, Justin was surprised to hear Laurie's direct question. "Dr. Donnelly, do you think I killed Professor Allan Grant?"

"Do you think I have reason to believe that?"

"I would guess that everyone has good reason to suspect me. I quite simply did not and would not kill any human being. The fact that Allan Grant could possibly link me to the sort of anonymous trash he'd received was humiliating. But we don't kill because someone misreads a nasty situation."

"*We*, Laurie?"

Was it embarrassment or guilt that flickered in her expression for a fleeting moment? When she did not answer, Justin said, "Laurie, Sarah has talked with you about the serious charges against you. Do you understand what they are?"

"Certainly. They're absurd, but I haven't listened to my father and Sarah talk about the cases she was prosecuting or the sentences the defendants got without knowing what this can mean."

"It would be pretty reasonable to be frightened of what's ahead for you, Laurie."

Her head went down. Her hair fell forward, shielding her face. Her shoulders rounded. She clasped her hands in her lap and drew up her feet so that they did not touch the floor but dangled above it. The soft weeping that Sarah had heard several times in the last few days began again. Instinctively, Sarah reached out to comfort Laurie, but Justin Donnelly shook his head. "You're so scared, aren't you, Laurie," he commented kindly.

She shook her head from side to side.

"You're not scared?"

Her head bobbed up and down. Then between sobs she said, "Not Laurie."

"You're not Laurie. Will you tell me your name?"

"Debbie."

"Debbie. What a pretty name. How old are you, Debbie?"

"I'm four."

Dear God, Sarah thought as she listened to Dr. Donnelly talking to Laurie as though he were speaking to a little child. He is right. Something terrible must have happened to her in those two years she was gone. Poor Mother, always determined to believe that some child-hungry couple took her and loved her. I knew there was a difference when she came home. If she had had help back then, would we be here now? Suppose Laurie has a totally separate personality that wrote those letters and then killed Allan Grant? Should I let him get to it? Suppose she confesses? What was Donnelly asking Laurie now?

"Debbie, you're very tired aren't you?"

"Yes."

"Would you like to go to your room and rest? I'll bet you have a pretty bedroom."

"No! No! No!"

"That's all right. You can stay right here. Why don't you nap sitting in that chair, and if Laurie's around will you ask her to come back and talk to me?"

Her breathing became even. A moment later she lifted her head. Her shoulders straightened. Her feet touched the floor and she brushed her hair back. "Of course I'm frightened," Laurie told Justin Donnelly, "but since I had nothing to do with Allan's death, I know I can count on Sarah to find the truth." She turned, smiled at Sarah and then looked directly at the doctor again. "If I were Sarah, I'd wish I'd stayed an only child. But here I am, and she's always been there for me. She's always understood."

"Understood what, Laurie?"

She shrugged. "I don't know."

"I think you do."

"I really don't."

Justin knew it was time to tell Laurie what Sarah already knew. Something terrible had happened during the two years that she had been missing, something so overwhelming that as a little child she could not handle it alone. Others came to help her, maybe one or two, maybe more, and she had become in effect a multiple personality. When she was returned home, the loving environment had made it unnecessary for the alter personalities to come forward except perhaps very occasionally. The death of her parents had been so painful that the alters were needed again.

Laurie listened quietly. "What kind of treatment are you talking about?"

"Hypnosis. I'd like to videotape you during the sessions."

"Suppose I confess that some part of me . . . some person, if you will—*did* kill Allan Grant? What then?"

It was Sarah's turn to answer. "Laurie, I'm very much afraid that as it stands a jury will almost inevitably convict you. Our only hope is to prove extenuating circumstances or that you were incapable of knowing the nature of the crime."

"I see. So it is possible that I killed Allan, that I wrote those letters? Not just possible. Probable. Sarah, have there been other people who claimed multiple personality as a defense against a murder charge?"

"Yes."

"How many of them got off?"

Sarah did not answer.

"How many of them, Sarah?" Laurie persisted. "One? Two? None? That's it, isn't it? Not one of them got off. Oh my God. Well, let's go ahead. We might as well know the truth even though it's very clear the truth won't set me free."

She seemed to be fighting back tears, then her voice became strident, angry. "Just one thing, Doctor. Sarah stays with me. I will *not* be alone with you in a room with a closed door and I will not lie on that couch. Got it?"

"Laurie, I'll do anything I can to make this easier for you. You're a very nice person who's had a very bad break."

She laughed, a jeering laugh. "What's nice about that stupid wimp? She's never done anything but cause trouble since the day she was born."

"Laurie," Sarah protested.

"I think Laurie's gone away again," Justin said calmly. "Am I right?"

"You're right. I've got my hands full with her."

"What is your name?"

"Kate."

"How old are you, Kate?"

"Thirty-three. Listen, I didn't mean to come out. I just wanted to warn you. Don't think you're going to hypnotize Laurie and get her to talk about those two years. You're wasting your time. See you."

There was a pause. Then Laurie sighed wearily. "Would it be all right if we stopped talking now? I have such a headache."

53

ON FRIDAY morning, Betsy Lyons received a firm offer of five hundred and seventy-five thousand dollars for the Kenyon home from the couple who wanted to move in quickly because the wife was expecting a baby. She called Sarah but could not reach her until the afternoon. To her dismay, Sarah told her the house was off the market. Sarah was sympathetic but firm. "I'm terribly sorry, Mrs. Lyons. First of all I wouldn't entertain an offer that low, but anyhow there is no way I can worry about moving at this time. I know how much work you've put into this sale, but you do understand."

Betsy Lyons did understand. On the other hand the real estate business was desperately slow and she was counting on the commission.

"I'm sorry," Sarah repeated, "but I can't see planning to leave this house before fall at the earliest. Now I do have someone here. I'll talk to you another time."

She was in the library with Brendon Moody. "I had decided it would be a good idea if Laurie and I moved to a condominium," she explained to the detective, "but under the circumstances . . ."

"Absolutely," Brendon agreed. "You're better to take the place off the market. Once this case comes to trial, you'll have reporters posing as potential buyers just to get a look inside."

"I never thought of that," Sarah confessed. Wearily she pushed back a strand of hair that had fallen on her forehead. "Brendon, I can't tell you how glad I am that you want to take on this investigation." She had just finished telling him everything, including what had happened during the session with Laurie at Justin Donnelly's office.

Moody had been taking notes. His high forehead puckered in concentration, his rimless glasses magnifying his snapping brown eyes, his precise bow tie and conservative dark brown suit gave him the air of a meticulous auditor. It was an image that Sarah knew was both accurate and dependable. When he was conducting an investigation, Brendon Moody missed nothing.

She waited while he reread his notes carefully. It was a familiar procedure. That was the way they had worked together in the prosecutor's office. She heard Sophie going up the stairs. Good. She was checking on Laurie again.

Sarah thought back for a moment to the drive home from Dr. Donnelly's office. Laurie had been deeply despondent, saying, "Sarah, I wish I had been in my car when that bus hit it. Mom and Dad would still be alive. You'd be working at the job you love. I'm a pariah, a jinx."

"No, you're not," Sarah had told her. "You were a four-year-old kid who had the hard luck to get kidnapped and be treated God only knows how badly. You're a twenty-one-year-old who's in a hell of a mess through no fault of her own, so stop blaming yourself!"

Then it was Sarah's turn to cry. Blinding tears

obscured her vision. Frantically she wiped them away, trying to focus on the heavy Route 17 traffic.

Now she reflected that in a way her outburst might have been a blessing in disguise. A shocked, contrite Laurie had said, "Sarah, I'm so damn selfish. Tell me what you want me to do."

She'd answered, "Do exactly what Dr. Donnelly asks. Keep a journal. That will help him. Stop fighting him. Cooperate with the hypnosis."

"All right, I think I have everything," Moody said briskly, breaking Sarah's reverie. "I have to agree. The *physical aspects* are pretty cut and dried."

It gave Sarah a lift to hear him accentuate "physical aspects." Clearly he understood where the defense was heading.

"You're going for stress, diminished mental capacity?" he asked.

"Yes." She waited.

"What kind of fellow was this Grant guy? He was married. Why wasn't his wife home that night?"

"She works for a travel agency in New York and apparently stays in the city during the week."

"Don't they have travel agencies in New Jersey?"

"I would think so."

"Any chance that the professor was the kind who compensated for the absence of his wife by leading on his students?"

"We're on the same wavelength." Suddenly the library, with its cheery mahogany bookcases, family pictures, paintings, blue Oriental rug, butter-soft leather couches and chairs, assumed the electric atmosphere of the stuffy cubicle that had been her domain in the prosecutor's office. Her father's antique English desk became the battered, shabby relic she'd worked at for nearly five years. "There's a recent case where a defendant was convicted of raping a twelve-year-old," she told Moody.

"I would hope so," he said.

"The legal issue was that the victim is chronologically twenty-seven years old. She suffers from multiple personality disorder and convinced a jury that she'd been violated when she was in her twelve-year-old persona and not capable of giving informed consent. He was found guilty of statutory rape of a person who was found to be mentally defective. The verdict was overturned on appeal, but the point is, a jury believed the testimony of a woman with multiple personality disorder."

Moody leaned forward with the swiftness of a hound catching its first scent of the prey. "You're talking about turning it around."

"Yes. Allan Grant was particularly solicitous of Laurie. When she fainted in church at the funeral mass, he rushed to be with her. He offered to take her home and stay with her. Looking back, I wonder if that wasn't pretty unusual concern." She sighed. "At least it's a starting point. We don't have much else."

"It's a good starting point," Moody said decisively. "I've got a few things to clear up, then I'll get down to Clinton and start digging."

The phone rang again. "Sophie will get it," Sarah said. "Bless her. She's moved in with us. Says we can't be alone. Now let's settle the terms . . ."

"Oh, we'll talk about that later."

"No, we won't," she said firmly. "I know you, Brendon Moody."

Sophie tapped on the door, then opened it. "I'm sorry to interrupt, Sarah, but that real estate agent is on the phone again and she says it's very important."

Sarah picked up the receiver, greeted Betsy Lyons, then listened. Finally she said slowly, "I suppose I owe this to you, Mrs. Lyons. But I have to be clear. That woman cannot keep looking at the house. We'll be out on Monday morning and you can bring her in between ten o'clock and one o'clock, but that is it."

When Sarah hung up she explained to Brendon Moody. "There's a prospective buyer who's been hemming and hawing about this place. Apparently she's pretty much decided on it at full price. She wants one more walk through and then indicates she'll be willing to wait to occupy it until it's available. She'll be here on Monday."

54

THE FUNERAL SERVICE for Professor Allan Grant was held on Saturday morning at St. Luke's Episcopal Church near the Clinton campus. Faculty members and students crowded together to pay their final respects to the popular teacher. The rector's homily spoke of Allan's intellect, warmth and generosity. "He was an outstanding educator . . . That smile would brighten the darkest day . . . He made people feel good about themselves . . .

He could sense when someone was having a tough time. Somehow he found a way to help."

Brendon Moody was at the service in the capacity of observer, not mourner. He was especially interested in studying Allan Grant's widow, who was wearing a deceptively simple black suit with a string of pearls. Somewhat to his surprise, Brendon had developed over the years a reasonably accurate sense of fashion. On a faculty salary, even with her travel agent job thrown in, Karen Grant would find it pretty tough to buy designer clothes. Did either she or Grant have family money? It was raw and windy out and she had not elected to wear a coat into church. That meant she must have left one in the car. The cemetery would be a damn cold place on a day like this.

She was weeping as she followed the casket from the church. Good-looking woman, Brendon thought. He was surprised to see the president of the college and his wife accompany Karen Grant into the first limousine. No family member? No close friend? Brendon decided to continue to pay his respects. He'd go to the burial service.

His question about Karen's coat was answered there. She emerged from the limousine wearing a full-length Blackglama mink.

55

THE CHURCH of the Airways had a twelve-member council that met on the first Saturday of the month. Not all of the members approved of the rapid changes the Reverend Bobby Hawkins was instituting on the religious hour. The Well of Miracles particularly was anathema to the senior member of the council.

Viewers were invited to write in explaining their need for a miracle. The letters were placed in the well, and just before the final hymn, Reverend Hawkins extended his hands over it and emotionally prayed that the requests be granted. Sometimes he invited a member of the studio congregation who was in need of a miracle to come up for a special blessing.

"Rutland Garrison must be spinning in his grave," the senior member told Bic at the monthly council meeting.

Bic eyed him coldly. "Have the donations increased substantially?"

"Yes, but—"

"But *what?* More money for the hospital and the retirement home, more for the South American orphanages that have always been my personal charity, more of the faithful voicing their needs to the Lord."

He looked around the table from one member to the other. "When I accepted this ministry I said that I must steer it into wider waters. I've studied the records. In the past several years donations have been steadily decreasing. Isn't that true?"

There was no answer.

"Isn't that true?" he thundered.

Heads nodded.

"Very well. Then I suggest that he who is not with me is against me and ought to resign from this august body. The meeting is adjourned."

He strode from the conference room and down the corridor into his private office where Opal was going through the Well of Miracles mail. Her system was to glance at the requests and separate any unusual ones for Bic to possibly read aloud on the program. The letters were then dropped in one pile to be placed in the Well of Miracles. The donations were in another pile for Bic to tabulate.

Opal dreaded having to show him one letter she had put aside.

"They're seeing the light, Carla," he informed her. "They're coming to understand that my way is the Lord's way."

"Bic," she said timidly.

He frowned. "In this office you must never—"

"I know. I'm sorry. It's just . . . Read this." She thrust Thomasina Perkins' rambling letter into his outstretched hand.

56

AFTER THE FUNERAL, Karen and the faculty members went to the home of the president of the college where a buffet luncheon was waiting. Dean Walter Larkin told Karen that he could not forgive himself for not realizing how sick Laurie Kenyon was. "Dr. Iovino, the Director of the Counseling Center, feels the same way."

"What has happened is a tragedy, and there's no use trying to place blame on ourselves or others," Karen said quietly. "I ought to have persuaded Allan to show those letters to the administration even before he was sure Laurie was writing them. Allan himself ought not to have left that bedroom window wide open. I should hate that girl, but all I can remember is how sorry Allan felt for her."

Walter Larkin had always thought that Karen was something of a cold fish but now he wondered if he'd been unfair. The tears in her eyes and her quivering lip certainly weren't faked.

At breakfast the next morning, he commented on that to his wife, Louise. "Oh, don't be such a romantic, Walter," she told him crisply. "Karen was bored stiff with campus life and faculty teas. She'd have been gone long ago if Allan hadn't been so generous with her. Look at the clothes she wears!

You know what I think? Allan was finally waking up to the truth about the woman he was married to. I bet he wouldn't have put up with it much longer. That poor Kenyon girl gave Karen a one-way, first-class ticket to New York."

57

OPAL APPEARED at the real estate office promptly at ten o'clock on Monday morning. Betsy Lyons was waiting for her. "Mrs. Hawkins," she said, "I'm afraid that this will be the only time I can bring you to the Kenyon house, so please, try to make a note of anything you want to see or ask about."

It was the opening Opal needed. Bic had told her to try to pump the real estate agent for any information about the case. "That family has so much tragedy." She sighed. "How is that poor girl?"

Betsy Lyons was relieved to see that Carla Hawkins did not seem to be linking the house to the shocking headlines of Laurie Kenyon's arrest on the murder charge. She rewarded her by being less closemouthed than usual. "As you can imagine, the whole town is buzzing. Everyone feels so sorry for them. My husband is a lawyer, and he says they'll have to go with a diminished capacity defense but it will be hard to prove. Laurie Kenyon never acted odd or crazy in all the years I've known her. Now we'd better be on our way."

Opal was quiet on the drive to the house. Suppose leaving this picture of Lee backfired and gave her a flash of memory? But even if it did, it would remind her of Bic's threat.

Bic had been pretty scary that day. He'd encouraged Lee to really love that silly chicken. Lee's eyes, usually downcast and sad, would brighten when she went in the backyard. She'd rush over to the chicken, put her arms around it and hug it. Bic had taken the butcher knife from the kitchen drawer and winked at Opal. "Watch this performance," he'd said.

He'd run outside, slashing the knife back and forth in front of Lee. She'd been terrified and hugged the chicken tighter. Then he'd reached down and grabbed it by the neck. It began to squawk, and Lee in an unusual show of courage tried to pull it from Bic. He'd slapped her so hard she fell backwards, then as she scrambled to her feet, he'd lifted his arm and swung it in an arc, cutting that chicken's head off in one blow.

Opal had felt her own blood go cold as he threw the body of the chicken at Lee's feet where it flapped around spattering her with blood. Then Bic had held up the head of the dead creature and pointed the knife at Lee's throat, chopping the air with it, his eyes fearsome and glittering. In a terrible voice, he'd sworn that that's what would happen to her if she ever talked about them. Bic was right. A reminder of that day would shut Lee up or drive her completely crazy.

Betsy Lyons was not displeased by her passenger's silence. It was her experience that when people were about to commit themselves to a purchase, they tended to become serious and introspective. It was a worry that Carla Hawkins had not brought her husband to see the house at least once though. As she steered the car into the Kenyon driveway, Betsy asked about that.

"My husband is leaving the decision entirely up to me," Opal said calmly. "He trusts my judgment. I know exactly what will make him happy."

"That's a compliment to you," Betsy assured her with fervent haste.

Lyons was about to insert the key in the lock when the door opened. Opal was dismayed to see the stocky figure in the dark skirt and cardigan who was introduced as the housekeeper, Sophie Perosky. If the woman trailed around the house with them, Opal might not be able to plant the picture.

But Sophie stayed in the kitchen, and planting the photo was easier than Opal expected. In every room, she stood by the windows to observe the view. "My husband asked me to be sure that we're not too near any other houses," she explained. In Lee's room, she spotted a spiral notebook on the desk. The cover was partially raised and the tip of a pen could be seen protruding from under it. "What are the exact dimensions of this room?" she asked as she leaned over the desk to look out the window.

As she had expected, Betsy Lyons fished in her briefcase for the house plan. Opal glanced down swiftly and flipped open the notebook. Just the first three or four pages had writing on them. The words "Dr. Donnelly wants me . . ." jumped out at her. Lee must be keeping a journal. With all her being, Opal wished she could read the entry.

It took only an instant to take the picture from her pocket and slip it about twenty pages back in the book. It was the photo Bic had taken of Lee that first day, just after they reached the farm. Lee had been standing in front of the big tree, shivering in her pink bathing suit, crying, hugging herself tightly.

Bic had cut Lee's head from the picture and stapled the fragment to the bottom. Now the picture showed Lee's face, eyes puffy with tears, hair tangled, staring up at her own decapitated body.

"You really do have a great deal of privacy from the other houses," Opal commented as Betsy Lyons announced that the room was twelve by eighteen feet, really a wonderful size for a bedroom.

58

*J*USTIN DONNELLY had arranged his schedule so that he could see Laurie every morning, Monday to Friday, at ten o'clock. He'd also set up appointments for her with the art and journal therapists. On Friday he had given her a half-dozen books on multiple personality disorder.

"Laurie," he'd said, "I want you to read these and understand that most of the patients with your problem are women who were abused as children. They blocked out what happened to them just as you're blocking it out. I think that the personalities who helped you to cope those two years you were missing were just about dormant until you lost your parents. Now they've come back in full force. When you read these books, you're going to see that alter personalities are often trying to help you, not hurt you. That's why I hope you'll do your best to consciously let me talk to them."

On Monday morning he had his video camera set up in his office. He knew that if Sarah decided to use any of the tapes at the trial, he had to be extremely careful not to look as though he was putting words in Laurie's mouth.

When Sarah and Laurie came in, he showed them the camera, explained that he was going to record the sessions and told Laurie, "After a while I'll play them back for you." Then he hypnotized her for the first time. Clinging to Sarah's hand, Laurie obediently riveted her attention on him, listened as he urged her to relax, closed her eyes, visibly settled back, let her hand slip from her sister's.

"How do you feel, Laurie?"

"Sad."

"Why are you sad, Laurie?"

"I'm always sad." Her voice was higher, hesitant, with a trace of a lisp.

Sarah watched as Laurie's hair fell forward, as her features seemed to become fluid and change until a childlike expression came over them. She listened as Justin Donnelly said, "I think I'm talking to Debbie. Am I right?"

He was rewarded by a shy nod.

"Why are you sad, Debbie?"

"Sometimes I do bad things."

"Like what, Debbie?"

"Leave that kid alone! She doesn't know what she's talking about."

Sarah bit her lip. The angry voice she'd heard on Friday. Justin Donnelly did not seem perturbed. "Kate, is that you?"

"You know it's me."

"Kate, I don't want to hurt Laurie or Debbie. They've been hurt enough. If you want to help them, why don't you trust me?"

An angry, bitter laugh preceded the statement that chilled Sarah. "We can't trust any man. Look at Allan Grant. He acted so nice to Laurie, and look at the fix he put her in. Good riddance to him, I say."

"You don't mean that you're glad he's dead?"

"I wish he'd never been born."

"Do you want to talk about that, Kate?"

"No, I don't."

"Would you write about it in your journal?"

"I was going to write this morning but that stupid kid had the book. She can't spell worth a damn."

"Do you remember what you were going to write about?"

A derisive laugh. "It's what I'm *not* going to write that would interest you."

On the way home in the car, Laurie was again visibly exhausted. Sophie had lunch waiting, and after Laurie picked at it she decided to lie down.

Sarah settled at the desk and went through her messages. The grand jury would consider the complaint against Laurie on Monday the seventeenth. That was only two weeks away. If the prosecutor was convening the jury that fast, he must be convinced he had a very strong case already. As indeed he did.

A stack of mail had piled up on her desk. She scanned the envelopes, not bothering to open any until she came to the one with the carefully printed return address in the corner. Thomasina Perkins! She was the cashier who long ago had spotted Laurie in the restaurant. Sarah could remember how her father's heartfelt gratitude to the woman had eroded when her frequent letters arrived, filled with increasingly lurid memories of the trauma Laurie exhibited in the restaurant. But there was no doubt Thomasina Perkins meant well. She had written a very kind note in September. This was probably another expression of sympathy. Sarah slit the envelope and read the single sheet of paper. In it, Perkins had given her phone number. Sarah dialed rapidly.

Thomasina picked up on the first ring. She was thrilled to realize it was Sarah calling. "Oh, wait till I tell you my news," she bubbled. "Reverend Bobby Hawkins phoned me himself. He doesn't believe in hypnosis. He invited me to be a guest on next Sunday's program. He's going to pray over me so that God will whisper in my ear the name of that terrible man who kidnapped Laurie."

59

REVEREND BOBBY HAWKINS skillfully turned the Thomasina Perkins problem into a potential advantage. A trusted staff member was instantly sent to Harrisburg to check on her. It was a reasonable thing to do. The Reverend Hawkins and the council needed to be sure there was no investigative reporter putting her up to writing the letter. Bic also wanted details of Thomasina's health, particularly her hearing and vision.

The results of the probe were gratifying. Thomasina wore trifocals and had been operated on for cataracts. Her description of the two people she'd seen with Laurie had been vague from the beginning.

"She clearly doesn't recognize us on the TV screen and won't in person," Bic told Opal as he read the report. "She'll be an inspiration to our congregation."

The following Sunday morning, a delighted Thomasina, her hands clasped together in the attitude of prayer, gazed worshipfully up into Bic's face. He laid his hands on her shoulders. "Years ago, this good woman brought about a miracle when the Lord gifted her with the ability to see that a child was in need. But the Lord did not grant

Thomasina the ability to remember the name of the villainous man who was accompanying Laurie Kenyon. Now Lee is in need again. Thomasina, I command you to listen and remember the name that has been drifting in your unconscious all these years."

Thomasina could hardly contain herself. Here she was, a celebrity on international television; there was no way she could fail to obey Reverend Bobby's command. She strained her ears. The organ was playing softly. From somewhere she heard a whisper: "Jim . . . Jim . . . Jim . . ."

Thomasina straightened her shoulders, threw out her arms and cried, "The name I have been seeking is Jim!"

60

*S*ARAH HAD TOLD Justin Donnelly about Thomasina Perkins and the reason for her appearance on the "Church of the Airways" program. At ten o'clock on Sunday morning Donnelly turned on the television set and at the last minute decided to tape the program.

Thomasina did not appear until the hour was almost over. Then, incredulously, Donnelly witnessed the Reverend Bobby's histrionics and Perkins' revelation that "Jim" was the abductor's name. That guy claims he can bring on miracles and he couldn't even get Laurie's name straight, Donnelly thought in disgust as he snapped off the set. He referred to her as *Lee*. Nevertheless he carefully labeled the video cassette and put it in his briefcase.

Sarah phoned a few minutes later. "I don't like to call you at home," she apologized, "but I have to ask. What did you think? Is there any chance that Miss Perkins was right about the name?"

"No," Donnelly said flatly. He heard her sigh.

"I'm still going to ask the Harrisburg police to run 'Jim' through the computers," she told him. "There might be a file on a child abuser by that name who was active seventeen years ago."

"I'm afraid you're wasting your time. The Perkins woman was taking a wild guess. After all, she had Almighty God on the line, didn't she? How's Laurie doing?"

"Pretty well." She sounded cautious.

"Did she watch the program?"

"No, she refuses to listen to any kind of gospel music. Besides, I'm trying to keep her mind off all this. We're going to play a round of golf. It's fairly pleasant out considering it's February."

"I always meant to try golf. That should be relaxing for both of you. Has Laurie been writing in the journal?"

"She's upstairs scribbling away now."

"Good. See you tomorrow." Donnelly hung up and decided that the best way to shake his feeling of restlessness was to take a long walk. He realized that for the first time since he'd lived in New York, the prospect of a totally unstructured Sunday was not appealing to him.

61

THOMASINA HAD HOPED that after the "Church of the Airways" program the Reverend Bobby Hawkins and his lovely wife, Carla, might invite her to lunch at a nice place like the Tavern on the Green and maybe suggest that they drive her around New York to see the sights. Thomasina hadn't been to New York in thirty years.

But something happened. The minute the cameras were turned off, Carla whispered something to Reverend Bobby and they both looked upset. The upshot of it was that they sort of brushed Thomasina off with a hurried goodbye and thank you and keep praying. Then an escort brought her to the car that would take her to the airport.

On the ride, Thomasina tried to console herself with the glory of her appearance on the program, of the new stories she'd have to tell. Maybe "Good Morning, Harrisburg" would want her back to talk about the miracle.

Thomasina sighed. She was tired. She'd barely closed her eyes last night for the excitement and now her head ached and she wanted a cup of tea.

She arrived at the airport with nearly two hours to wait for her plane and went into one of the cafeterias. Orange juice, oatmeal, bacon, eggs, a

Danish and a pot of tea restored her usual good nature. It had been a very exciting experience. The Reverend Bobby seemed so Godlike that she'd shivered when he prayed over her.

She pushed back her empty plate, poured a second cup of tea and, while she sipped it, thought of the miracle. God had spoken directly to her, saying, "Jim, Jim."

Not for the world would she contradict anything the Almighty told her, but as Thomasina dipped the paper napkin in her water glass and scrubbed away at a spot of bacon grease on her good blue dress she was ashamed of the guilty thought that imposed itself in her mind: That just isn't the name I remember hearing.

62

ON MONDAY MORNING, ten days after her husband's funeral, Karen Grant entered the travel agency, a heavy stack of mail in her arms.

Anne Webster and Connie Santini were already there. They had been discussing once again the fact that Karen had not invited them to join her at the reception even though they clearly heard the college president tell her to be sure to include any close friends who had attended the service.

Anne Webster still puzzled over the omission. "I'm certain it was just that Karen was so upset."

Connie had other ideas. She was sure Karen didn't want any of the faculty asking them about the travel agency. It would have been just like Anne to artlessly say that business had been terrible for several years. Connie would have bet her bottom dollar that at Clinton College, Karen had given the impression that Global Travel was on a level with Perillo Tours.

The discussion ended with Karen's arrival. She greeted them briefly and said, "The dean had someone pick up the mail at the house. There's an awful pile. Most of it sympathy cards, I suppose. I hate to read them, but I guess I can't avoid it."

With an exaggerated sigh, she settled at her desk and reached for a letter opener. Minutes later she gasped, "Oh, my God."

Connie and Anne jumped up and rushed to her. "What is it? What's wrong?"

"Call the police in Clinton," Karen snapped. Her face was the color of chalk. "It's a letter from Laurie Kenyon, signing herself 'Leona' again. Now that crazy girl is threatening to kill *me!*"

63

THE MONDAY MORNING SESSION with Laurie was unproductive. She'd been quiet and depressed. She told Justin about playing golf. "I was terrible, Dr. Donnelly. I just couldn't concentrate. So many loud thoughts." But he couldn't get her to discuss the loud thoughts. None of the alters would talk to him either.

When Laurie went into art therapy, Sarah told Donnelly that she had begun to prepare her for the grand jury hearing. "I think everything is really starting to sink in," she explained. "Then last night I caught her going through some photo albums she keeps in her room." Sarah's eyes began to fill with tears that she hastily blinked away. "I told her it wasn't a great idea to look at pictures of Mom and Dad just now."

They left at noon. At two o'clock, Sarah phoned. In the background, Justin Donnelly could hear Laurie screaming.

Her voice trembling, Sarah said, "Laurie's hysterical. She must have been going through the albums again. There's a picture she's torn to bits."

Now Donnelly could make out what Laurie was shrieking. "I promise I won't tell. I promise I won't tell."

"Give me directions to your house," he snapped. "And then get two Valiums into her."

Sophie let him in.

"They're in Laurie's room, Doctor." She led the way upstairs. Sarah was sitting on the bed, holding a sedated Laurie.

"I made her take the Valiums," Sarah told him. "She quieted down, but now she's almost out of it." She released Laurie and eased her head onto the pillow.

Justin bent over Laurie and began to examine her. Her pulse was erratic, her breathing shallow, her pupils dilated, her skin cold to the touch. "She's in shock," he said quietly. "Do you know what brought it on?"

"No. She seemed to be all right after we got home. She said she was going to write in her journal. Then I heard her screaming. I think she must have started going through the album because she tore up a picture. There are pieces of it all over her desk."

"I want those pieces collected," Justin said. "Try not to miss any of them." He began to tap Laurie's face. "Laurie, it's Dr. Donnelly. I want you to talk to me. Tell me your full name."

She did not respond. Donnelly's fingers tapped her face with greater force. "Tell me your name," he said insistently. Finally Laurie opened her eyes. As they focused on him, they took on a surprised expression followed by one of relief.

"Dr. Donnelly," she murmured. "When did you come?"

Sarah felt herself go limp. The last hour had been agony. The sedative had calmed Laurie's hysteria, but then her total withdrawal was even more frightening. Sarah had been terrified that Laurie was slipping so far away she would not make it back.

Sophie was standing in the doorway. "Would a cup of tea be good for her?" she asked softly.

Justin heard. He looked over his shoulder. "Please."

Sarah went over to the desk. The picture was virtually shredded. In those few moments from the time Laurie started shrieking till Sarah and Sophie reached her, she had managed to reduce it to minuscule pieces. It would be a miracle if it could be put together.

"I don't want to stay here," Laurie said.

Sarah whirled around. Laurie was sitting up, hugging herself. "I can't stay here. Please."

"Okay," Justin said calmly. "Let's go downstairs. We could all use a cup of tea." He supported Laurie as she got to her feet. They were halfway down the stairs, Sarah behind them, when the chimes rang in the foyer signaling someone was at the front door.

Sophie bustled to answer it. Two uniformed policemen were on the porch. They were carrying a warrant for Laurie's arrest. By contacting the widow of Allan Grant with a threatening letter, she had violated the terms of her bail and it had been revoked.

That evening, Sarah sat in Justin Donnelly's office in the clinic. "If you hadn't been there, Laurie would be in a jail cell right now," she told him. "I can't tell you how grateful I am."

It was true. When Laurie was brought before the judge, Donnelly had convinced him that she was under intense psychological stress and required hospitalization in a secured facility. The judge had amended his order, to permit inpatient hospitalization. On the drive from New Jersey to New York, she had been in a trance-like sleep.

Justin chose his words carefully. "I'm glad to have her here. She needs to be watched and monitored constantly right now."

"To keep her from sending threatening letters?"

"And to keep her from harming herself."

Sarah got up. "I've taken enough of your time for one day, Doctor. I'll be back first thing in the morning."

It was nearly nine o'clock. "There's a place around the corner where the menu is good and the service is fast," Donnelly told her. "Why don't you grab a quick bite with me and then I'll send for a car to take you home?"

Sarah had already phoned Sophie to tell her that Laurie was checked into the hospital and to be sure to keep her own plans for the evening. The thought of something to eat and a cup of coffee with Justin Donnelly instead of going home to the empty house was comforting. "I'd like that," she said simply.

Laurie was standing at the window of her room. She liked the room. It wasn't large, so she could see all of it in one glance. She felt safe in it. The outside window didn't open. She had tried it. There was an interior window that looked out on the hallway and the nurses' station. It had a drape but she'd left it partially open. She didn't ever want to be in the dark again.

What had happened today? The last thing she remembered was sitting at the desk writing. She'd turned the page and then . . .

And then it all went blank until I saw Dr. Donnelly bending over me, she thought. Then we were going down the stairs and the police came.

The police said she had written a letter to Allan Grant's wife. Why would I write to her? Laurie wondered. They said I threatened her. That's silly, she thought. When would I have written the letter? When would I have mailed it?

If Karen Grant had received a threatening letter in the last few days it was proof that somebody else must have sent it. She couldn't wait to point that out to Sarah.

Laurie leaned her forehead against the window. It felt so cool. She was tired now and would go to bed. A few people were on the sidewalk, hurrying down the block, their heads down. You could tell it was chilly out.

She saw a man and a woman cross the street in front of the clinic. Was that Sarah and the doctor? She couldn't be sure.

She turned, crossed the room and got into bed, pulling the covers around her. Her eyes were so heavy. It was good to drift away. It would be so good never to have to wake up again.

64

ON TUESDAY MORNING, Brendon Moody drove to the Clinton College campus. His plan was to canvas the residents of the building where Laurie had her studio apartment. After Allan Grant's funeral, he'd given it the once-over. Five years old, it had been erected to serve the needs of upperclassmen. The rooms were good-sized and included a kitchenette and private bath. It was popular housing for students like Laurie who could afford to pay the surcharge for privacy.

Laurie's apartment had been thoroughly searched and then released by lab technicians from the prosecutor's office. Brendon made it his first stop.

It was totally disheveled. The bed was stripped. The door of the closet was ajar and the clothing looked as though it had been examined and re-placed haphazardly on the hangers. The drawers of the dresser were partially open. The contents of the desk were strewn on its surface.

Moody knew that the investigators had taken the typewriter on which the letters to Allan Grant had been written and the rest of the stationery. He knew that the bed sheets and Laurie's bloodstained clothing and watchband and bracelet had been confiscated.

What then was he looking for?

If asked the question, Brendon Moody would have said "Nothing," and meant that he had no particular agenda in mind. He looked around, getting a feel for the premises.

It was obvious that in its normal condition the room was quite attractive. Tie-back, floor-length ivory curtains, an ivory dust ruffle on the bed, framed prints of Monet and Manet, paintings on the walls, a half-dozen golf trophies on a shelf over the bookcase. She had not stuck pictures of class-mates and friends in the mirror frame over the dresser, the way so many students did. There was only a single family picture on the desk. Brendon studied the photograph. The Kenyons. He'd known the parents. This shot must have been taken in the pool area behind their house. The family had obviously been happy and content together.

Put yourself in Laurie's place, Moody thought. The family is destroyed. You blame yourself. You're vulnerable and latch onto a guy who's kind to you, who's both an attractive man and old enough to be a sort of father figure, and then he rejects you. And you explode.

Open and shut. Brendon prowled around, exam-ining, evaluating. He stood over the tub in the bathroom. Traces of blood had been found in it. Laurie had been smart enough to wash the sheets and her clothing here, bring them down to the dryer, then fold and put them away. She'd tried to clean the watchband too. Brendon knew what the prosecutor could do with that evidence. Try to prove panic and confusion when the killer had systematically attempted to destroy evidence.

As Brendon was about to leave the room, he looked around one more time. He had found absolutely nothing, not one shred of evidence that could be used to help Laurie. Why did he have the nagging sense that somehow, someway, he was missing something?

65

SARAH HAD a sleepless night. The day kept replaying in her mind: Laurie's bloodcurdling screams; the torn picture; the policemen at the door; Laurie being taken out in handcuffs; Justin swearing he'd get her released in his custody as they followed the squad car to Clinton. It was dawn when Sarah finally slept, an uneasy, troubled sleep in which she dreamt of courtrooms and guilty verdicts.

She woke up at eight o'clock, showered, put on a tan cashmere shirt, matching slacks and dark brown ankle boots and went downstairs. Sophie was already in the kitchen. Coffee was brewing. In the breakfast area, a flowered pitcher held freshly squeezed orange juice. A compote of cut-up oranges, grapefruit, apples and cantaloupe was attractively arranged in a Tiffany bowl. An English toast rack was positioned next to the toaster.

Everything looks so normal, Sarah thought. It's just as though Mom and Dad and Laurie will come downstairs any minute. She pointed to the toast rack. "Sophie, remember how Dad used to call that thing a toast *cooler*. He was right."

Sophie nodded. Her round, unlined face showing distress, she poured juice into Sarah's glass. "I was worried last night—not being here when you got back. Was Laurie really willing to go into the hospital?"

"She did seem to understand that it was the clinic or jail." Wearily Sarah rubbed her forehead. "Something happened yesterday. I don't know what it was, but Laurie said she'll never spend another night in her bedroom. Sophie, if that woman who came back to see the house the other day wants it, I'm going to sell."

She did not hear the expected protest. Instead Sophie sighed. "I think maybe you're right. This isn't a happy home anymore. Maybe it's too much to expect it to be after what happened in September."

It was both a relief and a blow to realize that Sophie agreed with her. Sarah finished the juice, swallowing over the large lump in her throat. "I'll skip everything except the coffee." A thought struck her. "Do you think you found most of the pieces of that picture Laurie tore up yesterday?"

Sophie's lips creased in a triumphant smile.

"Better than that. I put it together." She produced it. "See, I assembled it on the sheet of paper and then, when I was sure it was right, I glued it. Only trouble is the pieces were so small that the glue ran all over them. It's kind of hard to tell much about it."

"Why it's just a picture of Laurie when she was a kid," Sarah said. "That certainly can't be what caused her to get so upset." She studied it, then shrugged helplessly. "I'll put it in my briefcase right now. Doctor Donnelly wants to see it."

With troubled eyes, Sophie watched Sarah push back her chair. She'd so hoped that pasting the picture together would somehow be helpful and show what had brought on Laurie's hysterical outburst. She remembered something and fished inside the pocket of her apron. It wasn't there. Of course it wasn't. The staple that she'd removed from one of the scraps of the picture was in the pocket of the housedress she'd been wearing yesterday. It certainly couldn't be important, she decided as she poured coffee into Sarah's cup.

66

*O*N TUESDAY MORNING, while listening to the eight o'clock CBS news, Bic and Opal heard about Laurie Kenyon's threatening letter to Karen Grant, the revoking of her bail and her confinement in the locked facility of a clinic for multiple personality disorder.

Nervously Opal asked, "Bic, do you think they'll get her to talk in that place?"

"Intense efforts will be made to have her recall her childhood," he said. "We must know what is going on. Carla, call that real estate woman."

Betsy Lyons caught Sarah as she was about to leave for New York. "Sarah," she bubbled, "have I got good news for you! Mrs. Hawkins phoned. She's crazy about the house, wants to close on it as soon as possible and is willing to give you up to a year to live in it. She only asks to be able to come in occasionally with her decorator, at your convenience. Sarah, remember I told you that in this market you might have to come down from seven hundred fifty thousand? My dear, she didn't bicker about the price at all and is paying cash."

"I guess it's meant to be," Sarah said quietly. "I'm glad people who want the house that much are going to have it. You can tell them they can move in by August. The condominium should be ready then. I don't care if they come in with their decorator. Laurie will be staying in the hospital, and if I'm home I'll be working in the library."

Betsy called Carla Hawkins. "Congratulations. It's all set. Sarah is perfectly willing for you to bring in your decorator. She says if she's home she'll be working in the library." Betsy's tone became confidential. "You know, she's going to defend her sister at the trial. Poor darling, she'll have her hands full."

Bic had picked up the extension and listened to

the conversation. After a final, "Congratulations again. I'm sure you'll be so happy in that beautiful house," Lyons said goodbye.

Smiling, Bic replaced the receiver. "I'm sure we'll be very happy together," he said and went to the desk. "My special phone book, Carla. Where is it?"

She hurried over. "Right here, Bic, in this drawer." She handed it to him. "Bic, what interior decorator do you want me to get?"

He sighed, "Oh, Carla." Thumbing through the book, he found the name he was looking for and dialed a number in Kentucky.

67

SARAH REMEMBERED that Laurie had gone into the clinic with only the clothes she was wearing. Grateful that she wasn't already on her way to New York, she went to Laurie's room and with Sophie's help packed a bag.

At the clinic the bag's contents were examined, and a nurse quietly removed a leather belt and laced sneakers. "Just a precaution," she said.

"You all think that she's suicidal," Sarah told Justin a few minutes later, then looked away from the understanding in his eyes. She knew she could bear anything except sympathy. I can't lose it, she warned herself, again swallowing over the constriction in her throat.

"Sarah, I told you yesterday that Laurie is fragile and depressed. But there is one thing I can promise you—and this is our great hope—she doesn't want you hurt anymore. She'll do anything to prevent that."

"Does she realize that the worst way she could hurt me would be to harm herself?"

"Yes, I do think she knows that. And I believe she is starting to trust me. She knows that I convinced the judge to let her come here instead of going to jail. Were you able to figure out what it was she tore up yesterday?"

"Sophie managed to put it together." Sarah removed the reconstructed photograph from her bag and showed it to him. "I don't understand why this picture would upset her," she said. "It's similar to a lot of others in the album and around the house."

Justin Donnelly studied it. "With all the cracks and glue, it's hard to tell much. I'll have the nurse bring her in."

Laurie was wearing some of the clothes Sarah had brought, jeans and a blue sweater that accentuated her cornflower blue eyes. Her hair was loose. She wore no makeup and looked to be about sixteen. Seeing Sarah, she ran to her and the sisters embraced. As Sarah smoothed down Laurie's hair, she thought, When we come to trial, this is the way she's got to look. Young. Vulnerable.

The thought helped her to get a grip on herself. She realized that when she concentrated on defending Laurie, her own emotions were safely harnessed.

Laurie sat in one of the armchairs. Clearly she had no intention of going near the couch. She made that apparent immediately.

"I'll bet you thought you'd coax her into lying down." It was the strident voice again.

"I think it's Kate who's talking, isn't it?" Justin asked pleasantly.

The look of a sixteen-year-old had vanished. Laurie's face had hardened. No, firmed, Sarah thought. She seems older.

"Yes, it's Kate. And I want to thank you for keeping the wimp out of jail yesterday. That really would have done her in. I tried to stop her from writing that crazy letter to Allan's wife the other day, but she wouldn't listen and see what happened."

"Laurie wrote the letter?" Justin asked.

"No, Leona wrote it. The wimp would have written a letter of condolence. That would have been just as bad. I swear I can't stand her, and as for those other two! One of them always mooning about Allan Grant, the other, the little kid, always crying. If she doesn't shut up soon, I'll throttle her."

Sarah could not take her eyes from Laurie. This alter personality who called herself Kate dwelt inside Laurie, directed or tried to direct Laurie's actions. If she came out on the witness stand with that arrogance and bullying attitude, no jury would ever acquit Laurie.

Justin said, "You know, I haven't turned on the video camera yet. You came out awfully fast this morning. Is it okay if I turn it on now?"

An annoyed shrug. "Go ahead. You will anyhow."

"Kate, Laurie got awfully upset yesterday, didn't she."

"You should know. You were there."

"I was there after she got upset. I just wondered if you could tell me what caused it?"

"That discussion is forbidden."

Donnelly did not seem fazed. "All right, so we won't discuss it. Could you show me what Laurie was doing when she got upset."

"No way, pal." She turned her head. "Oh shut up that sniffling."

"Is Debbie crying?" Justin asked.

"Who else?"

"I don't know. How many of you are there?"

"Not many. Some of the others went away after Laurie was back home. Just as well. It was getting crowded. I said, *shut up.*"

"Kate, maybe if I spoke to Debbie, I could find out what's bothering her."

"Go ahead. I can't do a thing with her."

"Debbie, please don't be afraid. I promise nothing will hurt you. Talk to me again, won't you?" Justin Donnelly's voice was gentle, coaxing.

The changeover happened in an instant. The hair falling forward, the features smoothed out, the mouth puckered, lips quivering, the hands clasped in her lap, the dangling legs. Tears began to gush down her cheeks.

"Hi, Debbie," Justin said. "You've been crying a lot today, haven't you."

She nodded vigorously.

"Did something happen to you yesterday?"

She nodded assent.

"Debbie, you *know* I like you. You know I keep you safe. Do you think you can trust me?"

A tentative nod.

"Then can you tell me what scared you?"

She shook her head from side to side.

"You can't tell me. Then maybe you can show me. Were you writing in the journal?"

"No. Laurie was writing." The voice was soft, childlike and sad.

"Laurie was writing, but you could tell what she was writing, couldn't you?"

"Not everything, I just started to learn how to read."

"All right. Show me what Laurie was doing."

She picked up an imaginary pen, made the motion of opening a book and began to write in the air. She hesitated, held up the pen as though thinking, looked around and then her hand reached down to turn another page.

Her eyes widened. Her mouth opened in a silent scream. She jumped up, threw the book away from her and began a tearing motion, both hands working vigorously, her face contorted in horror.

Abruptly she stopped, dropped her hands and shouted, "Debbie, get back inside! Listen, Doctor, I may be sick of that little kid, but I take care of her. You burn that picture, do you hear me? Just don't make her look at it again."

Kate had taken charge.

At the end of the session, an attendant came for Laurie. "Can you come back later?" Laurie begged Sarah as she was leaving.

"Yes. Whatever time Dr. Donnelly says is okay."

When Laurie was gone, Justin handed the picture to Sarah. "Can you see anything about this that might frighten her?"

Sarah studied it. "You can't see much with all those cracks and that glue drying over it. You can tell she looks cold, the way she's hugging herself. She's wearing that same bathing suit in the picture with me that we have in the library. It was taken a few days before she was kidnapped. In fact that's the bathing suit she was wearing when she disappeared. Do you think that might have triggered the fear?"

"Very possibly." Dr. Donnelly put the picture in the file. "We'll keep her busy today. She'll be in art therapy this morning and a journal-writing session this afternoon. She still refuses to take any of the standardized tests. I'll be available to see her between and around other patients. I hope the time will come when she's willing to talk to me without you. I think that may happen."

Sarah stood up. "What time shall I come back?"

"Right after she has dinner. Six o'clock work out for you?"

"Of course." As she left, Sarah was calculating the time. It was now nearly noon. With luck she'd be home by one. She'd have to be on her way back by four-thirty to avoid the worst of the commuter traffic. That still gave her three-and-a-half hours at her desk.

Justin walked her to the door of the reception area, then watched her go. Her slim back was straight, her tote bag over her shoulder, her head high. Chin up, he thought, good girl. Then as he watched her walk down the corridor he saw her shove both hands in her pockets as though seeking warmth from a chill only she could feel.

Part Four

68

THE GRAND JURY convened on February 17 and did not take long to indict Laurie for the purposeful and knowing murder of Allan Grant. A trial date was set for October fifth.

The next day Sarah met Brendon Moody in Solari's, the popular restaurant around the corner from the Bergen County courthouse. As lawyers and judges came in, they all stopped to speak to Sarah. She should be eating with them, joking with them, Brendon thought, not meeting them this way.

Sarah had spent the morning in the courthouse library researching insanity and diminished mental capacity defenses. Brendon could see the worry in her eyes, the way the smile faded as soon as anyone who greeted her turned away. She looked pale, and there were hollows in her cheeks. He was glad that she had ordered a decent lunch and commented on that.

"Everything tastes like sawdust, but there's no way I can let myself get sick at this stage of the game," Sarah said wryly. "How about you, Brendon? How's the food around the campus?"

"Predictable." Brendon took an appreciative bite of his cheeseburger. "I'm not getting very far, Sarah." He pulled out his notes. "The best and maybe the most dangerous witness is Susan Grimes, who lives across the hall from Laurie. She's the one you called a couple of times. Since October she's noticed Laurie going out regularly between eight and nine o'clock at night and not coming back till eleven or later. She said Laurie looked different on those occasions, pretty sexy, lots of makeup, hair kind of wild, jeans tucked into high-heeled boots—not her usual style at all. She was sure Laurie was meeting some guy."

"Is there any indication that she was ever actually *with* Allan Grant?"

"You can pinpoint specific dates from some of the letters she wrote to him, and they don't hold up," Moody said bluntly. He pulled out his notepad. "On November sixteenth, Laurie wrote that she loved being in Allan's arms the night before. The night before was Friday, November fifteenth, and Allan and Karen Grant were at a faculty party together. Same kind of fantasizing for December second, twelfth, fourteenth, January sixth and eleventh. I could go on right up to January twenty-eighth. The point is, I hoped to prove that Allan Grant had been leading her on. We know she was hanging around his house, but we haven't a shred of evidence that he was aware of it. In fact everything points the other way."

"Then you're saying that all this was in Laurie's mind, that we can't even suggest that Grant might have been taking advantage of her despondency?"

"There's someone else I want to talk to, a teacher who's been away on sick leave. Her name's Vera West. I'm picking up some rumors about her and Grant."

The pleasant background hum of voices and laughter and dishes being placed on tables, all the familiar sounds that had been part of her workday world seemed suddenly intrusive and foreign to Sarah. She knew what Brendon Moody was saying. If Laurie had fantasized all the encounters with Allan Grant, if in his wife's absence Allan had begun a romance with another woman and Laurie had learned about it, it gave more credence to the prosecutor's contention that she had killed him in a jealous rage. "When will you question Vera West?" she asked.

"Soon, I hope."

Sarah swallowed the rest of her coffee and signaled for the check. "I'd better get back. I'm going to meet the people who are buying our house. Guess what? This Mrs. Hawkins who's been coming out is none other than the wife of the Reverend Bobby Hawkins."

"Who's that?" Brendon asked.

"The hot new preacher on the 'Church of the Airways' program. That's the one Miss Perkins was on when she came up with the name 'Jim' as the man Laurie was with in the diner years ago."

"Oh, that guy. What a faker. How come he's buying your house? That's quite a coincidence with him being involved with the Perkins woman."

"Not really. His wife had been looking at the house before all this happened. The Perkins woman wrote to him, not the other way round. Have we gotten any feedback yet from the Harrisburg police on 'Jim'?"

Brendon Moody was hoping Sarah would not ask him about that. Choosing his words carefully, he said, "Sarah, as a matter of fact we just did. There's a Jim Brown from Harrisburg who's a known child molester. He has a record a mile long. He was in the area when Laurie was spotted in the diner. Miss

Perkins was shown his picture at that time but couldn't identify him. They wanted to bring him in for questioning. After Laurie was found, he disappeared without a trace."

"He never showed up again?"

"He died in prison six years ago in Seattle."

"What was the offense?"

"Kidnapping and assault of a five-year-old girl. She testified at his trial about the two months she was with him. I've read the testimony. Bright little kid. Came out with some pretty harrowing stuff. It was all over the papers at the time."

"Which means that even if he was Laurie's abductor it won't do us any good. If Laurie has a breakthrough and remembers him and is able to describe what he did to her, the prosecutor would bring the Seattle newspapers into court and claim that she'd just parroted that case."

"We don't know that this guy had anything to do with Laurie at all," Moody said briskly. "But, yes, if he did, no matter what Laurie remembers about him, it will sound as if she's lying."

Neither one of them spoke the thought that was in their minds. The way it was going, they might have to ask the prosecutor to consider plea-bargaining for Laurie. If that proved necessary, it would mean that by the end of the summer Laurie would be in prison.

69

BIC AND OPAL drove with Betsy Lyons to the Kenyon home. For this meeting they had both dressed conservatively. Bic was wearing a gray pin-striped suit with a white shirt and bluish gray tie. His topcoat was dark gray, and he carried gray kidskin gloves.

Opal's hair had just been lightened and shaped at Elizabeth Arden's. Her gray wool dress had a velvet collar and cuffs. Over it she wore a black fitted coat with a narrow sable collar. Her shoes and bag, purchased at Gucci, were black lizard.

Bic was sitting next to Lyons in the front seat of her car. As she chatted, indicating various points of interest in the town, Lyons kept glancing sideways at Bic. She'd been startled when another agent had asked, "Betsy, do you know who that guy *is?*"

She knew he was in television. She certainly hadn't realized he had his own program. She decided that the Reverend Hawkins was a terribly attractive and charismatic man. He was talking about moving to the New York area.

"When I was called to the Church of the Airways ministry, I knew that we'd want to have a home nearby. I'm just not a city person. Carla has had the undesirable job of scouting for us. And she has kept coming back to this town and this house."

Praise the Lord, Betsy Lyons thought.

"My one hesitation," the preacher was saying in his courteous, gentle voice, "is that I was so afraid that Carla was letting herself in for a disappointment. I honestly thought that the house might be taken off the market permanently."

So did I, Betsy Lyons thought, shivering at the prospect. "The girls will be happier in a smaller place," she confided. "Look, this is the street. You drive down Lincoln Avenue and pass all these lovely homes, then the road bends here and it's Twin Oaks Road."

As they turned onto Twin Oaks Road, she rattled off the names of the neighbors. "He owns the Williams Bank. The Kimballs live in the Tudor. She's Courtney Meier, the actress."

In the backseat, Opal clutched her gloves nervously. It seemed to her that every time they came to Ridgewood it was as though they were skating on thin ice and insistently, consistently testing it, pushing nearer and nearer the breaking point.

Sarah was waiting for them. Attractive, Opal decided, as for the first time she got a close look at her. The kind who gets better looking as she gets older. Bic would have passed her by when she was a little kid. Opal wished Lee hadn't had golden hair down to her waist. She wished Lee hadn't been standing by the road that day.

Mutton dressed as lamb, Sarah thought as she extended her hand to Opal. Then she wondered why in the name of God that old Irish expression, a favorite of her grandmother's, had jumped into her mind at this moment. Mrs. Hawkins was a well-dressed, fashionably coiffed woman in her mid-forties. It was the small lips and tiny chin that gave her a weak, almost furtive expression. Or maybe it was that the Reverend Bobby Hawkins had such a magnetic presence. He seemed to fill the room, to absorb all the energy in it. He spoke immediately about Laurie.

"I don't know if you're aware that we prayed on our holy hour that memory of the name of your sister's abductor would be returned to a Miss Thomasina Perkins."

"I saw the program," Sarah told him.

"Have you looked into the name, Jim, to see if there is any possible connection? The Lord works in strange ways, sometimes directly, sometimes indirectly."

"There is nothing we're not checking in my sister's defense," Sarah said with closure in her voice.

He took the hint. "This is a beautiful room," he said, looking around the library. "My wife kept saying how happy I'd be working here with the bookcases and those big windows. I like to be always in the light. Now I don't want to take any more of your time. If we can just go through the house with Mrs. Lyons one last time, then my lawyer can contact your lawyer about passing papers . . ."

Betsy Lyons took the couple upstairs, and Sarah returned to work, filing the notes she had made in the law library. Suddenly she realized she'd better get started for New York.

The Hawkinses and Betsy Lyons looked in to say they were leaving. Reverend Hawkins explained that he would like to bring his architect in as soon as possible but certainly didn't want to have him going over the library while Sarah was working. What would be a good time?

"Tomorrow or the next day between nine and twelve, or late afternoon," Sarah told him.

"Tomorrow morning, then."

When Sarah returned from the clinic and went into the library the next afternoon, she had no way of knowing that from now on every word spoken in that room would be turning on sophisticated voice-activated equipment and that all her conversations would be transmitted to a tape recorder hidden in the wall of the guest-room closet.

70

IN MID-MARCH, Karen Grant drove to Clinton for what she hoped would be the last time. In the weeks since Allan's death, she had spent Saturdays going through the house, weeding out the accumulation of six years of marriage, selecting the pieces of furniture she wanted in the New York apartment, arranging for a used-furniture dealer to pick up the rest. She had sold Allan's car and put the house in the hands of a real estate agent. Today there was going to be a memorial service for Allan in the chapel on campus.

Tomorrow she was leaving for four days in St. Thomas. It would be good to get away, she thought as she drove swiftly down the New Jersey Turnpike. The travel business perks were wonderful. She'd been invited to Frenchman's Reef, one of her favorite places.

Edwin would be going too. Her pulse quickened and unconsciously she smiled. By fall they wouldn't have to sneak around anymore.

The memorial service was like the funeral. It was overwhelming to hear Allan eulogized. Karen heard herself sobbing. Louise Larkin, seated next to her, put an arm around her. "If only he'd listened to me," Karen whispered to Louise. "I warned him that girl was dangerous."

There was a reception afterwards at the Larkin home. Karen had always admired this house. It was over one hundred years old and had been beautifully restored. It reminded her of the houses in Cooperstown where so many of her high school friends lived. She had grown up in a trailer park and could still remember when one of the kids in school asked derisively if her folks were going to have a sketch of their mobile home on their Christmas card.

The Larkins had invited not only faculty members and administrative staff but a dozen or so students. Some of them offered fervent condolences, some paused to tell a favorite story about Allan. Karen's eyes moistened as she told people that she missed Allan more and more each day.

Across the room, forty-year-old Vera West, newest member of the faculty, nursed a glass of white wine. Her round, pleasant face was framed by short, naturally wavy brown hair. Tinted glasses concealed her hazel eyes. She did not need the glasses for vision. She was afraid that the expression in her eyes was too revealing. She sipped her wine, trying not to remember that at a faculty party a few months ago Allan, not his wife, had been across the room. Vera had hoped that the sick leave would give her the time she needed to get a grip on her emotions—emotions no one must suspect her of having. As she pushed back the single strand of hair that always managed to fall on her forehead, she thought of the verse written by a nineteenth-century poet: "Sorrow which is never spoken is the heaviest load to bear."

Louise Larkin joined her. "It's so good to have you back, Vera. We've missed you. How are you feeling?" Larkin's eyes were inquisitive.

"Much better, thank you."

"Mononucleosis is so debilitating."

"Yes, it is." After Allan's funeral, Vera had fled to her cottage in Cape Cod. Mono was the excuse she'd used when she phoned the dean.

"Karen really looks quite marvelous for someone who's had such a devastating loss, don't you think, Vera?"

Vera raised the glass to her lips, sipped, then said calmly, "Karen's a beautiful woman."

"I mean, you've lost so much weight, and your face is so drawn. I swear, if I were a stranger and had to make a guess between the two of you, I'd pick you as the mourner." Louise Larkin squeezed Vera's hand and smiled sympathetically.

71

LAURIE AWAKENED to the faint murmur of voices in the corridor. It was a comforting sound, one she'd been hearing for three months now. February. March. April. It was the beginning of May. Outside, before coming here, whether on the street, on the campus, or even at home, she had begun to feel as though she was free-falling, unable to stop her descent. Here in the clinic, she felt suspended in time. Her plunge had been slowed. She was grateful for the reprieve even though she knew that in the end no one could save her.

She sat up slowly and hugged her legs. This was one of the best moments of the day, when she'd awaken to know the knife dream hadn't wrenched her awake during the night, that whatever stalked her was being held at bay.

It was the sort of thing that they wanted her to write in the journal. She reached over to the night table for the spiral notebook and pen. She had time to jot down a few thoughts before dressing and going to breakfast. She propped up the pillows, pulled herself up and opened the book.

There were pages of writing in it that hadn't been there last night. Over and over a childish hand had written, "I want my mommy. I want to go home."

* * *

Later that morning as she and Sarah sat across the desk from Justin Donnelly, Laurie carefully studied the doctor as he read the journal. He was such a big man, she thought, with those broad shoulders, those strong features, that mass of dark hair. She liked his eyes. They were intensely dark blue. She normally didn't like mustaches, but his seemed so right, especially above those even white teeth. She liked his hands too. Wide but with long fingers. Tanned but no hint of fuzz on them. Funny, she could think a mustache looked great on Dr. Donnelly, but she hated fuzz on a man's hands or arms. She heard herself saying that.

Donnelly looked up. "Laurie?"

She shrugged. "I don't know why I said that."

"Would you repeat it?"

"I said I hate fuzz on a man's hands or arms."

"Why do you think that just occurred to you?"

"She's not going to answer that."

Sarah had come to recognize Kate's voice immediately.

Justin wasn't fazed. "Come on, Kate," he said good-humoredly. "You can't keep getting away with bullying Laurie. She wants to talk to me. Or Debbie does. I think it was Debbie writing in the book last night. It looks like her handwriting."

"Well it certainly isn't mine." Over the past three months the tone had become less strident. A certain wary understanding had been struck between Justin and the alter personality, Kate.

"May I speak to Debbie now?"

"Oh, all right. But don't get her crying again. I'm sick of that kid's sniffling."

"Kate, you're a bluff," Justin said. "You protect Debbie and Laurie and we both know it. But you've got to let me help you. It's too big a job for you."

The hair falling forward was the usual signal. It wrenched Sarah's heart to hear the frightened child who called herself Debbie. Was this the way it was for Laurie those two years she was away, weeping, terrified, longing for the people she loved?

"Hi, Debbie," Justin said. "How's the big girl today?"

"Better, thank you."

"Debbie, I'm so glad you started writing in the journal again. Do you know why you wrote this last night?"

"I knew the book was empty. I shook it first."

"You shook the book? What did you expect to find?"

"I don't know."

"What were you afraid to find, Debbie?"

"More pictures," she whispered. "I have to go now. They're looking for me."

"Who? Who is looking for you?"

But she was gone.

A lazy laugh. Laurie had crossed her legs, slumped a little in the chair. In a deliberately provocative gesture, she ran her hand through her hair.

"There she goes, trying to hide, hoping they won't find her."

Sarah stiffened. This was Leona, the alter personality who wrote the letters to Allan Grant. This was the scorned woman who had killed him. She'd only come out twice before in these months.

"Hi, Leona." Justin leaned across the desk, his manner that of offering flattering attention to an attractive woman. "I've been hoping you'd pay us a visit."

"Well, a girl's got to live. You can't keep moping around forever. Got a cigarette?"

"Sure." He reached in the drawer, held out the pack, lit the cigarette for her. "Have you been moping around, Leona?"

She shrugged. "Oh, you know how it is. I was pretty crazy about Professor Kiss-and-Tell."

"Allan Grant?"

"Yes, but listen, it's over, right? I'm sorry for him, but these things happen."

"What things?"

"I mean him giving me away to the shrink and the dean at school."

"You were angry at him for that, weren't you."

"You bet I was. So was Laurie, but for different reasons. She really put on a class-A performance when she buttonholed him in the hall."

I'll have to plea bargain, Sarah thought. If this personality got on the stand, displaying not a shred of remorse about Allan Grant's death . . .

"You know that Allan's dead . . ."

"Oh, I'm used to that now. What a shock though."

"Do you know how he died?"

"Sure I do. Our kitchen knife." The bravado crumbled. "I sure wish to God I'd left it in my room when I dropped in on him that night. I really was crazy about him, you know."

72

IN THE THREE months between the beginning of February and the end of April, Brendon Moody had made frequent visits to Clinton College. He had become a familiar figure, chatting with students in the Rathskeller or the student center, talking to the faculty, falling in step with residents of Laurie's dormitory.

At the end of that time he had learned little that would be useful in Laurie's defense, although there were a few things he'd come up with that might possibly lighten her sentence. For the first three years of college she'd been an exemplary student, popular with both faculty and fellow students. "Well liked, but, if you know what I mean, not close," a student from the third floor of her apartment building volunteered. "It's just natural after a while for friends to talk pretty openly about their dates or their families or what's on their minds. Laurie never did that. She was with the crowd and agreeable, but if anyone teased her about Gregg Bennett, who obviously was crazy about her, she'd laugh it off. There was always something very private about her."

Brendon Moody had looked thoroughly into Gregg Bennett's background. Family money.

Bright. Had quit college to become an entrepreneur, gotten his ears pinned back and returned for his degree. Carried a double major with honors in both. Graduating in May. Would be starting Stanford next September in the master's program. The kind of guy you'd want your daughter to bring home to meet the family, Brendon thought, and then reminded himself they'd said the same thing about serial killer Ted Bundy.

All the students were in agreement that the change in Laurie after her parents' death was dramatic. Moody. Withdrawn. Complained of headaches. Skipped classes. Assignments late. "Sometimes she'd pass me right by and not even say hello, or she'd look at me as though she'd never seen me before," one junior explained.

Brendon did not tell anyone about Laurie's multiple personality disorder. Sarah was saving that for the trial and did not want a plethora of publicity on the subject.

A significant number of students had noticed Laurie regularly going out alone at night and returning late. They'd commented on it among themselves, trying to guess whom she was meeting. A few had started to put two and two together because of the way Laurie frequently arrived at Allan Grant's classes early and lingered to talk with him afterwards.

The dean's wife, Louise Larkin, enjoyed talking with Moody. It was from her that he got the hint that Allan Grant had become interested in one of the new teachers in the English department. Following Mrs. Larkin's lead, he spoke to Vera West, but she stonewalled him.

"Allan Grant was a good friend to everybody,"

West said when Brendon talked with her. She ignored any implication in his questions.

Start sifting again, Brendon thought grimly. The problem was that the school year would be over soon, and a lot of the seniors who knew Laurie Kenyon well would be graduating. People like Gregg Bennett.

With that thought in mind, Brendon called Bennett and asked if they could get together again for a cup of coffee. Gregg was on his way out for the weekend, however, so they agreed to meet on Monday. As always, Bennett asked how Laurie was doing.

"From what her sister tells me, she's coming along pretty well," Brendon told him.

"Remind Sarah to call me if there's anything I can do."

Another unproductive week, Brendon thought as he drove home. To his disgust, he learned that his wife was having a Tupperware party at their home that evening. "I'll grab something at Solari's," he said, planting an irritated kiss on the top of her forehead. "How you let yourself get roped into that nonsense, I can't fathom."

"Have fun, dear. It will do you good to catch up with the regulars."

That night Brendon got his long-awaited break. He was sitting at the bar, talking with some of the old crowd from the prosecutor's office. The talk led to Sarah and Laurie Kenyon. The general feeling was that Sarah would be better off to plea bargain. "If they drop the charge to aggravated manslaughter, Laurie might get between fifteen and thirty, probably serve one third . . . be out by the time she's twenty-six or -seven."

"Judge Armon has been assigned, and he doesn't cut deals," one of the other assistant prosecutors said. "Anyhow, the fatal attraction killers aren't popular with any judge at sentencing time."

"I'd hate to see a good-looking kid like Laurie Kenyon locked up with some of those tough babes," another commented.

Bill Owens, a private investigator for an insurance company, was standing next to Brendon Moody. He waited till the subject was changed. Then he said, "Brendon, it can't get around that I tipped you off."

Moody's head did not turn, but his eyes darted to the side. "What's up?"

"You know Danny O'Toole?"

"Danny the Spouse Hunter? Sure. Who's he been spying on lately?"

"That's the point. He was a little drunk here the other night, and as usual, something came up about the Kenyon case. Listen to this. After the parents were killed, Danny was hired to investigate the sisters. Something about an insurance claim. When the younger one was arrested, the job ended."

"Sounds fishy," Moody said. "I'll get right on it. And thanks."

73

"*THE PEOPLE* who bought our house are getting on Sarah's nerves," Laurie volunteered to Dr. Donnelly.

Justin was surprised. "I hadn't realized that."

"Yes, Sarah said they're around too much. They'll be taking over the house in August and asked permission to do some planting."

"Have you ever watched them on television, Laurie?"

She shook her head. "I don't like that kind of program."

Justin waited. On his desk he had the report from the art therapist. Little by little a pattern was forming in Laurie's sketches. The last half dozen had been collages, and in each she had included two specific scenes: one showed a rocking chair with a thick, deep cushion, and next to it a stick figure of a woman, the other, a thick-trunked tree with wide, heavy branches in front of a windowless house.

Justin pointed to those illustrations on each of the papers. "Remember doing these?"

Laurie looked at them indifferently. "Sure. I'm not much of an artist, am I?"

"You'll do. Laurie, look at that rocking chair. Can you describe it?"

He saw her start to slip away. Her eyes widened. Her body became tense. But he did not want one of the alter personalities to block him. "Laurie, try."

"I have a headache," she whispered.

"Laurie, you trust me. You've just remembered something, haven't you? Don't be afraid. For Sarah's sake, tell me about it, let it out."

She pointed to the rocking chair, then clamped her lips together and squeezed her arms against her sides.

"Laurie, show me. If you can't talk about it, show me what happened."

"I will." The lisping, childlike voice.

"Good girl, Debbie." Justin waited.

She hooked her feet under his desk and tilted back the chair. Her arms crushed against her sides as though held in place by an outside force. She brought down the chair onto the floor with a thud and tilted it back again. Her face was contorted in fear. "'Amazing grace, how sweet the sound,'" she sang in a frail, little-girl voice.

The chair thudded and tilted in perfect imitation of a rocker. With her body arched and arms immobile, she was miming a young child being held on a lap. Justin glanced down at the top drawing. That was it. The cushion looked like a lap. A small child held by someone and singing as she was being rocked. Back and forth. Back and forth.

"'. . . And grace will lead me home.'" The chair stopped. Her eyes closed again. Her breathing became quick, painful gasps. She stood and went up on her toes as though she was being lifted. "Time to go upstairs," she said in a deep voice.

74

"*HERE THEY COME* again," Sophie observed tartly as the familiar dark blue Cadillac pulled up into the driveway.

Sarah and Brendon Moody were in the kitchen waiting for the coffee to perk. "Oh God," Sarah said, her tone irritated. "It's my fault for letting it happen," she said to Brendon. "Tell you what. Sophie, bring the coffee into the library when it's ready and tell them I'm in a meeting. I'm just not in the mood to be prayed over."

Brendon scurried behind her and closed the library door as the chimes sounded through the house. "I'm glad you didn't give them a key," he said.

Sarah smiled. "I'm not that crazy. The thing is that there are so many things in this house that I can't use, and they're willing and anxious to buy them. I've been having appraisals. They're bringing in experts to have their own appraisals, and it's beginning to feel as though I have star boarders."

"Why not get it over with at once?" Brendon asked.

"Mostly my fault. I tell them what I'm willing to sell, then I take a look at all the stuff in this house and realize no way am I going to fit it into a condo, and so I tell them all this other stuff is available too.

Or they come to me and ask about that painting or that table or that lamp. And so it goes." Sarah pushed back her hair. The day was warm and humid, and her hair had frizzed into a cloud resembling dark autumn leaves around her face.

"That's something else," she added as she sat down at the desk. "Dad never went for air-conditioning, and they intend to put in a new system. They'd like to be able to move on it as soon as we close, and that means engineers and whatever now."

Keep your mouth shut, Brendon told himself as he settled in the leather chair opposite the desk. He knew that the Hawkinses had paid top dollar for the house, and if they were buying the furniture Sarah could not use, it meant she didn't have to try to find buyers or store it. Laurie's hospitalization was costing a fortune, and the student insurance policy she carried was covering only a small portion of it. To say nothing of the costs of preparing a defense, and Sarah not working, he thought.

"You've had a chance to go over your insurance policies?" he asked.

"Yes. Brendon, I don't get it. There is no outstanding or questionable claim. My father kept his records straight. His insurance went to Mother, and then, in the event of her predeceasing him, to us. Since he outlived her by a few minutes, it came directly to us. Unfortunately everything except the house is tied up in trusts, which would have made a lot of sense if all this hadn't happened. We get payouts of fifty thousand dollars each for five years for a total of a quarter of a million each, and there's no way we can invade the principal of those trusts."

"What about the bus company?" Brendon asked. "Have you filed suit against them?"

"Of course," Sarah said. "But why would they have us checked? We weren't involved in the accident."

"Oh, hell," Brendon said, "I was hoping to get somewhere with this angle. I'll get the investigator drunk and pump him, but that's probably what it's about. Just the bus company. How's Laurie?"

Sarah considered. "She's better in a lot of ways. I think she's coming to terms with losing Dad and Mom. Dr. Donnelly is wonderful."

"Any memory of Allan Grant's death?"

"Nothing. However, she is starting to let things out about what happened to her those years she was away. Just bits and pieces. Justin, I mean Dr. Donnelly, is sure that she was molested in that time. But even showing her the videotapes of her therapy sessions when her alter personalities come out isn't helping her to have a real breakthrough." Sarah's voice lost its calm tone and became desperate. "Brendon, it's May. In three months I have found nothing to use as a defense for her. She seems to have three alter personalities. Kate, who is kind of a protector, almost like a cross nanny. Calls Laurie a wimp and gets angry at her, but then tries to shield her. She keeps blocking memory. Leona is a sexpot. That personality did have a fatal attraction for Allan Grant. Just last week she told Dr. Donnelly that she's so sorry she brought the knife with her that night."

"Sweet Jesus," Brendon muttered.

"The last personality is Debbie, a four-year-old kid. She cries all the time." Sarah raised her hands, then let them fall. "Brendon, that's it."

"Will she ever remember what happened?"

"Possibly, but no one can predict how long it will take. She does trust Justin. She understands that

215

she can end up in prison. But she can't seem to make the breakthrough." Sarah looked at him. "Brendon, don't suggest I plea bargain."

"I have no intention of suggesting that," Brendon growled. "At least not yet."

Sophie entered the library, carrying a tray of coffee. "I left them alone upstairs," she said. "That's all right, isn't it?"

"Of course," Sarah said. "After all, Sophie, he's a preacher. Surely he's not stuffing trinkets in his pockets."

"Today they're having a big debate about combining your bathroom and Laurie's and putting in a Jacuzzi. I thought clergymen lived simply." She banged the tray on the desk.

"Not necessarily," Brendon commented. He dropped three lumps of sugar in the coffee and stirred it vigorously. "Sarah, Gregg Bennett honestly doesn't know what triggered Laurie's reaction to him last year. I think he's still pretty crazy about her. The evening before Grant died, some of the students were discussing Laurie's crush on the professor and Gregg overheard them. Stormed out of the student center."

"Jealous?" Sarah asked quickly.

Brendon shrugged. "If he was, it doesn't seem to have any bearing on Allan Grant's death unless . . ."

"Unless Laurie gets her memory back."

There was a tap on the door. Sarah raised her eyes. "Prepare yourself to be blessed," she murmured, then called, "come in."

Bic and Opal, their faces set in solicitous smiles, stood in the doorway. They were dressed casually. Bic had taken off his jacket, and his shortsleeved

T-shirt revealed muscular arms covered with soft graying hair. Opal wore slacks and a cotton blouse. "Not to disturb, just to see how it's going," she said.

Sarah introduced Brendon Moody to them. He grunted a greeting.

"And how is that little girl?" Bic asked. "You don't know how many people we have praying on her."

75

JUSTIN DONNELLY did not want to admit to Sarah that he now believed Laurie would not recover significant memory in time for the trial. With two members of his staff, Pat and Kathie, the art and journal therapists, he reviewed the tapes of his therapy sessions with Laurie. "Notice how the alter personalities trust me now and are willing to talk, but they all stonewall me when I try to go back to the night of January twenty-eighth or the years of Laurie's abduction. Let's discuss the three alter personalities again.

"Kate is thirty-three, which makes her fairly close to Sarah's age. I think she was created by Laurie to be a protector, which is how Laurie sees Sarah. Totally unlike Sarah, Kate is usually annoyed at Laurie, calls her a wimp, gets disgusted with her for getting in trouble. I think that shows Laurie's feeling that she deserves to have Sarah angry at her.

"Debbie, the four-year-old child, wants to talk but is too frightened or maybe just doesn't understand what happened. I suspect she is pretty much as Laurie was at that age. Sometimes she shows flashes of humor. Sarah Kenyon said that Laurie was a precociously funny child before she was kidnapped.

"Leona is a pretty sexy lady. There's no question she was crazy about Allan Grant and jealous of his wife. There's no question that she was so angry about what she perceived as his betrayal of her that she might have been capable of killing him, but now she talks about him with a kind of affection, the way you might talk about an old lover. The fight's over. The anger's faded and you remember the good parts."

They were in the staff room adjacent to Justin's office. The late spring sun was streaming in the windows. From where he sat, Justin could look over at the solarium. Several of the patients were there, enjoying the sunshine. As he watched, Laurie walked into the solarium, arm in arm with Sarah.

Pat, the art therapist, was holding several new drawings. "Have you got the snapshot that Laurie tore up at home?" she asked.

"Right here." Justin riffled through the file.

The therapist studied the photograph, compared it with some of Laurie's sketches, then laid them side by side. "Okay, see this." She pointed to a stick figure. "And this. And this. What do you make of it?"

"She's starting to put a playsuit or a bathing suit on the stick figure," Justin commented.

"Right. Now notice how in these three, the figure has long hair. In these two, look at the difference. Very short hair. She's drawn a face of sorts that gives me the impression of a boy's face. The arms are folded the way they are in the picture that's glued together. I think there's a possibility that she's recreating that image of herself but changing it to a boy. I wish to God the print wasn't so mutilated. She sure did a terrific job of shredding it."

Kathie, the journal therapist, was holding Laurie's latest composition. "This is the handwriting of her alternate Kate. But notice how different it is from the way it was in February. It's more and more like Laurie's penmanship. And listen to what it says. 'I'm getting so tired. Laurie will be strong enough to accept what has to be. She'd like to walk in Central Park. She'd like to take the golf clubs, drive to the club and tee off. It would have been fun for her to be on the golf circuit. Was it less than a year ago they called her the best young woman golfer in New Jersey? Maybe prison isn't much different than here. Maybe it's secure like this place. Maybe the knife dream will stay far away in prison. Nobody can sneak into prison with guards around. They can't come with knives in the night. They check all the incoming mail in prison. That means that pictures can't walk into books by themselves.'" The journal therapist handed the composition to Justin. "Doctor, this may be a sign that Kate is accepting guilt and punishment for Laurie."

Justin stared out the window. Sarah and Laurie were sitting side by side. Whatever Sarah was saying, Laurie was laughing. They could have been two very attractive young women on their terrace at home or at a country club.

219

The art therapist had followed his gaze. "I was talking to Sarah yesterday. I think she's going on sheer nerve now. The day the prison door closes behind Laurie, you may have a new patient, Dr. Donnelly."

Justin stood up. "They're due in my office in ten minutes. Pat, I think you're right. She's drawing different versions of the torn snapshot. Do you know anyone who might be able to take it apart, clean off all that glue, reassemble it and blow it up so we can get a better look?"

She nodded. "I can try."

He turned to Kathie. "Do you think that if Laurie or Kate realizes the effect her imprisonment will have on Sarah that she'll be less resigned to an automatic conviction?"

"Possibly."

"Okay. And there's something else I'm going to do. I'm going to talk to Gregg Bennett, Laurie's ex-boyfriend, and try to find out all the circumstances of the day she became so frightened of him."

76

As BRENDON MOODY slid onto a bar stool at Solari's next to Danny the Spouse Hunter, he noted that Danny's cherubic face was beginning to sag at the jawline. Broken capillaries on his nose and cheeks were tributes to his appreciation of dry Manhattans.

Dan greeted Moody with his usual exuberance. "Ah, there you are, Brendon. A sight for sore eyes."

Brendon grunted a greeting, resisting the urge to tell Dan what he could do with his acquired brogue. Then, reminding himself of the reason he was here and of Danny's fondness for dry Manhattans and the Mets, he ordered a round and asked Danny how he figured the team would do this season.

"Brilliant. A pennant," Danny crowed happily. "The lads have it together, by jingo."

I knew you when you could speak English, Brendon thought, but said, "Grand. Grand."

An hour later as Brendon nursed his first drink, Danny finished his third. It was time. Brendon directed the conversation to Laurie Kenyon. "I've been on the case," he said in a confidential whisper.

Danny's eyes narrowed. "So I've heard. Poor girl went bonkers, did she not?"

"Looks it," Brendon acknowledged. "Guess she went nuts after the parents were killed. Too bad she didn't get regular professional counseling then."

Danny glanced around. "Ah, but she did," he whispered. "And forget where you heard it. I hate to think they'd keep you in the dark."

Brendon looked shocked. "You mean she was seeing some shrink?"

"Right over in Ridgewood."

"How do you know, Danny?"

"Between the two of us?"

"Of course."

"Right after the parents died my services were engaged just to do a background check on the sisters and their activities."

"No kidding. Insurance company, I suppose.

Something about a claim against the bus company?"

"Now, Brendon Moody, you know the client-investigator relationship is strictly confidential."

"Of course it is. But that bus was going too fast; the brakes were bad. The Kenyons never had a chance. Naturally an insurance company would be pretty nervous and want to get a line on the potential plaintiffs. Who else would be checking on them?"

Danny remained stubbornly silent. Brendon signaled the bartender, who shook his head. "I'll drive my good friend home," Brendon promised. He knew it was time to change the subject. An hour later, after he hoisted Danny into the passenger seat of his car, he started talking about the Kenyons again. As he pulled up in the driveway of Danny's modest split level he hit pay dirt.

"Brendon, me lad, you're a good friend," Danny said, his voice thick and slow. "Don't think I don't know but that you've been pumping me. Between you and me and the lamppost, I don't know who hired me. All very mysterious. A woman it was. Called herself Jane Graves. Never did meet her. Called every week to get a progress report. Had it sent to a private mail drop in New York City. You know who I think it might be? The widow of the late professor. Wasn't the poor dingbat Kenyon girl writing mash notes to him? And didn't the demand for my services end the day after the murder?"

Danny pushed open the car door and staggered out. "A grand good night to ye, and next time ask me straight. It won't cost you so many drinks."

77

*T*HE "ARCHITECT" Bic had brought to the Kenyon home on one of his early visits was an ex-convict from Kentucky. It was he who wired the library and telephone with sophisticated, voice-activated equipment, and concealed a recorder in the guest bedroom above the study.

As Bic and Opal roamed upstairs with measuring tapes, fabrics and paint samples, it was an easy matter for them to change the cassettes. The minute they were in the car, Bic began playing the tapes and he continued to listen to them over and over in their Wyndham Hotel suite.

Sarah had begun to have regular evening telephone conversations with Justin Donnelly, and these were gold mines of information. At first Opal had to make a concerted effort to conceal her sullen annoyance at Bic's absolute passion for any news of Lee. But as the weeks went by she was torn between fear of discovery and fascination at the talk about Laurie's flashes of recall. Sarah's discussion with the doctor about the rocking chair memory especially gratified Bic.

"The little darlin'," he sighed. "Remember how pretty she was and how nice she could sing. We taught her well." He shook his head. "My, my." Then he frowned. "But, she's starting to talk."

Bic had opened the hotel windows, allowing the warm May air to fill the room, the faint breeze rippling the curtains. He was letting his hair grow a little longer, and today it was disheveled. He was wearing only old slacks and a T-shirt, which exposed the thick curly hair on his arms that Opal called her favorite pillow. She stared at him, worshipping him with her eyes.

"What are you thinking, Opal?" he asked.

"You'll say I'm crazy."

"Try me."

"It just occurred to me that right at this minute, with your hair mussed and you in your T-shirt and your jacket off, all you need is that gold earring you used to wear and the Reverend Hawkins would disappear. You'd be Bic the nightclub singer again."

Bic stared at her for a long minute. I shouldn't have told him that, she thought aghast. He won't want to think that's possible. But then he said, "Opal, the Lord directed you to that revelation. I was thinking on the old farmhouse in Pennsylvania and that rocking chair where I used to sit with that sweet baby in my arms, and a plan was forming. Now you've completed it."

"What is it?"

The benevolent expression faded. "No questions. You know that. Never any questions. This is between me and the Blessed Lord."

"I'm sorry, Bobby." She deliberately addressed him that way, knowing it would mollify him.

"That's all right. One thing I am learning from all that listening is that I don't wear short sleeves around those people. The business of fuzzy arm hair is coming up pretty regular. And did you notice something else?"

She waited.

Bic smiled coldly. "This whole situation may be starting a little romantic brush fire. Listen to the way that doctor and Sarah talk to each other. Tone of voice, warmer and warmer. He's more and more concerned about her. It will be nice for her to have someone for comfort after Lee joins the heavenly choir."

78

KAREN GRANT glanced up from her desk and smiled brightly. The small, balding man with the wrinkled forehead looked vaguely familiar. She invited him to sit down. He presented his card, and she understood why she had recognized him. He was the investigator working for the Kenyons, and he'd been at the funeral. Louise Larkin had told her that he had been questioning people on the campus.

"Mrs. Grant, if this isn't a good time, just say so." Moody glanced around the office.

"Absolutely fine," she assured him. "It's a quiet morning."

"I gather the travel business in general is pretty quiet these days," Moody said casually. "At least that's what my friends tell me."

"Oh, like everything else, it's gotten leaner and meaner. Can I sell you a trip?"

Sharp lady, Brendon thought, and just as attractive up close as across a grave site. Karen Grant was wearing a turquoise linen suit and matching blouse. The blue-green color brought out the green in her eyes. That outfit didn't come from K Mart, Brendon decided. Neither did the crescent of jade and diamonds on her lapel. "Not today," he said. "If I may I'd like to ask a few questions about your late husband."

The smile faded. "It's very hard to talk about Allan," she said. "Louise Larkin told me about you. You're working on Laurie Kenyon's defense. Mr. Moody, I'm terribly sorry for Laurie, but she did take my husband's life and she threatened mine."

"She doesn't remember anything about it. She's a very sick girl," Brendon said quietly. "It's my job to try to help a jury to understand that. I've been going over copies of the letters she, or someone, sent to Professor Grant. How long were you aware that he was receiving them?"

"At first, Allan didn't show them to me. I guess he was afraid I'd be upset."

"Upset?"

"Well, they were patently ludicrous. I mean some of the 'remembrances' were of nights when Allan and I were together. It was obvious they were all fantasy, but even so, they were certainly unpleasant. I happened to see the letters in his desk drawer and I asked about them."

"How well did you know Laurie?"

"Not well. She's a marvelous golfer, and I'd seen write-ups about her in the papers. I met her parents at some college affairs, that sort of thing. I felt terribly sorry for her after they died. I know Allan thought that she was heading for a breakdown."

226

"You were in New York the night he died?"

"I was at the airport meeting a client."

"When did you last speak to your husband?"

"I called him at about eight o'clock that night. He was terribly upset. He told me about the scene with Laurie Kenyon. He felt he hadn't handled the situation properly. He thought he should have sat down with Sarah and Laurie before having Laurie called in by the dean. He said that he honestly believed she had no recollection of writing those letters. She was so angry and shocked when she was accused."

"You do realize that if you testify to that on the witness stand it could be helpful to Laurie."

Now tears welled in Karen Grant's eyes. "My husband was the nicest, kindest human being I've ever known. He of all people would not want me to hurt that girl."

Moody's eyes narrowed. "Mrs. Grant, was there any point when you had a few doubts about whether or not your husband was falling in love with Laurie?"

She looked astonished. "That's ridiculous. She's twenty or twenty-one. Allan was forty."

"It's been known to happen. I certainly wouldn't blame you if you wanted to be sure, say maybe have it checked out."

"I don't know what you're talking about."

"I mean possibly hire a private investigator like myself . . ."

The tears dried. Karen Grant was visibly angry. "Mr. Moody, I wouldn't have insulted my husband like that. And you're insulting me." She stood up. "I don't think we have anything more to say to each other."

Moody rose slowly. "Mrs. Grant, please forgive

me. Try to understand that my job is to find some reason for Laurie's actions. You said that Professor Grant thought Laurie was nearing a breakdown. If there was something going on between them, if he then betrayed her to the administration and she then snapped . . ."

"Mr. Moody. Do not try to defend the girl who murdered my husband by ruining his reputation. Allan was a private man and intensely embarrassed by student crushes. You cannot change that fact to save his murderer."

As he nodded apologetically, Brendon Moody's glance was sweeping the office. Attractively furnished with a red leather settee and chairs. Framed posters of exotic travel scenes on walls. Fresh flowers on Karen Grant's desk and on the coffee table by the couch. Her desk, however, was clear of paperwork, and the phone had not rung since he'd been in the office. "Mrs. Grant, I'd like to leave on a happier note. My daughter is an American Airlines hostess. Loves the job. Says the travel business gets into your blood. I hope you feel that way and your job is helping you to adjust to the loss of your husband."

He thought she seemed slightly mollified. "I'd be lost without it."

There was no sign of anyone else. "How many people work here?" he asked casually.

"My secretary is on an errand. Anne Webster, the owner, is out ill today."

"Then you're in charge?"

"Anne is retiring soon. I'll be taking over completely."

"I see. Well, I've taken enough of your time."

Moody did not leave the hotel immediately. Instead he sat in the lobby and observed the travel agency. Two hours later not a single person had entered it. Through the glass wall he could see that Karen did not pick up the phone even once. Putting down the newspaper he had used to disguise his presence, he moseyed over to the bell captain's desk and began to chat with him.

79

GREGG BENNETT drove up the Turnpike to the exit for the Lincoln Tunnel. It was a warm, hazy day, more like July than the last week in May. He rode with the top down on his new Mustang convertible, a graduation gift from his grandfather. The gift made him uncomfortable. "Granpa, I'm twenty-five, old enough to earn the money for my own cars," he'd protested. Then his mother pulled him aside.

"For heaven's sake, Gregg, don't be such a stiffneck. Granpa is so proud that you've been accepted at Stanford that he's busting his buttons."

In truth, Gregg preferred the ten-year-old secondhand Ford he'd driven at Clinton. He could still see himself throwing the golf bags in the trunk, Laurie getting in beside him, teasing him about his game.

Laurie.

He turned the car onto the Route 3 approach to the tunnel. As usual traffic was backed up, and he glanced at the clock on the dashboard. Three-forty. It was okay. He'd left plenty of time to get to the clinic. He hoped he looked all right. He had debated about what to wear, then chosen a tan linen jacket, open-neck shirt, chinos and loafers. Laurie wouldn't know him if he got too gussied up. His mouth went dry at the thought that after all these months he would be seeing her again.

Sarah was waiting for him in the reception area. He kissed her cheek. It was obvious to him that she'd been going through hell. Deep circles underlined her eyes. Her dark brows and lashes made her skin seem transparent. She immediately brought him in to meet Laurie's doctor.

Donnelly was gravely honest. "Someday Laurie may be able to tell us about those years she was missing and about Allan Grant's death, but as it stands now, she can't tell us in time to prepare her defense. What we're trying to do is to in effect go around her, to recreate a scene in which she had a dissociative reaction and see if we can learn what set her off. You've told Sarah and Detective Moody about the episode in your apartment a year ago—we'd like to recreate it.

"Laurie's agreeable to the experiment. We're going to videotape you with her. We need you to describe in her presence, what you were doing, what you were saying, where you were in relation to each other. Please, for her sake don't edit or hide anything. I mean anything."

Gregg nodded.

Dr. Donnelly picked up the phone. "Will you bring Laurie in, please?"

Gregg didn't know what to expect. Certainly it wasn't the attractive Laurie dressed in a short cotton skirt and T-shirt, a narrow belt cinching her slender waist, sandals on her feet. She stiffened when she saw him. Some instinct made Gregg decide not to get up. He waved at her casually. "Hi, Laurie."

She watched him warily as she took a seat next to Sarah, then nodded but said nothing.

Justin turned on the camera. "Gregg, Laurie came to visit you about a year ago and for some unknown reason, she panicked. Tell us about it."

Gregg had gone over that morning so often in his mind that there was no hesitation. "It was Sunday. I slept late. At ten o'clock Laurie rang the bell and woke me up."

"Describe where you live," Justin cut in.

"A rented studio over a garage a couple of miles from the campus. Compact kitchen, countertop with stools, convertible sofa bed, bookcases, dresser, two closets, decent-sized john. Actually it's not bad as these things go."

Sarah watched Laurie close her eyes as though remembering.

"All right," Justin said. "Did you expect Laurie to drop in?"

"No. She was going home for the day. Actually she had invited me to go with her, but I had a term paper due. She'd been to the nine o'clock mass, then stopped at the bakery. When I opened the door, she said something like, 'Coffee for a hot bagel? Fair trade?'"

"What was her attitude?"

"Relaxed. Laughing. We'd played golf on Saturday and it had been a close round. She'd beaten me by only a stroke. Sunday morning she was wearing a white linen dress and looked terrific."

"Did you kiss her?"

Gregg glanced at Laurie. "On the cheek. I'd get signals from her. Occasionally she could be pretty responsive when I'd start to kiss her, but I was always careful. It was like you could scare her away. When I kissed her or put my arm around her, I'd do it slowly and casually and see if she'd tense up. If she did, I quit right away."

"Didn't you find that pretty frustrating?" Justin asked quickly.

"Sure. But I think I always knew there was something in Laurie that was afraid, and that I would have to wait for her to trust me." Gregg looked directly at Laurie. "I'd never hurt her. I'd kill before I let anyone else hurt her."

Laurie was staring at him, no longer avoiding his gaze. It was she who spoke next. "I sat next to Gregg at the counter. We had two cups of coffee and split the third bagel. We were talking about when we could get in another round of golf. I felt so happy that day. It was such a beautiful morning and everything felt so fresh and clean." Her voice faltered as she said "clean."

Gregg stood up. "Laurie said she had to be on her way. She kissed me and started to leave."

"There was no sign of fear or panic at that point?" Justin interjected.

"None."

"Laurie, I want you to stand near Gregg just as you did that day. Pretend you're about to leave his apartment."

Hesitantly Laurie stood up. "Like this," she whispered. She reached out for an imaginary doorknob, her back to Gregg. "And he . . ."

"And I started to pick her up . . ." Gregg said. "I mean jokingly. I wanted to kiss her again."

"Show me how," Justin commanded.

"Like this." Gregg stood behind Laurie, pressed his hands against her arms and started to raise her.

Her body stiffened. She began to whimper. Instantly Gregg released her.

"Laurie, tell me why you're afraid," Justin said swiftly.

The whimper changed into stifled, childlike weeping, but she did not answer.

"Debbie, you're the one crying," Justin said. "Tell me why."

She pointed down and to the right. A frail, small voice sobbed, "He's going to take me there."

Gregg looked shocked and puzzled. "Wait a minute," he said. "If we were in my apartment, she'd be pointing to the sofabed."

"Describe it," Justin snapped.

"I'd just gotten up, so it was still open and unmade."

"Debbie, why were you afraid when you thought Gregg was taking you to the bed? What might happen to you there? Tell us."

She had dropped her face in her hands. The soft childlike crying continued. "I can't."

"Why not, Debbie? We love you."

She looked up and ran to Sarah. "Sare-wuh, I don't know what happened," she whispered. "Whenever we got to the bed, I floated away."

80

V*ERA WEST* was counting the days until the term ended. She was finding it increasingly difficult to keep up the calm façade that she knew was absolutely necessary. Now as she walked across the campus in the late afternoon, her leather zipbag bulging with final term papers clasped in her arms, she found herself praying that she would reach the sanctuary of her rented cottage before she began to cry.

She loved the cottage. It was on a wooded cul-de-sac and at one time had been the home of the gardener of the large manor house nearby. She had taken the job in the English Department at Clinton because after going back to school for her doctorate at age thirty-seven and receiving it at forty, she'd felt restless, ready for a change from Boston.

Clinton was the kind of jewellike smaller college she loved. A theater buff, she also enjoyed the nearness to New York.

Along the way, a few men had been interested in her. At times she wistfully wished she could find someone who would seem special but had decided she was destined to follow in the footsteps of her unmarried aunts.

Then she'd met Allan Grant.

Until it was too late, it never occurred to Vera that she was falling in love with him. He was another faculty member, a very nice human being, a teacher whose intellect she admired, whose popularity she understood.

It had begun in October. One night Allan's car wouldn't start, and she'd offered him a ride home from a Kissinger lecture in the auditorium. He'd invited her in for a nightcap and she'd accepted. It hadn't occurred to her that his wife wasn't there.

His house was a surprise. Expensively furnished. Surprisingly so, considering what she knew to be his salary. But there was no sense of an effort having been made to pull it together. It looked as though it could stand a good cleaning. She knew that Karen, his wife, worked in Manhattan but didn't realize that she had an apartment there.

"Hi, Dr. West."

"What—oh, hello." Vera tried to smile as she passed a group of students. From the air of buoyancy about them it was obvious that the term was nearly over. None of these students would be dreading the emptiness of the summer, the emptiness of the future.

That first evening at Allan's home, she'd offered to get the ice while he prepared a scotch and soda for them. In the freezer individual packages of pizza, lasagna, chicken-pot pies and God knows what else were piled together. Good heavens, she'd wondered, is that the way this poor guy eats?

Two nights later, Allan dropped off a book at her place. She'd just roasted a chicken, and the inviting aroma filled the cottage. When he commented on it, she impulsively invited him to dinner.

Allan was in the habit of taking a long predinner

walk. He began to stop by occasionally, and then more often on the nights Karen was in New York. He would phone, ask if she wanted company and if so, what could he bring? Calling himself the man who came to dinner, he'd arrive with wine or a wedge of cheese or some fruit. He always left by eight or eight-thirty. His manner toward her was always attentive, but no different than if the room had been filled with people.

Even so, Vera began to lie awake at night wondering how long it would be before people started to gossip about them. Without asking, she was sure that he did not tell his wife about their time together.

Allan showed her the "Leona" letters as soon as they began to arrive. "I'm not going to let Karen see these," he said. "They'd only upset her."

"Surely she wouldn't put any stock in them."

"No, but underneath that sophisticated veneer, Karen is pretty insecure, and she does depend on me more than she realizes." A few weeks later he told her that Karen had found the letters. "Just what I expected. She's upset and worried."

At the time, Vera had thought that Karen sent some pretty mixed signals. Worried about her husband but away so much. Foolish lady.

At first, Allan seemed to deliberately avoid any kind of personal discussion. Then gradually he began to talk about growing up. "My dad split when I was eight months old. My mother and grandmother . . . what a pair. They did anything to make a dollar." He'd laughed. "I mean just *about* anything. My grandmother had a big old house in Ithaca. She rented rooms to old people. I always said I was raised in a nursing home. Four or five of them were retired teachers, so I had a lot of help with my homework. My mother worked in the local department store. They saved every penny they could for my education and invested it wisely. I swear they were disappointed when I won a full scholarship to Yale. They were both good cooks. I can still remember how great it was to get home on a cold afternoon after I finished my paper route, open the door, feel that blast of warmth and breathe in all the good smells from the kitchen."

Allan had told her all that a week before he died. Then he'd said, "Vera, that's the way I feel when I come here. Warmth and a sense of coming home to someone I want to be with and who I hope wants me." He'd put his arm around her. "Can you be patient with me? I've got to work something out."

The night he died, Allan had been with her for the last time. He'd been depressed and upset. "I should have spoken to Laurie and her sister first. I jumped the gun by going to the dean. Now the dean has as much as said that my manner with these kids is too friendly. He flat out asked me if Karen and I were having problems, if there was any reason she was away so much." At the door that night, he'd kissed her slowly and said, "It's going to change. I love and need you very much."

Some instinct had warned her to tell him to stay with her. If only she'd listened to it and to hell with the gossips. But she let him go. A little after ten-thirty she'd phoned him. He sounded remarkably cheerful. He'd spoken to Karen and it was all out on the table. He had taken a sleeping pill. Again he had said, "I love you," the last words she would ever hear from him.

Too restless to go to bed herself, Vera had watched the eleven o'clock news and started tidying up the living room, fluffing pillows, straightening magazines. In the wing chair she'd noticed something gleaming. The ignition key to Allan's car. It must have slipped out of his pocket.

She was filled with unreasoning worry about him. The key was an excuse to call again. She dialed his number, letting the phone ring and ring. There was no answer. The sleeping pill must really have taken effect, she'd reassured herself.

Today, suddenly reminded again of her loneliness, Vera hurried, head down, along her cobblestone walk, Allan's face filling her mind. Her arms ached for him. She reached the steps. *"Allan. Allan. Allan."*

Vera didn't realize she'd spoken his name aloud until she looked up into the keen eyes of Brendon Moody, who was waiting for her on the porch.

81

SEATED AT a corner table in Villa Cesare in Hillsdale, a few miles from Ridgewood, Sarah wondered why in heaven's name she had let herself get talked into having dinner with the Reverend Bobby and Carla Hawkins.

The couple had shown up at her door five minutes after she returned from New York. They'd been just driving around, they explained, getting to know their new neighborhood, and she'd passed them on Lincoln Avenue.

"You looked as though you needed a little help," the Reverend Bobby said. "I just felt the Lord telling me to turn around, drop by and say hello."

When she'd reached home at seven o'clock after leaving the clinic and saying goodbye to Gregg Bennett, Sarah had realized she was tired and hungry. Sophie was out, and the minute Sarah opened the door of the empty house she knew she didn't want to stay there.

Villa Cesare was a longtime favorite restaurant, a great place to eat. Clams casino, shrimp scampi, a glass of white wine, cappuccino; that always-friendly, welcoming atmosphere, she thought. She was walking out the door when the Hawkinses arrived; somehow they ended up joining her.

As she nodded to familiar faces at other tables, Sarah told herself, these are caring people and I'll accept any prayers I can get. Lost in her thoughts, she suddenly realized that Reverend Hawkins was asking about Laurie.

"It's all a matter of time," she explained. "Justin—I mean Dr. Donnelly—doesn't have any doubt that eventually Laurie will let down her defenses and talk about the night Professor Grant died, but it seems as though that memory is entwined with her fear of whatever happened to her in the past. The doctor feels that at some point she'll achieve a spontaneous breakthrough. Pray God she does."

"Amen," Bobby and Carla said in unison.

Sarah realized her guard was down. She was talking about Laurie too much. These people were, after all, strangers whose only connection to her was that they had bought the house.

The house. Safe ground. "Mother planned the landscaping so we'd always have color," she said as she selected a crusty roll. "The tulips were marvelous. You saw them. The azaleas will be out in a week or so. They're my favorites. Ours are great, but the D'Andreas' are spectacular. They're in the corner house."

Opal smiled brightly. "Which house is that? The one with green shutters or the white one that used to be pink?"

"The one that used to be pink. God, my father hated it when the old owners painted it that color. I remember he said he was going to go to the town hall and petition to have his taxes lowered."

Opal felt Bic's eyes glaring at her. The enormity of her mistake almost made her gasp. Why had the pink corner house popped into her mind now? How many years since it had been painted?

But fortunately Sarah Kenyon did not seem to notice the slip. She began talking about the condominium and how well it was coming along. "It will be ready by August first," she said. "So we'll be on target to vacate the house for you. You've been very kind to wait so long to occupy it."

"Is there any chance that Laurie may get home?" Bic asked casually as the waiter served him veal piccata.

"Pray for that, Reverend Hawkins," Sarah told him. "Dr. Donnelly has said she is absolutely no threat to anyone. He wants a psychiatrist appointed by the prosecutor's office to examine her and agree that she should become an outpatient. He believes that in order to cooperate in her defense, Laurie must overcome the feeling that she needs to be behind locked doors in order to feel safe."

"There is nothing I want more than to see your little sister at home in Ridgewood," Bic said as he patted Sarah's hand.

That night when Sarah settled in bed, she had the nagging feeling that something she should have noticed had escaped her attention.

It must have been something Laurie said, she decided as she drifted off to sleep.

82

*J*USTIN DONNELLY walked from the clinic to his Central Park South apartment, so engrossed in his own meditation today that for once he did not drink in the changing panorama of New York. At seven o'clock, the sun was still forty minutes from setting. The hazy warmth had brought out a steady stream of people, strolling along Fifth Avenue, browsing through the book-stands on the sidewalk flanking the park or apprais-ing the amateurish art.

The pungent smell of souvlaki that wafted to his nostrils as the weary vendors pushed their carts to overnight shelters, the sight of the patient horses as they stood fastened to festively decorated carriages at the corner of Fifth and Central Park South, the line of limousines in front of the Plaza Hotel—all these things escaped him. Justin's thoughts were totally on Laurie Kenyon.

She was by far the most interesting patient he'd ever encountered. It was common for women who had been molested as small children to feel that they had somehow invited or caused the abuse. Most of them at some point came to understand they had been powerless to prevent what had happened to them. Laurie Kenyon was resisting that knowledge.

But there was progress. He'd stopped in to see her before he left the clinic. Dinner was over, and she was sitting in the solarium. She'd been quiet and pensive. "Gregg was awfully nice to have come today," she'd volunteered and then added, "I know he'd never hurt me."

Justin had taken a chance. "He did more than not hurt you, Laurie. He helped you to see that by jokingly picking you up, he triggered a memory that, if you let it out, will help you to get well. The rest is up to you."

She'd said, "I know it is. I'll try. I promise. You know, Doctor, what I'd like to do more than anything in the world?" She hadn't waited for an answer. "I'd like to fly to Scotland and play golf at St. Andrews. Does that seem crazy to you?"

"It sounds terrific to me."

"But of course it will never happen."

"Not unless you help yourself."

As Justin turned in to his building, he wondered if he'd pushed her too far. He wondered if calling the psychiatrist appointed by the prosecutor's office and asking him to reevaluate Laurie for the purpose of reinstating bail was a mistake.

A few minutes later he was sitting on the terrace of his apartment, sipping his favorite Australian Chardonnay, when the phone rang. It was the clinic. The head nurse apologized for calling. "It's Miss Kenyon. She says she must speak to you at once."

"Laurie!"

"Not Laurie, Doctor. Her alter Kate. She wants to tell you something terribly important."

"Put her on!"

The strident voice said, "Dr. Donnelly, listen, you ought to know. There's a kid who wants to talk to you something fierce, but Laurie's afraid to let him."

"Who is the kid, Kate?" Justin asked quickly. I'm right, he thought. Laurie does have another alter who hasn't surfaced yet.

"I don't know his name. He won't tell me what it is. But he's nine or ten and smart and took a hell of a lot for Laurie. He's tired of shutting his mouth. Keep working on her. You're wearing her down. He came within inches of talking to you today."

The receiver clicked in Justin's ear.

83

ON JUNE 15 the Reverend Bobby Hawkins received a phone call from Liz Pierce of *People* magazine requesting an interview. She'd been assigned to do a feature on him for a September issue, she said.

Bic protested, then said that he was flattered and pleased. "It will be a joy to spread the word of my ministry," he assured Pierce.

But when he hung up the phone, the warmth disappeared from his voice. "Opal, if I refuse, that reporter might think I was hiding something. At least this way I can influence what she writes."

84

BRENDON MOODY looked compassionately at Sarah. The mid-June day was sticky, but she still had not turned on the window air conditioner in the library. She was wearing a dark blue linen jacket with a white collar and a white skirt. It was only eight-thirty, but she was already dressed to go to New York. Four months of this, Brendon thought, eating, drinking, breathing a defense that's going nowhere; spending the day in a psychiatric clinic and being grateful her sister is there instead of in the Hunterdon County jail. And he was about to shoot down her last hope for a viable defense.

Sophie knocked and without waiting for a response opened the door and came in carrying a tray with cups of coffee, rolls and orange juice. "Mr. Moody," she said, "I hope you can make Sarah swallow this roll. She's at the point where she eats nothing and is becoming skin and bones."

"Oh, Sophie," Sarah protested.

"Don't, 'oh, Sophie,' me—it's the truth." Sophie put the tray down on the desk, her face puckered with worry. "Is the miracle man going to show up today?" she asked. "I swear, Sarah, you should charge those people rent."

"They should charge me rent," Sarah said. "They've owned this house since March."

"And the agreement was that you'd move out in August."

"They don't bother me. In fact they've been very nice to me."

"Well, I've been watching them on TV every Sunday lately, and let me tell you, they are some pair. As far as I'm concerned that man is taking the name of the Lord in vain what with promising miracles in return for cash and talking as though God drops in to chat with him every day."

"Sophie," Sarah protested.

"All right, all right, you're busy." Shaking her head, Sophie marched from the library, her heavy footsteps signaling her disapproval.

Sarah handed Brendon a coffee cup. "As we were saying, or did we get around to saying anything?"

Brendon took the coffee, added three heaping teaspoons of sugar and stirred noisily. "I wish I had good news," he said, "but I don't. Our best hope was that Allan Grant was taking advantage of Laurie's depression and grief and then drove her over the edge by giving her letters to the administration. Well, Sarah, if he was taking advantage of her, we'll never be able to prove it. His marriage was rotten. I could sense that and I've followed up on the wife. She's a piece of goods. According to the hotel staff, she's had quite a variety of different male friends. For the past year or so, however, she's stuck to the same one and seems pretty crazy about him. Name is Edwin Rand. He's one of those polished, good-looking types who's lived off women

245

all his life. About forty or forty-five. A travel writer who doesn't make enough money to live on but gets invited to resorts all over the world. He's made an art of the freebie."

"Did Allan Grant know about him?" Sarah asked.

"Can't be sure. When Karen was at home they seemed okay together."

"But suppose he did know and was hurt and rejected and turned to Laurie, who was crazy about him?"

Sarah seemed to come alive as she spoke. Poor kid, Brendon thought, grabbing at anything that would be the basis for a defense.

"It doesn't wash," he said flatly. "Allan had been seeing a member of the faculty, Vera West. West broke down when she told me that the last time she spoke to him was at about ten-thirty the night he died. He was in good spirits and said that he was relieved because it was all out on the table."

"Meaning?"

"She took it to mean that he'd told his wife he wanted a divorce."

Brendon looked away from the despair in Sarah's eyes. "Actually, you could make a prima facie case against the wife," he told her. "Allan Grant's mother left him a trust fund. He got in the neighborhood of $100,000 a year income from it. Couldn't touch the principal—and that's close to a million and a half and still growing—until he was sixty. The mother obviously realized he had no money sense.

"From what I hear, Karen Grant was treating that income as her personal allowance. In the event of a divorce, that trust was not community property. Whatever she makes at the travel agency wouldn't support her pricey apartment and designer clothers. The writer boyfriend would have been history. With Allan's death, however, she got it all.

"The only problem," Brendon concluded, "is that Karen Grant certainly didn't borrow the knife, kill her husband and then return the knife to Laurie afterwards."

Sarah didn't notice that her coffee was barely lukewarm. Sipping it helped to release the tightened muscles in her neck and throat.

"I've heard from the Hunterdon County prosecutor's office," she told him. "The psychiatrist they sent to examine Laurie reviewed the tapes of her therapy sessions. They accept the possibility that she suffers from multiple personality disorder."

She ran her hand over her forehead as though trying to brush away a headache. "In return for Laurie's pleading guilty to manslaughter, they won't press for the maximum penalty. She'd probably be out in five years, maybe less. But if we go to court, the charge will be purposeful and knowing murder. There's a good chance they could make it stick."

85

"IT'S BEEN a month since Kate phoned to tell me that there's another alter personality, a nine- or ten-year-old boy, who wants to talk to me," Justin Donnelly told Sarah. "As you know, since then, Kate disclaims any knowledge of that personality."

Sarah nodded. "I know." It was time to tell Justin Donnelly that she and Brendon Moody had agreed that it was in Laurie's best interest that they accept the offer of a plea bargain. "I've reached a decision," she began.

Justin listened, his eyes never leaving Sarah's face. If I were an artist, he thought, I would sketch that face and caption it "Grief."

"So you see," Sarah concluded, "the psychiatrists for the state do believe that Laurie was abused as a child and there is substantial indication of multiple personality disorder. They know the jury is going to sympathize with her, and it's unlikely she'd be convicted of murder. But the penalty for aggravated manslaughter is also a possible thirty years. On the other hand, if she pleads guilty to second-degree manslaughter, intentionally killing in the heat of passion with reasonable provocation, at worst she could be sentenced to a maximum of ten years. It would be up to the judge if she got a mandatory five years without parole. He could also give her as little as a five-year flat term with no parole ineligibility stipulation, and she could be out in a year or two. I don't have the right to gamble with nearly thirty years of Laurie's life."

"How can she plead guilty to a crime she doesn't remember committing?" Justin asked.

"It's legal. Her statement will be something to the effect that while she has no memory of the crime, she and her lawyer, having reviewed the evidence, are satisfied that she committed it."

"How long can you hold off?"

Sarah's voice became unsteady. "What would be

the point? I think if anything, taking the pressure off Laurie to remember might in the long run be beneficial to her. Let it go."

"No, Sarah." Justin pushed back his chair and walked over to the window, then was sorry he had. Across the garden, Laurie was standing in the solarium, her hands resting on the glass wall, looking out. Even from where he was, he could sense the feeling of a trapped bird longing to fly. He turned to Sarah. "Give me a little longer. How soon do you think the judge will allow her to go home?"

"Next week."

"All right. Are you busy tonight?"

"Well, let's see." Sarah spoke rapidly, obviously trying to rein in her emotions. "If I go home, one of two things will happen. The Hawkinses will come bursting in to deposit more of their possessions and want to take me to dinner. Or else Sophie, whom I love dearly, will be there, sorting through my parents' closets and relieving me of the job I've put off—giving away their clothes. The third alternative is that I'll try to figure out a brilliant defense for Laurie."

"Surely you have friends who ask you out."

"I have lots of friends," Sarah said. "Good friends, cousins too, terrific people who want to help. But, you see, at the end of the day I can't start explaining to everyone what's going on. I can't stand listening to the empty promises that something will turn up, that it's all going to be just fine. I can't bear to hear that none of this would have happened if Laurie hadn't been kidnapped all those years ago. I know that. That knowledge is driving me mad. Oh yes, I also don't want to hear that after all Dad was in his seventies and Mother had that operation a few years ago and the prognosis wasn't great and maybe it was a blessing they went together. You see, I do accept that. *But I don't want to hear it.*"

Justin knew that one comforting word would reduce Sarah to tears. He didn't want that to happen. Laurie would be joining them momentarily. "I was going to suggest that you have dinner with me tonight," he said mildly. "Here's something I want you to see now."

From Laurie's file, he pulled out an eight-by-ten photograph. Faint lines crisscrossed back and forth over it.

"This is an enlargement of the picture Laurie tore up the day she was admitted here," he explained. "The man who reconstructed it did a good job. Tell me what you see in it."

Sarah looked down at the photograph, and her eyes widened. "The way this was before, I didn't see that Laurie was crying. That tree. That dilapidated house. And what's that, a barn behind it? There's nothing like that in Ridgewood. Where was this taken?"

Then she frowned. "Oh, wait a minute. Laurie went to a nursery school three afternoons a week. They used to take the kids on excursions to parks and lakes. There are farmhouses like this around Harriman State Park. But why would this picture have upset her the way it did?"

"I'm going to try to find out," Justin said, switching on the video camera as Laurie opened the door.

Laurie forced herself to look at the picture. "The chicken coop behind the farmhouse," she whispered. "Bad things happen there."

"What bad things, Laurie?" Justin asked.

"Don't talk, you jerk. He'll find out and you know what he'll do to you."

Sarah dug her nails into her palms. This was a voice she had never heard before, a young, strong, boyish voice. Laurie was frowning. Even though her face seemed to have lost its contours, her mouth was set in a determined line. One hand was smacking the other.

"Hi," Justin said casually. "You're new. What's your name?"

"Get back inside, you!" It was Leona's catlike tone. "Listen, Doctor, I know that bossy Kate has been trying to go around me. It won't happen."

"Leona, why are you always the troublemaker?" Justin demanded.

Sarah realized he was trying a new tactic. His voice was belligerent.

"Because people are always pulling things on me. I trusted Allan and he made a fool of me. I trusted you when you told us to keep a journal, and you stuck that picture in it."

Laurie's hair was tumbling over her face. She was brushing it back with an unconsciously seductive gesture.

"That's impossible. You didn't find this picture in your journal, Leona."

"I certainly did. Just the way I found that damn knife in my tote bag. I was so nice when I went to Allan's for the showdown and he looked so peaceful I didn't even wake him up, and now people are blaming me because he's dead."

Sarah held her breath. Don't react, she told herself. Don't distract her.

"Did you try to wake him up?" Justin might have been commenting on the weather.

"No. I was going to show him. I mean there's no

251

way I can escape. The kitchen knife that was missing. Sarah. Sophie. Dr. Carpenter. Everybody wants to know why I took it. I did *not* take the knife. Then Allan makes a fool of me. You know what I decided to do?" She did not wait for an answer. "I was going to show that guy. Kill myself right in front of him. Let him be sorry for what he did to me. No use going on living. Nothing's ever going to be good for me."

"You went to his house and the big window was open?"

"No. I don't go in windows. The terrace door to the study. The lock doesn't catch. He was already in bed. I went into his room. For Pete's sake, have you got a cigarette?"

"Of course." Donnelly waited until Leona had settled back, the lit cigarette between her fingers, before he asked, "What was Allan doing when you went in?"

Her lips curved in a smile. "He was snoring. Can you believe it? My big scene wasted. He's curled up in bed like a little kid, arms all wrapped around the pillow, hair sort of tousled, and he's snoring." Her voice softened and became hesitant. "My daddy used to snore. Mommy used to say that was the only thing about him she'd change. He could wake up the dead when he started snoring."

Yes, Sarah thought, yes.

"And you had the knife?"

"Oh, that. I put my tote bag down on the floor by the bed. I had the knife in my hand by then. I laid the knife on top of the bag. I was so tired. And you know what I thought?"

"Tell me."

The voice changed completely, became that of

four-year-old Debbie. "I thought of all the times I wouldn't let my daddy hold me or kiss me after I came back from the house with the chicken coop and I laid down on the bed next to Allan and he never knew, he just kept on snoring."

"Then what happened, Debbie?"

Oh please, God, Sarah thought.

"Then I got scared, afraid he'd wake up and be mad at me and tell the dean on me again, so I got up and tiptoed out. And he never even knew I was there."

She giggled happily like a little girl who had played a trick and gotten away with it.

Justin took Sarah to dinner at Neary's Restaurant on East Fifty-seventh Street.

"I'm a regular here," he told her, as a beaming Jimmy Neary rushed to greet them. Justin introduced Sarah. "Here's someone you've got to fatten up, Jimmy."

At the table he said, "I think you've had a tough enough day. Want to hear about Australia?"

Sarah wouldn't have believed that she could eat every bite of a sliced steak sandwich and french fries. When Justin had ordered a bottle of Chianti, she'd protested. "Hey, you can walk home. I've got to drive."

"I know. It's only nine o'clock. We're going to take a long walk back to my place and have coffee there."

New York on a summer evening, Sarah thought as they sat on his small terrace, sipping espresso. The lights on the trees surrounding the Tavern on the Green, the lush foliage, the horses and carriages, the strollers and joggers. All this was a world away from locked rooms and prison bars.

"Let's talk about it," she said. "Is there any chance that what Laurie, or rather Debbie, told us today—about lying down with Allan Grant and then leaving him sleeping—is true?"

"As far as Debbie knows it's probably true."

"You mean that Leona might have taken over when Debbie started to leave?"

"Leona or an alter personality we haven't met so far."

"I see. I thought Laurie remembered something when she saw that picture. What could it be?"

"I believe there probably was a chicken coop wherever Laurie was kept during those two years. That picture reminded her of something that happened there. As time goes on we may be able to learn what it was."

"But time is running out." Sarah did not know she was going to cry until she felt the tears gushing down her cheeks. She held her hands over her mouth, trying to stifle racking sobs.

Justin put his arms around her. "Let it out, Sarah," he said tenderly.

86

IT WAS Brendon Moody's theory that if you waited long enough you'd get a break. His break came on June 25, from an unexpected source. Don Fraser, a junior at Clinton, was arrested for selling drugs. Realizing he'd been caught red-handed, he hinted that in exchange for leniency, he could tell them something about Laurie Kenyon's whereabouts the night she killed Allan Grant.

The prosecutor guaranteed nothing but said he'd do what he could. Dealing drugs within a thousand feet of a high school could mean a mandatory three-year sentence. Since the place where Fraser was picked up was just at the edge of the thousand-foot zone, the prosecutor agreed that he would not press for the within-school-zone offense if Fraser came up with something significant.

"And I want immunity from prosecution for what I'm telling you," Fraser insisted.

"You'd have made a good lawyer," the prosecutor told him sourly. "I'll say it again. You give us something helpful, and we'll help you. That's as far as I'll go right now. Take it or leave it."

"All right. All right. I happened to be on the corner of North Church and Maple the night of January twenty-eighth," Fraser began.

"Happened to be! What time was that?"

"Ten after eleven."

"All right. What happened then?"

"I'd been talking to a couple of friends. They'd left and I'd been waiting for someone else who never showed up. It was cold, so I figured I'd take off and go back to the dorm."

"This is ten after eleven."

"Yes." Fraser picked his words carefully. "All of a sudden this chick comes out of nowhere. I knew it was Laurie Kenyon. Everybody knows who she is. She was always getting her picture in the paper because of golf and then when her folks died."

"How was she dressed?"

"Ski jacket. Jeans."

"Was there any sign of blood on her?"

"No. Not a bit."

"Did you talk to her?"

"She came over to me. The way she was acting, I thought she was going to try to pick me up. There was something real sexy about her."

"Back up a minute. North Church and Maple is about ten blocks from the Grant home, isn't it?"

"About that. Anyhow she came up to me and said she needed a cigarette."

"What did you do?"

"Now this doesn't get used against me?"

"No. What did you do?"

"I thought she meant grass, so I pulled some out."

"And then?"

"She got mad. She said she didn't like that stuff and wanted a real cigarette. I had some with me and told her I'd sell her a pack."

"You didn't offer her one?"

"Hey, why should I?"

"Did she buy cigarettes from you?"

"No. She went to reach for her purse and then said something funny. She said, 'Damn it. I'll have to go back. That stupid kid forgot to bring it.'"

"What kid? Forgot to bring what?"

"I don't know what kid. I'm sure she was talking about her purse. She said to wait twenty minutes. She'd be back."

"Did you wait?"

"I figured why not? Maybe my other friend would show up too."

"You stood there."

"No. I didn't want to be seen. I got off the sidewalk and stood between two bushes on the lawn of the corner house."

"How long before Laurie got back?"

"Maybe fifteen minutes. But she never stopped. She was running like hell."

"This is very important. Was she carrying her bag?"

"She was hanging onto something with both hands, so I guess so."

87

*B*IC AND OPAL listened with rapt attention to the tape of Sarah's conversation with Brendon Moody about the testimony of the student drug dealer. "It's consistent with what Laurie told us," Sarah explained to Moody. "Debbie, the child alter, remembers leaving Allan Grant. None of Laurie's personalities will talk about what happened after she went back."

Bic remarked ominously, "Sneaking out of a man's house—going back and committing murder —terrible."

Opal tried to stifle her jealousy, comforting herself with the knowledge that it wasn't going to go on much longer. Sarah Kenyon would be out of the house in a matter of weeks, and Bic wouldn't have access to the condominium.

Bic was replaying the last part of the tape. "The judge is going to allow Lee to leave the clinic on July eighth. That's next Wednesday," he said. "We're going to pay a visit to Ridgewood to welcome Lee home."

"Bic, you don't mean to face her."

"I know what I mean, Opal. We'll both be conservatively dressed. We won't talk about prayer or God, much as it hurts me not to bring the Lord into our every activity. The point is, we must befriend her. Then, just in case she does get too much memory back, we'll be all mixed up in her mind. We won't stay long. We'll apologize for intruding and take our leave. Now try this on and let's see how cute you look."

He handed her a box. She opened it and took out a wig. She went to the mirror, put it on and adjusted it, then turned for him to see. "My Lord, it's just perfect," he observed.

The phone rang. Opal picked it up.

It was Rodney Harper from station WLIS in Bethlehem.

"You remember me?" he asked. "I was the station manager when you broadcast from here all those years ago. Proud to say I own the place now."

Opal motioned for Bic to pick up the extension as she said, "Rodney Harper. Of course I remember you."

"Been meaning to congratulate you on all your success. You folks have sure gone a long way. Reason I called today is that a woman from *People* magazine was in here talking to me about you."

Opal and Bic exchanged glances. "What did she ask?"

"Oh just about what kind of folks you were. I said Bobby was the best damn preacher we ever had in these parts. Then she wanted to know if I had a picture of you from those days."

Opal saw the sudden alarm on Bic's face and knew it mirrored her own. "And did you?"

"I'm sorry to say we can't find a one. We moved the station to a new facility about ten years ago and got rid of a heap of stuff. I guess your pictures got caught in the throwaway bags."

"Oh that doesn't matter," Opal said as she felt her stomach muscles begin to relax. "Wait a minute. Bobby's on the line and wants to say hello."

Bic cut in with a robust greeting. "Rodney, my friend, it's a treat to hear your voice. I'll never forget you gave us our first big break. If we hadn't been in Bethlehem on your station and getting known, I don't know we'd be on the 'Church of the Airways' today. Even so, if you do come across some old picture, I'd appreciate if you just tore it up. Looked too darn much like a hippie in those days, and it kind of doesn't go with preaching to the older folks in the 'Church of the Airways.'"

"Sure, Bobby. Just one thing I hope you won't mind. I did take that reporter from *People* to see the farmhouse where you lived those two years you were with us. Son of a gun. I missed the fact it had burned down. Kids or some bum, I suppose, broke in and got careless with matches."

Bic rounded his thumb and first finger, then winked at Opal.

"These things happen, but I'm real sorry to hear that. Carla and I loved that snug little place."

"Well, they took a couple of pictures of the property. I heard the reporter say she wasn't sure if she'd even use them in the article, but at least the chicken coop was still standing and that was proof enough for anyone that you came from humble beginnings."

88

KAREN GRANT reached her desk at nine o'clock and sighed with relief that Anne Webster wasn't already in the office. Karen was having a hard time hiding her anger at the agency's retiring owner. Webster did not want to complete the sale of the agency to Karen until mid-August. She had been invited on an inaugural flight of New World Airlines to Australia and didn't intend to miss it. Karen had been hoping to go on that one. Edwin had been invited too, and they'd planned to enjoy it together.

Karen had told Anne that there was really no need for her to come in to the office anymore.

Business was slow and Karen could handle it herself. After all, Anne was almost seventy, and the trip from Bronxville to the city was taxing. But Anne was proving unexpectedly stubborn about hanging on and was making a crusade of taking regular clients out to lunch and assuring them that Karen would take just as good care of them as she had.

Of course there was a reason for that. For three years Webster would get a percentage of the profits, and there was no question that even though the travel business had been abysmal for nearly two years, the mood was changing and people were starting to do more traveling.

As soon as Anne was totally out of the way, Edwin could use her office. But they'd wait until the late fall to move in together. It would look better for Karen to testify as the grieving widow at Laurie Kenyon's trial. Except for Anne hanging around and that damn detective dropping in so much, Karen was blissfully happy. She was so crazy about Edwin. Allan's trust fund was now in her name. One hundred thousand or better a year for the next twenty years, and in the meantime those stocks were increasing in value. In a way she wasn't sorry not to get the principal now. She might not always be crazy about Edwin, and if anything, his tastes were more expensive than hers.

She loved jewelry. It was hard to pass the L. Crown boutique in the lobby without looking in the showcase. It used to be that when she bought something that caught her eye she'd worry that one day Allan would come out of his dreamworld and ask to see the bankbook. He believed she was putting the bulk of the trust fund money in a savings account. Now she didn't have that worry, and between Allan's life insurance and the trust fund, he'd left her in great shape. When that damn house in Clinton sold, she was going to treat herself to an emerald necklace. Trouble was, a lot of people were squeamish about buying a house where someone had been murdered. She'd already reduced the selling price twice.

This morning she was debating about what to give Edwin for his birthday. Well, she still had two weeks to make up her mind.

The door opened. Karen forced a welcoming smile as Anne Webster came in. Now I'll hear how she didn't sleep well last night but got her usual nap on the train, she thought.

"Good morning, Karen. My, don't you look lovely. Is that another new dress?"

"Yes, I just got it yesterday." Karen couldn't resist telling the designer's name. "It's a Scaasi."

"It looks it." Anne sighed and brushed back a strand of gray hair that had escaped from the braid that circled the top of her head. "My, I'm feeling my age this morning. Awake half the night and then, as usual, dead asleep on the train. I was sitting next to Ed Anderson, my next-door neighbor. He always calls me the sleeping beauty and says that someday I'll wake up in the freight yard."

Karen laughed with her. My God, how many times more do I have to hear the sleeping beauty story? she thought. Only three weeks, she promised herself. The day we close the deal, Anne Webster will be history.

On the other hand . . . This time she gave Anne a genuinely warm smile. "You *are* a sleeping beauty!"

They chuckled together.

89

BRENDON MOODY was watching when, at quarter of ten, Connie Santini, the secretary, came in and Karen Grant left the travel agency office. Something was bothering him about Anne Webster's account of the evening she had spent with Karen Grant at Newark Airport. He had talked to Webster a week ago, and today he wanted to talk to her again. He walked over to the agency. As he opened the door, he attempted to plaster on his face the smile of a casual visitor. "Good morning, Mrs. Webster. I was passing this way and thought I'd drop by. You're looking well. It's good to see you again. I was afraid that by now you'd be retired."

"How nice of you to remember, Mr. Moody. No, I decided to wait and have the closing in mid-August. Frankly right now business is really picking up and I sometimes wonder if I should have held off selling. But then when I get up in the morning and rush for a train and leave my husband reading the papers over coffee, I say, enough's enough."

"Well, you and Karen Grant certainly know how to give custom service," Moody commented as he sank into a chair. "Remember you told me that the night Professor Grant died, you and Karen were at

Newark Airport? Not too many travel agents will personally go to the airport to meet even the very best client."

Anne Webster looked pleased at the compliment. "The lady we met is quite elderly," she said. "She loves to travel and usually has a contingent of friends and relatives with her, at her expense. Last year we booked her and eight others at full first-class fare on a round-the-world cruise. The night we met her, she had cut short a trip and returned alone because she wasn't feeling well. Her chauffeur happened to be away, so we volunteered to pick her up at the airport. It's little enough to do to keep her happy. Karen drove and I sat in back talking to her."

"The plane arrived at nine-thirty, as I remember," Brendon said casually.

"No. It was supposed to arrive at nine-thirty. We got to the airport at nine. The flight had been delayed in London. They said it would get in at ten, so we went to the VIP Lounge."

Brendon consulted his notes. "Then, according to your statement, it did arrive at ten."

Anne Webster looked embarrassed. "I was wrong. I thought about it later and realized it was nearly twelve-thirty."

"Twelve-thirty!"

"Yes. When we reached the lounge they said that the computers were down and there would be that long a delay. But Karen and I were watching a film on the TV in the lounge, so the time passed very quickly."

"I'll bet it did." The secretary laughed. "Now Mrs. Webster, you know you probably slept through the whole thing."

"I certainly did not," Anne Webster said indignantly. "They had *Spartacus* on. That was my favorite movie years ago, and now they've restored the footage that had been cut out. I never closed an eye."

Moody let it go. "Karen Grant has a friend Edwin who's a travel writer, doesn't she?" He did not miss the expression on the secretary's face, the tightened lips. She was the one he wanted to question when she was alone.

"Mr. Moody, a woman in business meets many men. She may have lunch or dinner with them, and it does offend me that in this day and age anyone can read anything improper in their meetings." Anne Webster was adamant. "Karen Grant is an attractive, hardworking young woman. She was married to a brilliant professor who understood her need to carve out her own life. He had an independent income and was extremely generous to her. She always talked about Allan in the most glowing terms. Her relationships with other men were totally on the up-and-up."

Connie Santini's desk was behind and to the right of Webster's. Catching Brendon's glance, she raised her eyes to heaven in the classic expression of total disbelief.

90

THE JULY 8 staff meeting at the clinic was almost over. There was only one patient left to discuss—Laurie Kenyon. As Justin Donnelly well knew, her case was the one that had engrossed everyone.

"We're making breakthroughs," he said. "Maybe even significant breakthroughs to what happened to her in those missing two years. The problem is that we don't have enough time. Laurie will go home this afternoon and will be an outpatient from now on. In a few weeks she'll go to court and plead guilty to manslaughter. The deadline from the prosecutor on the plea offer to manslaughter expires then."

The room was quiet. In addition to Dr. Donnelly, there were four others at the conference table: two psychiatrists, the art therapist, and the journal therapist. Kathie, the journal therapist, shook her head. "Doctor, it doesn't matter which alter personality writes in the journal, not one of them admits killing Allan Grant."

"I know that," Justin said. "I've asked Laurie to let us take her to Grant's house in Clinton to act out what happened that night. She certainly gave us a vivid picture of being in that rocking chair on someone's lap during abreaction, but she's stonewalling me on doing the same thing with Grant's death."

"Which suggests that neither she nor her alters want to remember what happened there?"

"Possibly."

"Doctor, her recent drawings have been much more detailed when she does the stick figure of a woman. Look at these." Pat, the art therapist, passed some of them around. "Now they really look as though the figure of the woman is wearing a pendant of some sort. Will she talk about that?"

"No. All she says is that's it's clear she's no artist."

When Laurie came to Justin's office an hour later, she was wearing a pale pink linen jacket and pleated white skirt. Sarah was with her and acknowledged Justin's compliment on the outfit with quiet pleasure. "It caught my eye when I was shopping last night," she explained, "and this is an important day."

"Freedom," Laurie said quietly, "brief, frightening, but still welcome."

Then Laurie unexpectedly said, "Maybe it's about time I tried your couch, Doctor."

Justin tried to sound offhand. "Be my guest. Any reason why today?"

She kicked off her shoes and stretched out. "Maybe it's just that I'm so comfortable with you two, and I feel like my old self in this new outfit, plus it will be nice to see the house again before we move." She hesitated. "Sarah tells me that after I plead guilty I'll have about six weeks before sentencing. The prosecutor has agreed to consent before the judge to my remaining free on bail till the sentence. I know that the minute I'm sentenced

I have to go to prison, so I'm going to have a wonderful time for those six weeks. We're going to play golf and we're going to fix up the condominium so I'll be able to think about it while I'm away."

"I hope you're not going to forget to come in for your sessions with me, Laurie."

"Oh no. We'll come in every day. It's just that there's so much I want to do. I'm dying to drive again. I used to love driving. Gregg has a new convertible. I'm going golfing with him next week." She smiled. "It's nice to look forward to going out with him and not be afraid that he'll hurt me. That's why I'm able to lie down. I know you won't hurt me either."

"No, I won't," Justin said. "Are you in love with Gregg, Laurie?"

She shook her head. "That's too strong. I'm too mixed up to love anybody, at least the way you mean. But the first step is just enjoying being with someone, isn't it?"

"Yes, it is. Laurie, could I speak to Kate?"

"If you want." She sounded indifferent.

For weeks now, Justin had not had to hypnotize Laurie to summon the alter personalities. Now Laurie sat up, thrust back her shoulders, narrowed her eyes. "What is it this time, Doctor?" It was Kate's voice they were hearing.

"Kate, I'm a bit troubled," Justin said. "I want Laurie to make her peace with herself and with everything that happened, but not until the whole truth has come out. She's burying it deeper, isn't she?"

"Doctor, I am getting thoroughly sick of you! Can't you get it straight? She's willing to take her medicine. She swore she'd never sleep in the house again, but now she's looking forward to going back to it. She knows that her parents' death was a terrible accident and not her fault. That guy in the service station where she had the appointment to have her car checked had hairy arms. It wasn't her fault he scared the bejesus out of her. She really understands that. Aren't you ever satisfied?"

"Hey, Kate, all along you've known the reason Laurie broke that appointment to have her car inspected, yet you never told me. Why are you telling me now?"

Sarah thought of Sam, the attendant at the service station in town. She'd just filled the car with gas there yesterday. Sam had started work at the end of last summer. He was a big guy with thick arms. Yesterday he'd been wearing a short-sleeved shirt, and she'd noticed that even the backs of his hands were covered by a mass of thick curly hair.

Kate shrugged. "I'm telling you because I'm tired of keeping secrets. Besides, the wimp will be safe in prison."

"Safe from what? Safe from whom?" Justin asked urgently. "Kate, don't do this to her. Tell us what you know."

"I know that while she's out they can get to her. She can't escape and she knows it too. If she doesn't go to prison soon, they'll make it happen."

"Who threatened her? Kate, please." Justin was cajoling, pleading.

She shook her head. "Doctor, I'm tired of telling you that I don't know everything and the kid who does isn't going to talk to you. He's the smart one. You wear me out."

Sarah watched as the aggressive look faded from

Laurie's features, as she slipped down and stretched out again on the couch, as her eyes closed and her breathing became even again.

"Kate isn't going to be around much longer," Justin whispered to Sarah. "For some reason she'll feel her job is done. Sarah, look at these." He held out Laurie's drawings. "See this stick figure. Do you make anything of this necklace she's wearing?"

Sarah frowned. "It looks familiar. I feel as though I've seen it."

"Compare these two," Justin said. "They're the most detailed of the batch. You see how the center seems to be oval-shaped and set in a square with brilliants. Does that mean anything to you?"

"I wonder . . ." Sarah said. "My mother had some nice pieces of jewelry. They're all in the safe-deposit box. One of them is a pendant. It has small diamonds all around the center stone—what is it—an aquamarine . . . no, it's not that. I can see it . . . it's—"

"Don't say that word. That's a forbidden word." The command was spoken in a young, alarmed but sturdy boyish voice. Laurie was sitting up, staring intently at Sarah.

"What's a forbidden word?" Justin asked.

"Don't say it." The boyish voice coming from Laurie's lips was part pleading, part commanding.

"You're the little boy who came to talk to us last month," Justin said. "We still don't know your name."

"It's not allowed to say names."

"Well, maybe it's forbidden for you, but Sarah can. Sarah, do you remember the stone that was in the center of your mother's pendant?"

"It was an opal," Sarah said quietly.

"What does *opal* mean to you?" Justin demanded, turning to Laurie.

On the couch, Laurie shook her head. Her expression became her own. She looked puzzled. "Did I drop off? I'm suddenly so sleepy. What did you ask me? Opal? Well, that's a gemstone, of course. Sarah, didn't Mama have a pretty opal pendant?"

91

AS ALWAYS, Opal felt the tension building inside her as they passed the sign that read ENTERING RIDGEWOOD. We look totally different, she assured herself, smoothing down the skirt of her navy-and-white print dress, a conservatively cut outfit with a V neck, long sleeves and a narrow belt. With it she wore navy shoes and a matching purse. Her only jewelry was a single strand of pearls and her wedding ring. She'd had her hair trimmed and colored a few hours ago. Now every ash blond strand was coiffed sleekly against her head. Large, blue-tinted sunglasses covered her eyes and subtly redefined the contours of her face.

"You look real classy, Carla," Bic had said approvingly before they left the Wyndham. "Don't worry. There isn't a snowball's chance in hell that Lee will recognize you. And what do you think of me?"

He was dressed in a crisp, white, long-sleeved shirt, a tan, single-breasted summer suit, and a tan-and-white tie with flecks of brown. His hair was now completely silver. Even though he'd let it grow a little longer, he had it combed back so that there was no suggestion of the wavy curls that he'd been so proud of in the early days. He'd also shaved the hair from the backs of his hands. He was very much the image of a distinguished clergyman.

Their car turned into Twin Oaks Road. "That used to be the pink house," Bic said sarcastically as he pointed. "Try not to refer to it again, and don't call the little girl Lee. Call her Laurie when you speak to her, which shouldn't be much at all."

Opal wanted to remind Bic that he was the one who had referred to her as Lee on the program, but she didn't dare. Instead she went over the few words she would exchange with Laurie when they came face to face with her.

There were three cars in the driveway. One they recognized as belonging to the housekeeper. The second, a BMW, was Sarah's. But the third, an Oldsmobile with New York plates—whose car was that?

"There's someone visiting," Bic said. "That might be the Lord's way of providing us with a witness who can testify that Lee met us, should the need arise."

It was just five o'clock. The afternoon sun's slanting rays brightened sections of the deep green lawn and glistened through the brilliant blue hydrangeas that bordered the sides of the house.

Bic pulled into the driveway. "We'll just stay a minute even if they encourage us to linger."

It was the last thing on Sarah's mind to encourage the Hawkinses to linger. She and Laurie and

Justin were sitting in the den, and a smiling Sophie, having embraced Laurie for a full minute, was making tea.

While Laurie was packing her bags, Justin had surprised Sarah by suggesting he accompany them.

"I think it might be wise for me to be with you when Laurie gets home," he explained. "I don't necessarily anticipate an adverse reaction, but she hasn't been there in five months, and a lot of memories are going to come flooding in. We can swing by my apartment building in your car, I'll pick up mine and follow you out."

"And you also want to be there to see if you can catch any breakthroughs," Sarah had added.

"That too."

"Actually, I'd be glad if you'd come. I think I'm as frightened as Laurie is of this homecoming."

Unconsciously Sarah had stretched out her hand, and Justin had taken it. "Sarah, when Laurie begins serving that sentence, I want you to promise that you'll get some counseling yourself. Don't worry. Not from me. I'm sure you don't want that. But it's going to be rough."

For an instant, feeling the warmth of his hand closing over hers, Sarah had felt less afraid of everything—of Laurie's reaction to being at home, of the day in court next week when she would stand next to Laurie and hear her plead guilty to manslaughter.

When the doorbell rang, Sarah was especially grateful to have Justin there. Laurie, who had happily showed the doctor around the house, suddenly looked alarmed. "I don't want to see anyone."

Sophie muttered, "Ten to one it's that pair."

Sarah bit her lip in exasperation. God, these

273

people were getting to be omnipresent. She could hear Reverend Hawkins explaining to Sophie that they had been looking for a box containing important papers and realized it had been mistakenly included in the things they'd shipped to New Jersey. "If I could just run down to the basement and get it, we'd be so grateful," he said.

"It's the people who bought the house," Sarah explained to Justin and Laurie. "Don't worry. I'm not going to invite them to so much as sit down, but I suppose I should speak to them. I'm sure they've noticed my car."

"I don't think you'll have to bother going to them," Justin said as footsteps came across the foyer. A moment later, Bic was standing in the doorway, Opal behind him.

"Sarah, my dear, my apologies. Some business records my accountant needs desperately. And, is this Laurie?"

Laurie had been sitting next to Sarah on the sofa. She stood up. "Sarah has told me about you and Mrs. Hawkins."

Bic did not leave the doorway. "We are delighted to meet you, Laurie. Your sister is a wonderful girl and talks about you a great deal."

"A wonderful girl," Opal echoed, "and we're so happy to be buying this lovely house."

Bic turned to look at Justin. "Reverend and Mrs. Hawkins, Dr. Donnelly," Sarah murmured.

To her relief, after an acknowledgment of the introduction, Hawkins said, "We will not intrude on your reunion. If we may we'll just go down and get the material we need and let ourselves out the side door. Good day one and all."

In that minute or two, Sarah realized that the Hawkinses had managed to spoil the temporary happiness of Laurie's homecoming. Laurie fell silent and did not respond when Justin talked breezily about growing up in Australia on a sheep station.

Sarah was grateful when Justin accepted the invitation to dinner. "Sophie has cooked enough for an army," she said.

Laurie clearly wanted Justin to stay as well. "I feel better that you're here, Dr. Donnelly."

Dinner was unexpectedly pleasant. The chill that the Hawkinses had brought to the house vanished as they ate Sophie's delicious dinner of pheasant and wild rice. Justin and Sarah sipped wine, Laurie had Perrier. As they were finishing coffee, Laurie quietly excused herself. When she came back downstairs, she was carrying a small bag. "Doctor," she said, "I can't help it. I have to go back with you and sleep in the clinic. Sarah, I'm so sorry, but I know something terrible is going to happen to me in this house and I just don't want it to be tonight."

92

*W*HEN BRENDON MOODY phoned Sarah the next morning, he could hear the sounds of doors opening and closing, of furniture being moved. "We're getting out of here," Sarah told him. "It's not good for Laurie to be in this house. The condo isn't quite ready, but they can complete the finishing touches sometime later." She told him how Laurie had returned to the clinic the night before.

"I'm going to pick her up late this afternoon," she said, "and when I do, we'll go straight to the condo. She can help me put it together. The activity might be good for her."

"Just don't give the Hawkinses a key to your new place," Brendon said sourly.

"I don't intend to. Those two set my teeth on edge. But remember . . ."

"I know. They paid top dollar. They let you stay after the closing. How did you ever get a mover that fast?"

"It took a lot of doing."

"Let me come over and help. I can at least pack books or pictures."

The moving was well under way when Brendon arrived. Sarah, her hair held back by a bandana, and dressed in a pair of khaki shorts and a cotton blouse, was busily tagging the furniture the Hawkinses had purchased.

"I won't get everything out today," she told Brendon, "but turnabout is fair play. I'm supposed to have the use of this place till August twenty-fifth. I'll feel free to come in and out and sort the things I'm not sure of now."

Sophie was in the kitchen. "Never thought I'd see the day I'd be glad to leave this house," she told Brendon. "The nerve of those two Hawkins people. They asked if I'd help them get settled when they move in for good. The answer is no."

Brendon felt his antennae going up. "What don't you like about them, Sophie? You've heard Sarah say that they've done her a big favor."

Sophie snorted. Her round, usually pleasant face grimaced in disgust. "There's something about them. Mark my words. How many times do you have to study rooms and closets to decide if you're going to enlarge them or cut them up? Too much talk as far as I'm concerned. I swear these last months their car has been on radar to this place. And all those boxes they left in the basement. Pick up one of them. They're light as a feather. I bet they're not half-full. But that hasn't stopped them from delivering another and another. Just an excuse for dropping in, is what I call it. What do you want to bet, the Reverend uses Laurie's story on one of his programs?"

"Sophie, you're a very clever woman," Brendon said softly. "You may have hit the nail on the head."

Sarah entrusted Brendon with packing the contents of her desk, including the deep drawer that contained all of Laurie's files. "I need them in the same order," she told him. "I just keep going through them hoping and hoping that something will jump out at me."

Brendon noticed the top file was marked "Chicken." "What's this?"

"I told you that the photograph of Laurie Dr. Donnelly had restored and enlarged had a chicken coop in the background and that something about it terrified Laurie."

Moody nodded. "Yes, you did."

"That's been nagging me particularly, and I've just realized why. Last winter Laurie was seeing Dr. Carpenter, a Ridgewood psychiatrist. A few days before Allan Grant died, she was leaving Carpenter's office and went into shock. What seems to have set her off is that she stepped on the head of a chicken in the lobby of his private entrance."

Moody's head tilted up in the position of a bird dog picking up a scent. "Sarah, are you telling me that the severed head of a chicken just *happened* to be on the floor at the entrance to a psychiatrist's office?"

"Dr. Carpenter had been treating a very disturbed man who would come by unexpectedly and who the police thought was involved in cult worship. Moody, it never occurred to me or Dr. Carpenter at the time that this could be in any way connected to Laurie. Now I wonder."

"I don't know what I think," he told her. "But I do know that some woman had Danny O'Toole reporting on your activities. Danny knew that Laurie had been seeing a psychiatrist in Ridgewood. He mentioned it to me. That means whoever was paying him knew it too."

"Brendon, is it possible that someone who knew the effect it would have on Laurie actually *planted* that chicken head?"

"I don't know. But I'll tell you this much. I felt in my bones that the idea of an insurance company hiring Danny didn't ring true. Danny thought his client was Allan Grant's wife. I never quite bought that."

He could see that Sarah was trembling with fatigue and emotion. "Take it easy," he said. "Tomorrow I'll drop in on Danny O'Toole, and I can promise you, Sarah, before I get finished we'll both know who ordered that report on you and Laurie."

93

ON THE DRIVE back to the clinic the night before, Laurie had been very quiet. The night nurse reported to Justin the next morning that she had slept fitfully and had talked aloud in her sleep.

"Did you hear what she said?" Justin asked.

"A word here or there, Doctor. I went in several times. She kept mumbling something about the tie that binds."

"The tie that binds?" Justin frowned. "Wait a minute. That's a phrase from a hymn. Let's see." He hummed a few notes. "Here it is. 'Blest be the tie that binds . . .'"

When Laurie came in later for the therapy session, she looked calm but tired. "Doctor, Sarah just phoned. She won't be here till late this afternoon. Guess what? We're moving into the condo today. Isn't that terrific?"

"Hey, that's fast." Smart of Sarah, Justin thought. That house has too many memories now. He still wasn't sure what had changed Laurie so drastically yesterday. It had happened when the Hawkins couple stopped in. But they'd barely stayed a minute. Was it the fact that they were strangers and therefore represented some sort of threat to Laurie?

"What I like about the condo is that there's a

security guard at the gate," Laurie said. "If anyone rings the bell, there's a television monitor so you'll never make a mistake and let a stranger in."

"Laurie, yesterday you said that something terrible was going to happen to you in the house. Let's talk about that."

"I don't want to talk about it, Doctor. I'm not going to stay there anymore."

"All right. Last night, in your sleep, you were apparently quite a chatterbox."

She looked amused. "Was I? Daddy used to say that if there was something I didn't get out during the day, I'd manage to have my say at night."

"The nurse couldn't understand a lot of it, but she did hear you say 'the tie that binds.' Do you remember what you were dreaming when you said that?"

The doctor watched as Laurie's lips became ashen, her eyelids drooped, her hands folded, her legs dangled. "'Blest be the tie that binds . . .'" The childlike voice, true and clear, sang the words then faded into silence.

"Debbie, it's you, isn't it? Tell me about the song. When did you learn it?"

She resumed singing. "'Our hearts in Christian love . . .'"

Abruptly she clamped her mouth shut. "Chill out and leave her alone, mister," a boyish voice ordered. "If you must know, she learned that one in the chicken coop."

94

THIS TIME Brendon Moody did not ply Danny the Spouse Hunter with liquor. Instead, he went to Danny's Hackensack office at 9 A.M., determined to get him at his most sober. Whatever condition that may be, Brendon thought as he sat across the shabby desk from him.

"Danny," he said. "I'm not going to mince words. You may have heard Laurie Kenyon is home."

"I heard."

"Anyone contact you to run a check on her again?"

Danny looked pained. "Brendon, you know perfectly well that the client-investigator relationship is as sacred as the confessional."

Brendon slammed his fist on the desk. "Not in this case. And not in any case where a person may be in jeopardy thanks to the good offices of the investigator."

Danny's florid complexion paled. "What's that supposed to mean?"

"It means that someone who knew Laurie's schedule may have deliberately tried to frighten her by putting the severed head of a chicken where she'd be sure to find it. It means that I'm damn sure no insurance company hired you and I don't believe Allan Grant's widow did either.

"Danny, I have three questions for you, and I want them answered. First, who paid you and how were you paid? Second, where did you send the information you gathered on the Kenyon sisters? Third, where is the copy of that information? After you've answered the questions, give a copy of your report to me."

The two men exchanged glares for a moment. Then Danny got up, took out a key, unlocked the file and riffled through the folders. He pulled out one and handed it to Brendon. "All the answers are in here," he said. "I was called by a woman who introduced herself as Jane Graves and said she represented one of the possible defendants in the Kenyon accident case. Wanted an investigation of the sisters. As I told you, that began right after the parents' funeral and continued until Laurie Kenyon was arrested for the murder of Allan Grant. I sent the reports to a private mail drop in New York City, enclosing my bill. The original retainer as well as all further bills were paid by a cashier's check from a bank in Chicago."

"A cashier's check," Brendon snorted. "A private mail drop. And you didn't think that was fishy?"

"When you're chasing spouses the way I do, you find the one who retains you often goes to great lengths to avoid being identified," Danny retorted. "You can make a copy of that file on my Xerox machine. And remember, you didn't get it from me."

The next day, Brendon Moody stopped by the condo. Sarah was there with Sophie, but Laurie had gone into New York. "She drove herself. She really wanted to. Isn't that great?"

"She's not nervous?"

"She locks the car doors at all times. She'll park next door to the clinic. She has a carphone now. That makes her feel safe."

"It's always best to be cautious," Brendon said, then decided to change the subject. "Incidentally, I like this place."

"So do I. It will be great when we get it in shape, which shouldn't take too long. I want Laurie to be able to enjoy it, really enjoy it before . . ." Sarah did not finish the sentence. Instead she said, "With all these levels, we do get our exercise. But this top floor makes a terrific study, don't you think? The bedrooms are the next floor down, then the living room, dining room, kitchen are entry level and the rec room opens out to the back."

It was clear to Brendon that Sarah welcomed the work involved in moving to take her mind off Laurie's problems. Unfortunately, there were some things Sarah had to know. He laid the file on her desk. "Take a look at this."

She began to read, her eyes widening in astonishment. "My God, it's our lives down to our every movement. *Who* would want this kind of information about us? Why would *anyone* want it?" She looked up at Moody.

"I intend to find out who it is if I have to blast open the records of that bank in Chicago," Moody said grimly.

"Brendon, if we can prove Laurie was under extraordinary duress from someone who knew how to terrify her, I'm sure the judge will be swayed."

Brendon Moody turned away from the look of naked hope on Sarah's face. He decided not to tell her that on gut instinct alone he was beginning to circle around Karen Grant. There are a number of things rotten in Denmark, he thought, and at least one of them has to do with that lady. Whatever it was, he was determined to find the answer.

95

THE PRIVATE postal box in New York had been rented under the name J. Graves. Rental payments had been made in cash. The clerk in charge of the boxes, a small man with slicked-back hair and an unpressed suit, had absolutely no memory of whoever made the pickups. "That box changed hands three times since February," he told Moody. "I'm paid to sort mail, not run Club Med."

Moody knew that this kind of mail drop was retained by purveyors of porno literature and get-rich-quick schemes, none of whom wanted to leave a paper trail that might lead back to them. His next call was to the Citizen's Bank in Chicago. He was keeping his fingers crossed on that one. In some banks it was possible to walk in, plunk down money and buy a cashier's check. Other institutions would only issue that kind of check for depositors. Muttering a prayer, he dialed the number.

The bank manager told Moody that it was bank policy that cashier's checks could only be sold to depositors who withdrew the funds from their savings or checking accounts. Bingo, Brendon thought. Then, predictably, the manager told him that without a subpoena no information would be forthcoming about any depositors or accounts. "I'll get the subpoena, don't worry," Moody told the manager grimly.

He dialed Sarah.

"I have a friend from law school who practices in Chicago," she said. "I'll get him to request the court for the subpoena. It will take a couple of weeks, but at least we're *doing* something."

"Don't get too excited about it yet," Moody cautioned. "I do have one theory. Karen Grant certainly had the money to hire Danny. We know that in her own personality Laurie liked and trusted Professor Grant. Suppose she told him something about things that frightened her and he discussed them with his wife."

"You mean Karen Grant may have believed there was something between Allan and Laurie and tried to scare Laurie off?"

"It's the only explanation I can come up with, and I could be all wet. But Sarah, I'll tell you this: That woman is a cold-blooded phony."

96

ON JULY 24, with Sarah at her side, Laurie pled guilty to manslaughter in the death of Professor Allan Grant.

The press rows of the courtroom were packed with reporters from television and radio networks, newspapers and magazines. Karen Grant, in a black sheath and gold jewelry, was seated behind the prosecutor. From the visitors' section, students from Clinton and the usual contingent of courtroom junkies watched the proceedings, hanging on every word.

Justin Donnelly, Gregg Bennett and Brendon Moody sat in the first row behind Laurie and Sarah. Justin felt an overwhelming sense of helplessness as the clerk called, "All rise for the Court," and the judge strode in from his chambers. Laurie was wearing a pale blue linen suit that accentuated her delicate beauty. She looked more like eighteen than twenty-two as she answered the judge's questions in a low but steady voice. Sarah was the one who seemed the more fragile of the two, Justin thought. Her dark red hair flamed against her pearl gray jacket. The jacket hung loosely on her, and he wondered how much weight she had lost since this nightmare had begun.

There was an air of pervasive sadness throughout

the courtroom as Laurie calmly answered the judge's questions. Yes, she understood what her plea meant. Yes, she had carefully reviewed the evidence. Yes, she and her lawyer were satisfied that she had killed Allan Grant in a fit of anger and passion after he turned her letters over to the school administration. She finished by saying, "I am satisfied from the evidence that I committed this crime. I don't remember anything about it but I know I must be guilty. I'm so terribly sorry. He was so good to me. I was hurt and angry when he turned those letters in to the administration, but that was because I didn't remember writing them either. I'd like to apologize to Professor Grant's friends and students and fellow members of the faculty. They lost a wonderful human being because of me. There's no way I can ever make that up to them." She turned to look at Karen Grant. "I'm so very, very sorry. If it were possible I would gladly give my life to bring your husband back."

The judge set the sentencing date for August 31. Sarah closed her eyes. Everything was moving too fast. She had lost her parents less than a year ago, and now her sister was to be taken away from her too.

A sheriff's officer led them to a side exit to escape the media. They drove away quickly, Gregg at the wheel, Moody beside him, Justin in the backseat with Laurie and Sarah. They were heading for Route 202 when Laurie said, "I want to go to Professor Grant's house."

"Laurie, you've been adamant about not going there. Why now?" Sarah asked.

Laurie pressed her head with her hands. "When I

287

was in court before the judge, the loud thoughts were pounding like tom-toms. A little boy was shouting that I was a liar."

Gregg made an illegal U-turn. "I know where it is."

The realtor's multiple-listing sign was on the lawn. The white ranch-style house had a closed and shuttered look. The grass was in need of cutting. Weeds were sprouting around the foundation shrubbery. "I want to go in," Laurie said.

"There's a phone number for the real estate agent," Moody pointed out. "We could call and find out about getting the key."

"The lock doesn't catch on the sliding glass door to the den," Laurie said. She chuckled. "I should know. I opened it often enough."

Chilled, Sarah realized that the sultry laugh belonged to Leona.

They followed silently as she led them around the side of the house onto the flagstone patio. Sarah noticed the privacy screen of tall evergreens that shielded the patio from the side road. In her letters to Allan Grant, Leona had written about watching him through this door. No wonder she had not been noticed by passersby.

"At first it seems to be locked, but if you just jiggle it a little . . ." The door slid open, and Leona stepped inside.

The room smelled musty. There was still some furniture scattered haphazardly in it. Sarah watched as Leona pointed to an old leather chair with an ottoman in front of it. "That was his favorite chair. He'd sit there for a couple of hours. I used to love to watch him. Sometimes after he went to bed, I'd curl up in it."

"Leona," Justin said. "You came back for your pocketbook the night Allan Grant died. Debbie told us you had left him sleeping, and your tote bag and the knife were on the floor beside him. Show us what happened."

She nodded and began to walk with careful, silent footsteps to the hallway that led to the bedroom. Then she stopped. "It's so quiet. He isn't snoring anymore. Maybe he's awake." On tiptoe she led the way to the door of the bedroom, then stopped.

"The door was open?" Justin asked.

"Yes."

"Was there a light on?"

"The night-light in the bathroom. Oh no!"

She stumbled to the center of the room and gazed down. Immediately her stance changed. "Look at him. He's dead. They're going to blame Laurie again." The young boyish voice that came from Laurie's throat was shocked. "Got to get her out of here."

The boy again, Justin thought. I must get to him. He's the key to all this.

Sarah watched horrified as Laurie, who was not Laurie, her feet wide apart, her features somehow reassembled with fuller cheeks and narrowed lips, closed her eyes, bent down and with both hands made a yanking gesture.

She's taking the knife from the body, Sarah thought. Oh dear God. Justin, Brendon and Gregg were standing in a line with her like spectators at a surrealistic play. The empty room suddenly seemed to be furnished by Allan Grant's deathbed. The carpet had been cleaned, but Sarah could imagine it spattered with blood as it had been that night.

Now the boy alter personality was reaching for something on the carpet. Her tote bag, Sarah thought. He's hiding the knife in it.

"Got to get her out of here," the frightened young voice said again. The feet that were not really Laurie's feet rushed to the window, stopped. The body that was not her body turned. The eyes that were not her eyes swept the room. She bent down as though picking up something and mimed shoving it in a pocket.

That's why the bracelet was found with Laurie's jeans, Sarah thought.

The window was being cranked open. Still clutching the imaginary bag, the boy alter stepped over the low sill into the backyard.

Justin whispered, "Follow him out."

It was Leona who was waiting for them. "That night the kid didn't have to open the window," she said matter-of-factly. "It was already open when I went back. That's why the room had gotten so cold. I hope you brought cigarettes, Doctor."

97

BIC AND OPAL did not attend Laurie's court appearance. For Bic the temptation had been great, but he realized that he would undoubtedly be recognized by the media. "As a minister of the

Lord and family friend it would be appropriate for me to be present," he said, "but Sarah is refusing all our invitations to share dinner or to visit with Lee."

They spent a lot of time in the New Jersey house now. Opal hated it. It upset her to see how often Bic would go into the bedroom that had been Lee's. The room's only piece of furniture was a decrepit rocking chair similar to the one they'd had on the farm. He'd sit in it for hours, rocking back and forth, fondling the faded pink bathing suit. Sometimes he'd sing hymns. Other days he'd listen to Lee's music box playing the same tinkling song over and over again.

"'All around the town ... Boys and girls together ...'"

Liz Pierce, the *People* magazine reporter, had been in touch with Bic and Opal several times, checking on facts and dates. "You were in upstate New York and that's where you found your calling. You were preaching on the radio station in Bethlehem, Pennsylvania, then in Marietta, Ohio; Louisville, Kentucky; Atlanta, Georgia, and finally New York. That's right, isn't it?"

It always chilled Opal that Pierce had the dates in Bethlehem so accurately. But at least no one there had ever seen Lee. There wasn't a person who wouldn't swear that they'd lived alone. It would be all right, she told herself.

The same day Lee pled guilty to manslaughter, Pierce called to arrange for more photographs. They'd been chosen as the *People* magazine cover story for the August 31 issue.

98

BRENDON MOODY had driven to the Hunterdon County courthouse in his own car. He'd planned to go home from there, but after what he'd witnessed in Allan Grant's bedroom he wanted a chance to talk quietly to Dr. Justin Donnelly. That was why when Sarah suggested he join them for lunch at the condo, Brendon readily accepted.

He got his opening when Sarah asked Donnelly to start a fire in the barbecue. Moody followed him onto the patio. In a low voice, he asked, "Is there any chance that Laurie or the alter personalities were telling the truth, that she'd left Allan Grant alive and came back to find him dead?"

"I'm afraid it's more probable that an alter personality we haven't met is the one who took Grant's life."

"Do you think there is any possibility at all that she is totally innocent?"

Donnelly carefully arranged the charcoal briquettes in the barbecue and reached for the lighter fluid. "Possibility? I suppose anything is possible. You observed two of Laurie's alter personalities today, Leona and the boy. There may be a dozen more who haven't surfaced yet, and I'm not sure that they ever will."

"I still have a gut feeling—" Brendon clamped his lips together as Sarah came out to the patio from the kitchen.

99

"THANK YOU for going to the courthouse with us Friday, Dr. Donnelly," Laurie told Justin. She was lying on the couch; she seemed calm, almost tranquil. Only the way she clasped her hands together hinted at inner turmoil.

"I wanted to be with you and Sarah, Laurie."

"You know, when I was making the statement I was more worried about Sarah than myself. She's suffering so much."

"I know she is."

"This morning at about six o'clock I heard her crying and went into her room. Funny, all these years she's been the one to come to me. You know what she was doing?"

"No."

"Sitting up in bed making a list of more people she'd ask to write to the judge for me. She's been hoping that I'll only have to serve two years before I'm eligible for parole, but now she's worried that Judge Armon might give me five years without parole. I hope you'll stay in touch with Sarah when I'm in prison. She's going to need you."

"I intend to stay in touch with Sarah."

"Gregg is terrific, isn't he, Doctor."

"Yes, he is."

"I don't want to go to prison," Laurie burst out. "I want to stay home. I want to be with Sarah and Gregg. *I don't want to go to prison.*"

She sat bolt upright, swung her feet down onto the floor and clenched her hands into fists. Her face hardened. "Listen, Doctor, you can't let her get those ideas. Laurie's got to be locked up."

"Why, Kate, why?" Justin asked urgently.

She did not answer.

"Kate, remember a couple of weeks ago, you told me the boy was ready to talk to me. He came out yesterday in the Grants' house. Were he and Leona telling the truth about what happened? Is there someone else I should talk to?"

In an instant Laurie's face changed again. The features became smooth, the eyes narrowed. "You shouldn't be asking so many questions about me." The boyish voice was polite but determined.

"Hi," Justin said easily. "I was glad to see you again yesterday. You took very good care of Laurie the night the professor died. You're very smart for a nine-year-old. But I'm grown up. I think I could help you take care of Laurie. Isn't it about time you trusted me?"

"You don't take care of her."

"Why do you say that?"

"You let her tell people she killed Dr. Grant, and she didn't do it. What kind of friend are you?"

"Maybe someone else who hasn't talked to me yet did it?"

"There are just four of us, Kate and Leona and Debbie and me, and none of us killed anyone. That's why I kept trying to make Laurie stop talking to the judge yesterday."

100

*B*RENDON MOODY could not let go of his gut reaction to Karen Grant. The last week of July, as he impatiently waited for the subpoena to be issued by the Chicago court, he wandered around the lobby of the Madison Arms Hotel. It was obvious that Anne Webster had finally retired from the agency. Her desk had been replaced by a handsome cherrywood table, and in general the decor of the agency had become more sophisticated. Moody decided it was time to pay another visit to Karen Grant's ex-partner, this time at her home in Bronxville.

Anne was quick to let Brendon know that she had been deeply offended by Karen's attitude. "She kept after me to move up the sale. The ink wasn't dry on the contract when she told me that it was not necessary for me to come into the office at all, that she would handle everything. Then immediately she replaced my things with new furniture for that boyfriend of hers. When I think of how I used to stick up for her when people made remarks about her, let me tell you, I feel like a fool. Some grieving widow!"

"Mrs. Webster," Moody said, "this is very important. I think there is a chance that Laurie Kenyon is not guilty of Allan Grant's murder. But she'll go to prison next month unless we can prove that someone else did kill him. Will you please go over that evening again, the one you spent at the airport with Karen Grant? Tell me every detail, no matter how unimportant it seems. Start with the drive out."

"We left for the airport at eight o'clock. Karen had been talking to her husband. She was terribly upset. When I asked her what was wrong, she said some hysterical girl had threatened him and he was taking it out on her."

"Taking it out on her? What did she mean by that?"

"I don't know. I'm not a gossip and I don't pry."

If there's anything I'm sure of, it's that, Brendon thought grimly. "Mrs. Webster, what did she mean?"

"Karen had been staying at the New York apartment more and more these last months, ever since she met Edwin Rand. I have the feeling that Allan Grant let her know he was mighty sick of the situation. On the way to the airport, she said something like, I should be straightening this out with Allan, not running a driving service.

"I reminded her that the client was one of our most valuable, and that she had a real aversion to hired cars."

"Then the plane was late."

"Yes. That really upset Karen. But we went to the VIP lounge and had a drink. Then *Spartacus* came on. It's my—"

"Your favorite movie of all time. Also a very long

one. And you do tend to fall asleep. Can you be sure that Karen Grant sat and watched the entire movie?"

"Well, I do know she was checking on the plane and went to make some phone calls."

"Mrs. Webster, her home in Clinton is forty-two miles from the airport. Was there any span of time when you did not see her for somewhere between two to two-and-a-half hours? I mean was it possible that she might have left you and driven to her home?"

"I really didn't think I slept but . . ." She paused.

"Mrs. Webster, what is it?"

"It's just that when we picked up our client and left the airport, Karen's car was parked in a different spot. It was so crowded when we arrived that we had quite a walk to the terminal, but when we left it was right across from the main door."

Moody sighed. "I wish you had told me this before, Mrs. Webster."

She looked at him, bewildered. "You didn't ask me."

101

IT WAS just like it had been in those months before Lee was locked up in the clinic, Opal thought. In rented cars, she and Bic began to follow her again. Some days they'd be parked across the street and watch Lee hurry from the garage to the clinic entrance, then wait however long it took until she came out again. Bic would spend the time staring at the door, so afraid of missing even one glimpse of her. Beads of perspiration would form on his forehead, his hands would grip the wheel when she reemerged.

"Wonder what she's been talking about today?" he'd ask, fear and anger in his voice. "She's alone in the room with that doctor, Opal. Maybe he's being tempted by her."

Weekdays Lee went to the clinic in the morning. Many afternoons she and Sarah would golf together, usually going to one of the local public courses. Afraid that Sarah would notice the car following them, Bic began to phone around to the starters to inquire about a reservation in the name of Kenyon. If there was one, he and Opal would occasionally drive to that course and try to run into Sarah and Lee in the coffee shop.

He never lingered at the table, just greeted them casually and kept going, but he missed nothing about Lee. Afterwards, he'd emotionally comment about her appearance. "That golf shirt just clings to her tender body . . . It was all I could do not to reach over and release the clip that was holding back that golden hair."

Because of the "Church of the Airways" program, they had to be in New York the better part of the weekend. Opal was secretly grateful for that. If they did get a glimpse of Lee and Sarah on Saturday or Sunday, the doctor and the same young man, Gregg Bennett, were always with them. That infuriated Bic.

One mid-August day he called to Opal to join him in Lee's room. The shades were drawn, and he was sitting in the rocker. "I have been praying for guidance and have received my answer," he told her. "Lee always goes to and returns from New York alone. She has a phone in her car. I have been able to get the number of that phone."

Opal cringed as Bic's face contorted and his eyes flashed with that strange compelling light. "Opal," he thundered, "do not think I have not been aware of your jealousy. I forbid you to trouble me with it again. Lee's earthly time is almost over. In the days that are left, you must allow me to fill myself with the sight and sound and scent of that pretty child."

102

*T*HOMASINA PERKINS was thrilled to receive a note from Sarah Kenyon asking her to write a letter on Laurie's behalf to the judge who was going to sentence her.

You remember so clearly how terrified and frightened Laurie was, Sarah wrote, *and you're the only person who ever actually saw her with her abductors. We need to make the judge understand the trauma Laurie suffered when she was a small child. Be sure to include the name you thought you heard the woman call the man as they rushed Laurie from the diner.* Sarah concluded by writing that a known child abuser by that name had been in the Harrisburg area then and, while of course they couldn't prove it, she intended to suggest the possibility that he was the kidnapper.

Thomasina had told the story of seeing Laurie and calling the police so often that it could practically write itself. Until she got to the sticking point.

That day the woman had *not* called the man Jim. Thomasina knew that now with absolute certainty. She couldn't give that name to the judge. It would be like lying under oath. It troubled her to know that Sarah had wasted time and money tracking down the wrong person.

Thomasina was losing faith in Reverend Hawkins. She'd written to him a couple of times thanking him for the privilege of being on his show and explaining that, while she would never suggest that God had made a mistake, maybe they should have waited and kept listening to Him. It was just that God had given her the name of the counter boy first. Could they try again?

Reverend Hawkins hadn't bothered to answer her. Oh, she was on his mailing list, that was for sure. For every two dollars she donated, she got a letter asking for more.

Her niece had taped Thomasina's appearance on the "Church of the Airways" program, and Thomasina loved to watch it. But as her resentment of Reverend Hawkins grew she noticed more and more things about the taped segment. The way his mouth was so close to her ear when she heard the name. The way he didn't even get Laurie's name straight. He had referred to her at one point as Lee.

Thomasina's conscience was clear when she mailed a passionate letter to the judge, describing Laurie's panic and hysteria in lurid terms but without mentioning the name *Jim*. She sent a copy of the letter and an explanation to Sarah, pointing out the mistake the Reverend Hawkins himself had made by referring to Laurie as Lee.

103

"*IT'S GETTING CLOSER,*" Laurie told Dr. Donnelly matter-of-factly as she kicked off her shoes and settled back on the couch.

"What is, Laurie?"

He expected her to talk about prison, but instead she said, "The knife."

He waited.

It was Kate who spoke to him now. "Doctor, I guess we've both done our best."

"Hey, Kate," he said, "that doesn't sound like you." Was Laurie becoming suicidal? he wondered.

A wry laugh. "Kate sees the handwriting on the wall, Doctor. Got a cigarette?"

"Sure. How's it going, Leona?"

"It's pretty nearly gone. Your golf is getting better."

"Thank you."

"You really like Sarah, don't you?"

"Very much."

"Don't let her be too unhappy, will you?"

"About what?"

Laurie stretched. "I have such a headache," she murmured. "It's as though it isn't just at night anymore. Even yesterday when Sarah and I were on the golf course I could suddenly see the hand that's holding the knife."

"Laurie, the memories are coming closer and closer to the surface. Can't you let them out?"

"I can't let go of the guilt." Was it Laurie or Leona or Kate speaking? For the first time Justin couldn't be sure. "I did such bad things," she said, "disgusting things. Some secret part of me is remembering them."

Justin made a sudden decision. "Come on. We're going to take a walk in the park. Let's sit in the playground for a while and watch the kids."

The swings and slides, the jungle gym and see-saws were filled with young children. They sat on a park bench near the watchful mothers and nannies. The children were laughing, calling to each other, arguing about whose turn it was to be on the swing. Justin spotted a little girl who looked to be about four. She was happily bouncing a ball. Several times the nanny called to the child, "Don't go so far away, Christy." The child, totally absorbed in keeping the ball bouncing, did not seem to hear. Finally the nanny got up, hurried over and firmly caught the ball. "I said, stay in the playground," she scolded. "If you chased that ball in the road, one of those cars would hit you."

"I forgot." The small face looked forlorn and repentant, then, turning and seeing Laurie and Justin watching her, immediately brightened. She ran to them. "Do you like my beautiful sweater?" she asked.

The nanny came up. "Christy, you mustn't bother people." She smiled apologetically. "Christy thinks everything she puts on is beautiful."

"Well, it is," Laurie said. "It's a perfectly beautiful new sweater."

A few minutes later they started back for the clinic. "Suppose," Justin said, "that little girl, very absorbed in what she was doing, wandered too close to the road and someone grabbed her, put her in a car, disappeared with her and abused her. Do you think that years later she should blame herself?"

Laurie's eyes were welling with tears. "Point taken, Doctor."

"Then forgive yourself as readily as you would forgive that child if something she couldn't help had happened to her today."

They went back into Justin's private office. Laurie stretched out on the couch. "If that little girl had been picked up today and put in a car . . ." she hesitated.

"Maybe you can imagine what might happen to her," Justin suggested.

"She wanted to go back home. Mommy would be angry that she went down to the road. There was a new neighbor whose son was seventeen years old and a fast driver. Mommy said the little girl must not run out in front anymore. She might get hurt by the car. They loved the little girl so much. They called her their miracle."

"But the people wouldn't take her home?"

"No. They drove and drove. She was crying, and the woman slapped her and said shut up. The man with the fuzzy arms picked her up and put her on his lap." Laurie's hands clenched and unclenched.

Justin watched as she clutched her shoulders. "Why are you doing that?"

"They told the little girl to get out of the car. It's so cold. She has to go to the bathroom, but he wants to take her picture so he makes her stand by the tree."

"The picture you tore up the day you first came to stay at the clinic made you remember that, didn't it."

"Yes. Yes."

"And the rest of the time the little girl stayed with him . . . the rest of the time *you* stayed with him . . ."

"He raped me," Laurie screamed. "I never knew when it would happen, but always after we sang the songs in the rocking chair he took me upstairs. Always then. Always then. He hurt me so much."

Justin rushed to comfort the sobbing girl. "It's okay," he said. "Just tell me this. Was it your fault?"

"He was so big. I tried to fight him. I couldn't make him stop," she shrieked. *"I couldn't make him stop."*

It was the moment to ask. "Was Opal there?"

"She's his wife."

Laurie gasped and bit her lip. Her eyes narrowed.

"Doctor, I told you that was a forbidden word." The nine-year-old boy would not allow any more memories to escape that day.

104

ON AUGUST 17, while Gregg took Laurie
to dinner and a play, Sarah and Brendon went to
Newark Airport. They arrived at 8:55. "This is
approximately the time Karen Grant and Anne
Webster got here the night Allan Grant died,"
Moody told Sarah as they drove into the parking
area. "The plane their client was on was more than
three hours late, as were a lot of other planes that
night. That means that the parking lot would be
pretty full. Anne Webster said they had to walk
quite a distance to the terminal."

Deliberately he parked his car almost at the end
of the facility. "It's a pretty good hike to the United
terminal," he observed. "Let's clock it at a normal
pace. It should take five minutes at least."

Sarah nodded. She had told herself not to grasp
at straws, not to be like so many family members of
defendants she had prosecuted. Denial. Their husband or daughter or sister or brother was incapable
of committing a crime, they'd argue. Even in the
face of overwhelming evidence they'd be convinced
there'd been some kind of horrible mistake.

But when she'd talked to Justin, he had been
cautiously encouraging about Moody's theory that
Karen Grant had both the opportunity and the
motive to kill her husband. He said that he was

beginning to accept the possibility that Laurie had no more than the four alter personalities they had met, all of whom consistently told him that Laurie was innocent.

As Sarah walked with Moody into the air-conditioned terminal, she welcomed the coolness and the relief from the muggy mid-August evening. The check-in lines reminded her of the wonderful trip to Italy she and Laurie had taken with their parents a little more than a year ago. Now it seemed as if that had been several lifetimes ago, she thought sadly.

"Remember, it was only after Karen Grant and Mrs. Webster got here that they learned the computer system had gone down and the plane was rescheduled for twelve-thirty arrival." Moody paused as he looked up at the listings of arrivals and departures. "What's your reaction if you're Karen Grant and edgy about your relationship with your husband? Maybe more than edgy if when you phoned him he'd told you he wanted a divorce?"

An image of Karen Grant came to Sarah's mind. In all these months she'd thought of Karen Grant as a grieving widow. In court at Laurie's plea bargain she'd been wearing black. It was odd, Sarah thought now as she remembered the scene. Maybe she was carrying it a bit far—not many people in their early thirties wear black as a sign of mourning anymore.

Sarah remarked on this fact to Brendon as they walked toward the VIP lounge. He nodded. "The widow Grant is always playing a part, and it shows. We know she and Anne Webster went up to the lounge and had a drink. The movie *Spartacus* started at nine o'clock that night on The Movie

Channel. The receptionist who was here that night is on duty now," he told Sarah. "We'll talk to her."

The receptionist did not remember the night of January 28, but she did know and like Anne Webster. "I've been on the job ten years," she explained, "and I've never known a better travel agent. Only problem with Anne Webster is that whenever she kills time here, she takes over the television. She always puts on one of the movie stations and gets mighty stubborn if someone else wants to watch the news or something."

"Real problem," Brendon said sympathetically.

The receptionist laughed. "Oh, not really. I always tell the people who want to watch something different to just wait five minutes. Anne Webster can conk out faster than anyone I know. And once she's asleep, we change the channel."

They drove from the airport to Clinton. On the way, Moody theorized. "Let's say Karen was hanging around the airport that night, getting more and more worried that she can't talk her husband out of wanting a divorce. Webster is either engrossed in a movie or asleep and won't miss her. The plane won't be in until twelve-thirty."

"So she got in her car and went home," Sarah said.

"Exactly. Assume she let herself into the house with her key and went to the bedroom. Allan was asleep. Karen saw Laurie's tote bag and the knife and realized that if he were found stabbed to death, Laurie would be blamed for it."

On the way they discussed the fact that the subpoena to the bank in Chicago had not, so far, helped them.

The account had been opened in the name of Jane Graves, using an address in the Bahamas that turned out to be another mail drop. The deposit had been a draft from a numbered bank account in Switzerland.

"Almost impossible to get any information about Swiss depositors," Brendon said. "I'm inclined to think now that it was Karen Grant who hired Danny. She may have been stashing some of Allan Grant's trust fund away, and as a travel agent, she knows her way around."

When they reached Clinton, the realtor's sign was still on the lawn of Allan Grant's home.

They sat in the car for several minutes, looking at the house. "It could happen. It makes sense," Sarah said. "But how do we prove it?"

"I talked to the secretary, Connie Santini, again today," Moody said. "She confirms everything we know. Karen Grant was living her own life exactly as she wanted to live it, using Allan Grant's income as a personal allowance. Putting on a show as the grieving widow, but it *is* a show. Her spirits have never been better, according to the secretary. I want you with me on August twenty-sixth when Anne Webster gets back from Australia. We're going to talk to that lady together."

"August twenty-sixth," Sarah said. "Five days before Laurie goes to prison."

105

"IT'S THE LAST WEEK," Laurie told Justin Donnelly on August 24.

He watched as she leaned back on the couch, her hands clasped behind her head.

"Yesterday was fun, wasn't it, Justin? I'm sorry. I'd rather call you Doctor in here."

"It was fun. You really are a terrific golfer, Laurie. You beat us all hands down."

"Even Gregg. Well, I'll be out of practice soon enough. Last night I was awake for a long time. I was thinking about that day when I was kidnapped. I could see myself in my pink bathing suit, going down the driveway to watch the people in the funeral procession. I thought it was a parade.

"When the man picked me up, I was still holding my music box. That song keeps going through my head . . . 'Eastside, westside, all around the town . . . Boys and girls together . . .'" She stopped.

Justin waited quietly.

"When the man with the hairy arms put me in the car, I asked him where we were going. The music box was still playing."

"Did anything special bring on those thoughts?"

"Maybe. Last night after you and Gregg left, Sarah and I sat up for a long time talking about that day. I told her that when we drove past the corner house, the one that was that ugly pink color, old Mrs. Whelan was on the porch. Isn't it funny to remember something like that?"

"Not really. All the memories are there. Once they're all out, the fear that they cause will go away."

" 'Boys and girls together . . .' " Laurie sang softly. "That's why the others came to be with me. We were boys and girls together."

"Boys? Laurie, is there another boy?"

Laurie swung her feet off the couch. One hand began smacking the other. "No, Doctor. There's only me." The young voice dropped to a whisper. "She didn't need anyone else. I always sent her away when Bic hurt her."

Justin had not caught the whispered name.

"Who hurt her?"

"Oh, gee," the boy alter said. "I didn't mean to tell. I'm glad you didn't hear me."

After the session, Justin Donnelly reminded himself that even though he had not been able to hear the name the boy alter had unintentionally said aloud, it was very near the surface. It would come out again.

But next week at this time Laurie would be in prison. She'd be lucky if she saw a counselor every few months.

Justin knew that many of his colleagues did not believe in multiple personality disorder.

106

ANNE WEBSTER and her husband returned from their trip early on August 26. Moody managed to reach Webster at noon and persuaded her to see him and Sarah immediately. When they arrived in Bronxville, Webster was unexpectedly direct. "I've been thinking a lot about the night Allan died," she said. "You know nobody likes to feel like a fool. I let Karen get away with claiming that she hadn't moved the car. But you know something? I have proof that she did."

Moody's head tilted up. Sarah's lips went dry. "What kind of proof, Mrs. Webster?" she asked.

"I told you that Karen was upset on the drive to the airport. Something I didn't remember to tell you was that she snapped at me when I pointed out that she was very low on gas. Well she didn't get any on the way to the airport and she didn't get any on the way back from the airport and she didn't get any the next morning when I drove down to Clinton with her."

"Do you know if Karen Grant charges her gas, or pays cash?" Moody asked.

Webster smiled grimly. "You can bet if she bought gas that night it went on the company credit card."

"Where would last January's statements be?"

"In the office. Karen will never let me march in and go through the files, but Connie will do it if I ask. I'll give her a call."

She talked at length to her former secretary. When she hung up she said, "You're in luck. Karen's at an outing American Airlines is sponsoring today. Connie will be glad to look up the statements. She's mad clean through. She asked for a raise, and Karen turned her down."

On the way to New York, Moody warned Sarah, "You know of course that even if we could prove Karen Grant had been in the Clinton area that night there isn't a shred of proof that links her with her husband's death."

"I know," Sarah told him. "But Brendon, there must be something tangible we can put our hands on."

Connie Santini had a triumphant smile for them. "January statement from an Exxon station just off Route 78 and four miles from Clinton," she said, "and a copy of the receipt with Karen's signature. Boy, I'm going to quit this job. She's so darn cheap. I didn't take a raise all last year because business wasn't good. Now it's really picking up and she still won't part with an extra cent. I'll tell you this: She spends more money on jewelry than I make in a year."

Santini pointed across the lobby to L. Crown Jeweler. "She shops over there the way some people go to the cosmetics counter. But she's cheap with them too. The very day her husband died she'd bought a bracelet, then lost it. She had me on my hands and knees searching for it. When the call came about Allan she was in Crown's raising hell that the bracelet had a lousy clasp. She'd lost it again. This time for good. Listen, there was nothing wrong with the clasp. She just didn't take the time to fasten it right, but you can be sure she made them replace it."

A bracelet, Sarah thought, *a bracelet!* In Allan Grant's bedroom the day of the plea bargain, Laurie, or rather, the boy alter, had acted out picking up something and shoving it in his pocket. It never occurred to me that the bracelet found with Laurie's bloodstained jeans might not be one of her own, she thought. I never asked to see it.

"Miss Santini, you've been a great help," Moody told her. "Will you be here for a little while?"

"Until five. I don't give her one extra minute."

"That's fine."

A young clerk was behind the counter of L. Crown Jewelers. Impressed by Moody's insinuation that he was from an insurance company and wanted to inquire about a certain lost bracelet, the clerk willingly looked up the records.

"Oh yes, sir. Mrs. Grant purchased a bracelet on January twenty-eighth. It was a new design from our showroom, twisted gold with silver going through it, giving the effect of diamonds. Quite lovely. It cost fifteen hundred dollars. But I don't understand why she'd put in a claim for it. We replaced it for her. She came in the next morning, most upset. She was sure it had fallen off her wrist shortly after she bought it."

"Why was she so sure of that?"

"Because she told us it had slipped off once at her desk before she lost it for good. Frankly, sir, the problem was that it had a new kind of catch, very secure, but not if you don't take the time to fasten it properly."

"Do you have the sales record?" Moody asked.

"Of course, but we did decide to replace it, sir. Mrs. Grant is a good customer."

"By any chance do you have a picture of the bracelet or a similar one?"

"I have both a picture and a bracelet. We've made several dozen of them since January."

"All alike? Was there anything different about that particular one?"

"The catch, sir. After the incident with Mrs. Grant we changed it on the others. We didn't want any repeat problems." He reached under the counter for a notebook. "You see the original catch clasped like this . . . the one we now use snaps this way and has a safety bar."

The clerk was a good artist.

A copy of the January 28 sales slip, a color photo of the bracelet and the signed and labeled sketch in hand, Sarah and Moody went back to the Global Travel Agency. Santini was waiting, her eyes alive with curiosity. She willingly dialed Anne Webster's number, then handed the phone to Moody, who pressed the speaker button.

"Mrs. Webster," he asked, "was there something about a missing bracelet the night you were at Newark airport with Karen Grant?"

"Oh yes. As I told you, Karen was driving the client and me back to New York. Suddenly she said, 'Damn it, I've lost it again.' Then she turned to me and, very upset, demanded to know whether or not I had noticed her bracelet in the airport."

"And had you?"

Webster hesitated. "I told a teeny-weeny fib. Actually I know she was wearing it in the VIP lounge, but after the way she carried on when she thought she'd lost it in the office . . . Well, I didn't want her to explode in front of the client. I said very positively that she hadn't been wearing it at the airport and that it was probably around her desk somewhere. But I did phone the airport that night, just in case someone turned it in. It's really all right. The jeweler replaced it."

Dear God, dear God, Sarah thought.

"Would you recognize it, Mrs. Webster?" Moody asked.

"Certainly. She showed it to Connie and me and told us about it being a new design."

Santini nodded vigorously.

"Mrs. Webster, I'll be back to you shortly. You've been a big help." In spite of yourself, Moody thought as he hung up the phone.

One last detail to put in place. Please, please, Sarah prayed as she dialed the office of the Hunterdon County prosecutor. She was put through to the prosecutor and told him what she needed. "I'll hold on." As she waited she told Moody, "They're sending someone to the evidence room."

They waited in silence for ten minutes, then Moody watched Sarah's face light up like a sunburst and then a rainbow as tears welled from her eyes. "Twisted gold with silver," she said. "Thank you. I need to see you first thing in the morning. Will Judge Armon be in his chambers?"

107

KAREN GRANT was thoroughly annoyed on Thursday morning to find that Connie Santini was not at her desk. I'm going to fire her, Karen thought as she snapped on lights and listened for messages. Santini had left one. She had an urgent errand but would be in sometime later. What's urgent about anything in *her* life? Karen thought as she opened her desk and took out the first draft of the statement she was planning to deliver in court at Laurie Kenyon's sentencing. It began: "Allan Grant was a husband beyond compare."

Karen should only know where I am right now, Connie Santini thought as she sat with Anne Webster in the small waiting area outside the prosecutor's private office. Sarah Kenyon and Mr. Moody were in talking to the prosecutor. Connie was fascinated by the charged atmosphere of the place. Phones ringing. Young attorneys rushing by, arms loaded with files. One of them looked over her shoulder and called, "Take a message. Can't talk now. I'm due in court."

Sarah Kenyon opened the door and said, "Will you come in now, please. The prosecutor wants to talk to you."

A moment later as she acknowledged the introduction to Prosecutor Levine, Anne Webster glanced down at his desk and noticed the object in a tagged plastic bag. "Oh for heaven's sake, there's Karen's bracelet," she said. "Where did you find it?"

An hour later, Prosecutor Levine and Sarah were in Judge Armon's chambers. "Your Honor," Levine said, "I don't know where to begin, but I'm here with Sarah Kenyon to jointly request an adjournment of Laurie Kenyon's sentencing for two weeks."

The judge's eyebrows raised. "Why?"

"Judge, I've never had anything like this happen before, especially where the defendant pled guilty. We now have reason to seriously question whether Laurie Kenyon committed this homicide. As you know, Miss Kenyon indicated to you that she didn't remember committing the homicide but was satisfied from the state's investigation that she had done so.

"Now some new and quite astonishing evidence has come to light that casts serious doubt on her culpability."

Sarah listened quietly as the prosecutor told the judge about the bracelet, the jewelry salesman's statement, the purchase of gas at the Clinton service station and then gave him the written affidavits of Anne Webster and Connie Santini.

They sat in silence for the three minutes it took Judge Armon to read the affidavits and examine the receipts. When he had finished, he shook his head and said, "Well, I've been on the bench for twenty years and I've never seen anything like this happen.

Of course, under the circumstances, I'll adjourn the sentencing."

He looked at Sarah sympathetically as she sat gripping the arms of the chair, the mixture of emotions obvious in her face.

Sarah tried to keep her voice steady as she said, "Judge, on one level I'm obviously ecstatic and on another I'm devastated that I allowed her to plead guilty."

"Don't be so hard on yourself, Sarah," Judge Armon said. "We all know you've turned yourself inside out to defend her."

The prosecutor stood up. "I was going to talk with Mrs. Grant before the sentencing about the statement she wanted to make in court. Instead I think I'm going to have a little talk with her about how her husband died."

"What do you mean the sentencing isn't going to take place on Monday?" Karen asked indignantly. "What kind of snag? Mr. Levine, I think you should realize that this is a terrible ordeal for me. I don't want to have to face that girl again. Just preparing the statement I'm going to make to the judge is upsetting."

"These technicalities come up," Levine said soothingly. "Why don't you come in tomorrow around ten. I want to go over it with you."

Connie Santini arrived in the office at two o'clock fully expecting to have Karen Grant's wrath descend on her. The prosecutor had warned her to say nothing to Karen about her meeting with him. Karen was preoccupied, however, and asked the secretary no questions. "You handle the phones," she told Connie. "Say I'm out. I'm working on my statement. I want that judge to know all I've been through."

The next morning, Karen dressed carefully for her meeting. It might be a little much to wear black today to the courtroom. Instead she chose a dark blue linen and matching pumps. She kept her makeup subdued.

The prosecutor did not keep her waiting. "Come in, Karen. I'm glad to see you."

He was always so pleasant and really a very attractive man. Karen smiled up at him. "I've prepared my statement for the judge. I think it really gets across everything I feel."

"Before we get to that, a couple of things have come up that I want to go over with you. Want to step in here?"

She was surprised that they did not go into his private office. Instead he took her into a smaller room. Several men and a stenotypist were already there. She recognized two of the men as the detectives who had spoken to her in the house the morning Allan's body was found.

There was something different about Prosecutor Levine. His voice was businesslike and remote as he said, "Karen, I'm going to read you your constitutional rights."

"What?"

"You have the right to remain silent. Do you understand that?"

Karen Grant felt the blood drain from her face. "Yes."

"You have a right to an attorney . . . anything you say can be used against you in a court of law . . ."

"Yes, I understand, but what the hell is going on? I'm the widow of the victim."

He continued to read her her rights, to ask if she understood them. Finally he requested, "Will you read and sign the waiver-of-rights form and speak to us?"

"Yes, I will, but I think you're all crazy." Karen Grant's hand shook as she signed the paper.

The questions began. She became oblivious to the video camera, barely aware of the faint clicking of the keys as the stenographer's fingers flew over the keyboard.

"No, of course I didn't leave the airport that night. No. I wasn't parked in a different spot. That old bag Webster is always half-asleep. I sat through that lousy movie with her snoring beside me."

They showed her the charge card receipt for the gas she had purchased at the service station.

"That's a mistake. The date's a mistake. Those people never know what they're doing."

The bracelet.

"They sell plenty of those bracelets. What do you think, I'm the only customer that store has? Anyhow I lost it in the office. Even Anne Webster said I didn't have it on at the airport."

Karen's head started to pound and the prosecutor pointed out that the catch on her bracelet was one of a kind, that Anne Webster's sworn statement was that she *had* seen the bracelet on Karen's wrist in the airport and had called to report it missing.

Time passed as she snapped answers to their questions.

Her relationship with Allan? "It was perfect. We were crazy about each other. Of course he didn't ask me for a divorce on the phone that night."

Edwin Rand? "He's just a friend."

The bracelet? "I don't want to talk about the bracelet anymore. No, I didn't lose it in the bedroom."

The veins in Karen Grant's neck were throbbing. Her eyes were watering. She was twisting a handkerchief in her hands.

The prosecutor and detectives could sense that she was beginning to realize she could not talk her way out of it. She was beginning to feel the net closing around her.

The older detective, Frank Reeves, took the sympathetic approach. "I can understand how it happened. You went home to make up with your husband. He was asleep. You saw Laurie Kenyon's bag on the floor beside the bed. Maybe you thought that Allan had been lying to you after all about being involved with her. You snapped. The knife was there. A second later you realized what you'd done. It must have been a shock when I told you that we'd found the knife in Laurie's room."

As Reeves spoke, Karen's head bowed, her whole body sagged. Her eyes welling with tears, she said bitterly, "When I saw Laurie's bag I thought he had been lying to me. He had told me on the phone that he wanted a divorce, that there was someone else. When you told me she had the knife, I couldn't believe it. I couldn't believe Allan was really dead either. I never meant to kill him."

She looked imploringly into the faces of the prosecutor and detectives. "I really loved him, you know," she said. "He was so generous."

108

"IT'S BEEN QUITE a weekend," Justin said to Laurie as she settled herself on the couch.

"I still can't get it through my head," Laurie said. "Do you realize that this is the very hour I expected to be standing in court being sentenced?"

"How do you feel about Karen Grant?"

"I honestly don't know. I guess I'm having trouble believing that I had nothing to do with her husband's death."

"Believe it, Laurie," Justin said gently. He studied her carefully. The euphoria of the swiftly moving events had vanished. The aftershock of all the strain was going to show for a while. "I think it's a great idea for you and Sarah to get away on vacation for a couple of weeks. Do you remember that not long ago you told me you'd give anything to play the golf course at St. Andrews in Scotland? Now you can do it."

"Can I?"

"Of course. Laurie, I'd like to thank the little boy who's taken such good care of you. He was the one who knew you were innocent. Can I talk to him?"

"If you like."

She closed her eyes, paused, sat up as she opened them again. Her lips tightened. Her features softened. Her posture altered. A polite boyish voice said, "All right, Doctor. I'm here now."

"I just wanted to let you know that you've been great," Justin said.

"Not that great. If I hadn't taken that bracelet, Laurie wouldn't have been blamed for everything."

"That's not your fault. You did your best, and you're only nine years old. Laurie is twenty-two and she's really getting strong. I think that soon you and Kate and Leona and Debbie ought to start thinking about joining her completely. I've hardly seen Debbie in weeks. I haven't seen that much of Kate or Leona either. Don't you think it's time to release all the secrets to Laurie and help her to get well?"

Laurie sighed. "Gosh I have a headache today," she said in her normal voice as she settled back on the couch. "Something's different today, Doctor. The others seem to want me to do the talking."

Justin knew it was an important moment, one that must not be wasted. "That's because they want to become part of you, Laurie," he said carefully. "They always have been part of you, you know. Kate is your natural desire to take care of yourself. She's self-preservation. Leona is the woman in you. You've frozen your normal womanly responses so long they had to come out another way."

"In a sex kitten," Laurie suggested with a half smile.

"She is, or was, pretty sexy," Justin agreed. "Debbie is the little girl lost, the child who wanted to go home. You're home now, Laurie. You're safe."

"Am I?"

"You will be if you'll only let that nine-year-old boy put the rest of the puzzle together. He's admitted that one of the names you're forbidden to say is

Opal. Let go a little more. Have him surrender his memories to you. Do you know the boy's name?"

"Now I do."

"Tell it to me, Laurie. Nothing will happen, I promise."

She sighed. "I hope not. His name is Lee."

109

THE PHONE would not stop ringing. Congratulations were pouring in. Sarah found herself saying the same thing over and over. "I know. It's a miracle. I don't think it's really sunk in yet."

Bouquets and baskets of flowers were arriving. The most elaborate basket came with the prayers and congratulations of the Reverend Bobby and Carla Hawkins.

"It's big enough to be from the chief mourner at a funeral," Sophie sniffed.

The words sent a clammy shock through Sarah. "Sophie, when you leave, take it with you, please. I don't care what you do with it."

"You're sure you don't need me anymore today?"

"Hey, give yourself a break." Sarah walked over to Sophie, hugged her. "We wouldn't have made it through all this without you. Gregg is coming over. His classes start next week, so he's leaving for

Stanford tomorrow. He and Laurie are taking off for the day."

"And you?"

"I'm staying home. I need to collapse."

"No Dr. Donnelly?"

"Not tonight. He's got to drive to Connecticut for some meeting."

"I like him, Sarah."

"So do I."

Sophie was starting out the door when the phone rang. Sarah waved her off. "Don't worry, I'll get it."

It was Justin. There was something in his quick greeting that set off a warning signal to Sarah. "Is anything wrong?" she demanded.

"No, no," he said soothingly. "It's just that Laurie came up with a name today and I'm trying to remember in what context I heard it recently."

"What is it?"

"Lee."

Sarah frowned. "Let's see. Oh, I know. The letter Thomasina Perkins wrote me a couple of weeks ago. I told you about it. She's decided that she's stopped believing in Reverend Hawkins's miracles. In the letter she pointed out that while he was praying over her, he referred to Laurie as 'Lee.'"

"That's it," Justin said. "I noticed it myself the day I watched that program."

"How did Laurie use the name?" Sarah asked.

"It's what her nine-year-old boy alter calls himself. Of course it's probably just coincidence. Sarah, I've got to run. They need me upstairs. Laurie's on her way home. I'll call you later."

Sarah hung up slowly. A thought so frightening, so incredible and still so plausible burned in her

325

mind. She dialed Betsy Lyons at the real estate agency. "Mrs. Lyons, please get out the file on our house. I'll be right over. I need to know the exact dates that the Hawkinses were in our house."

Laurie was on her way home. Gregg would be along any minute. As she ran from the apartment, Sarah remembered to hide the key under the mat for him.

110

*L*AURIE DROVE across Ninety-sixth Street, up the West Side Drive, over the George Washington Bridge, west on Route 4, north on Route 17. She knew why she had this terrible sense that her time was running out.

It was forbidden to tell the names. It was forbidden to tell what he had done to her. Her car phone rang. She pushed the ANSWER button.

It was the Reverend Hawkins. "Laurie, Sarah gave me your number. Are you on your way home?"

"Yes. Where is Sarah?"

"Right here. She's had a minor accident but she's all right, dear."

"Accident! What do you mean?"

"She came over to pick up some mail and

has twisted her ankle. Can you come directly
here?"

"Of course."

"Hurry, dear."

111

THE ISSUE of *People* magazine with the
Reverend Bobby and Carla Hawkins on the cover
arrived in mailboxes all over the country.

In Harrisburg, Thomasina Perkins oohed at the
sight of that picture of the Hawkinses and almost
forgave them their neglect of her. She opened to the
cover story and gasped at the totally different
picture of the Hawkinses taken twenty years ago.
His gold earring; the powerful hairy arms; the
beard. Her stringy, dark, straight hair. They were
holding guitars. Memory flooded Thomasina as she
read: "Bic and Opal, the would-be rock stars." *Bic.*
The name that had haunted her for so many years.

Fifteen minutes after he spoke to Sarah, Justin
Donnelly left his office to drive to Connecticut for
the seminar he was attending. As he passed his
secretary, he noticed the open magazine on her
desk. He happened to glance at one of the pictures
in the spread, and his blood ran cold. He grabbed
the magazine. That heavy tree. The house was gone

but the chicken coop in the rear . . . The caption read: "Site of the home from which Reverend Hawkins launched his ministry."

Justin raced back to his office and from Laurie's file grabbed the reconstructed picture and held it next to the one in the magazine. The tree, heavier in this new picture, but with that same gnarled, wide trunk; the edge of the chicken coop in the old picture, exactly the same as the side of the now-visible structure. The stone wall that ran beside the tree.

He raced from the clinic. His car was parked on the street. He'd call Sarah from the car phone. In his mind he could see the television program and the Reverend Bobby Hawkins praying over Thomasina Perkins, praying that she would be able to name the people who had abducted Lee.

In Teaneck, Betty Moody happily settled down to read the new issue of *People* magazine. An unusually relaxed Brendon was taking a couple of days off. His lip curled when he saw the picture of the Hawkinses on the cover. "Can't stand those two," he muttered as he looked over her shoulder. "What did they find to write about them?"

Betty flipped the pages to the cover story. "Sweet Jesus," Moody muttered as he read: "Bic and *Opal*, the would-be rock stars . . ."

"What's the matter with me?" Brendon shouted. "It was plain as the nose on my face." He dashed for the foyer, stopping only long enough to grab his gun from the drawer.

112

S_{ARAH} SAT at Betsy Lyons's desk and analyzed the Kenyon-Hawkins file. "The first time Carla Hawkins came into this office was after our place went on the market," Sarah commented.

"But I didn't show it to her immediately."

"How did you happen to show it to her?"

"She was going through the book and noticed it."

"Did you ever leave her alone in our house?"

"Never," Lyons bristled.

"Mrs. Lyons, a knife disappeared from our kitchen around the end of January. I see Carla Hawkins was looking at the house several times just before that. It isn't easy to steal a carving knife from a wall bracket unless you have at least a little time alone. Do you remember if you left her in the kitchen by herself?"

Lyons bit her lip. "Yes," she said reluctantly. "She dropped her glove in Laurie's room, and I left her sitting in the kitchen while I retrieved it."

"All right. Something else. Isn't it pretty unusual for people not to bargain on the price of a house?"

"You were lucky, Sarah, to get that price in this market."

"I'm not sure about how much luck is involved. Isn't it highly unusual to offer to close, then allow the former owners to stay on until they decide to move and not even charge them rent?"

"It's extraordinary."

"I'm not surprised. One last observation. Look at these dates. Mrs. Hawkins often came out on Saturday around eleven."

"Yes."

"That was just the time Laurie was in therapy," Sarah said quietly, "and they knew it." The chicken head that had so terrified Laurie. The knife. The picture in her journal. Those people in and out of the house with the boxes that hardly weighed a pound. Laurie's insistence on going back to the clinic the night she came home, right after the Hawkinses had stopped by. And . . . The *pink* house! Sarah thought. Carla Hawkins mentioned it that night I had dinner with them.

"Mrs. Lyons, did you ever tell Mrs. Hawkins that the corner house on our street used to be a garish pink?"

"I didn't know it had been pink."

She grabbed the phone. "I have to call home." Gregg Bennett answered.

"Gregg, I'm glad you're there. Make sure you stay with Laurie."

"She's not here," Gregg said. "I'd hoped she was with you. Sarah, Brendon Moody is here. Justin is on his way out. Sarah, the Hawkinses are the people who abducted Laurie. Justin and Moody are sure of it. Where is Laurie?"

With a certainty that went beyond reason, Sarah knew. "The house," she said. "I'm going to the house."

113

LAURIE DROVE down the familiar street, resisting the impulse to floor the accelerator. There were children playing on the lawn of one of the houses. Years ago Mama hadn't allowed her out front alone because of that boy who drove so fast.

Sarah. A twisted ankle isn't so bad, she tried to tell herself. But it wasn't that. There was something terribly wrong. She knew it. She'd sensed it all day.

She steered the car from the street into the driveway. Already the house seemed different. Mama's blue tieback draperies and scalloped shades had been so pretty. The Hawkinses had replaced them with blinds that, when closed, were totally black on the outside, giving the house a shuttered, unwelcoming look. Now it reminded her of another house, a dark, closed house where terrible things happened.

She hurried across the driveway, along the walk, up the porch steps to the door. An intercom had been installed. She must have been seen, because as she touched the bell she heard a woman say, "The door is unlocked. Come in."

She turned the handle, stepped into the foyer and closed the door behind her. The foyer, usually brightened by the light from the adjoining rooms, was now in semidarkness. Laurie blinked and looked around. There was no sound. "Sarah," she called. "Sarah."

"We're in your old room, waiting for you," a voice responded from a distance.

She began to climb the stairs, at first quickly, then with dragging footsteps.

Perspiration broke out on her forehead. The hand that clung to the railing became soaking wet, leaving a damp trail on the banister. Her tongue felt thick and dry. Her breathing became quick, short gasps. She was at the top of the stairs, turning down the hallway. The door to her room was closed.

"Sarah!" she called.

"Come in, Lee!" This time the man's voice was impatient, as impatient as it used to be long ago when she didn't want to obey the command to go upstairs with him.

Despairingly she stood outside the bedroom door. She knew Sarah was not there. She had always known that someday they'd be waiting for her. Someday was now.

The door swung inward, opened by Opal. Her eyes were cold and hostile, just as they had been when Laurie first met her; a smile that was not a smile slashed her lips. Opal was wearing a short black skirt and a T-shirt that hugged her breasts. Her long, stringy dark hair, tousled and uncombed, hung limp on her shoulders. Laurie offered no resistance as Opal took her hand and led her across the room to where Bic was sitting in an old rocking chair, his feet bare, his shiny black chinos unbuttoned at the waist, his soiled T-shirt exposing his curly-haired arms. The dull gold earring in his ear swayed as he leaned forward, reaching out for her. He took her hands in his, made her stand before him, a truant child. A scrap of pink material was on his knee. Her bathing suit. The only light was from the night-light in the floor socket that Mama had always left on because Laurie was so afraid of the dark.

The loud thoughts were shrieking in her head.

An angry voice, scolding, *You little fool, you shouldn't have come.*

A child crying, *Don't make me do it.*

A boy's voice yelling, *Run. Run.*

A weary voice saying, *It's time to die for all the bad things we did.*

"Lee," Bic sighed. "You forgot your promise, didn't you? You talked about us to that doctor."

"Yes."

"You know what's going to happen to you?"

"Yes."

"What happened to the chicken?"

"You cut its head off."

"Would you rather punish yourself?"

"Yes."

"Good girl. Do you see the knife?"

He pointed to the corner. She nodded.

"Pick it up and come back to me."

The voices shouted at her as she walked across the room: *Don't!*

Run.

Get it. Do what he says. We're both tramps and we know it.

Closing her palm around the handle of the knife, she returned to him. She flinched at the vision of the chicken flopping at her feet. It was her turn.

He was so close to her. His breath was hot on her face. She had known that someday she would walk into a room and find him just like this, in the rocking chair.

His arms closed around her. She was on his lap, her legs dangling, his face brushing hers. He began to rock back and forth, back and forth. "You have been my temptation," he whispered. "When you die you will free me. Pray for forgiveness as we sing the beautiful song we always sang together. Then you will get up, kiss me goodbye, walk to the corner, put the knife against your heart and plunge it in. If you disobey, you know what I have to do to you."

His voice was deep but soft as he began, "'Amazing Grace, how sweet the sound . . .'"

The rocking chair thudded back and forth on the bare floor. "Sing, Lee," he ordered sternly.

"'That saved a wretch like me . . .'" His hands were caressing her shoulders, her arms, her neck. In a minute it will be all over, she promised herself. Her soprano voice rose clear and sweet. "'I once was lost, but now am found . . . was blind but now I see.'" Her fingers pressed the blade of the knife against her heart.

We don't have to wait, Leona urged. *Do it now.*

114

J USTIN DROVE FROM New York to New Jersey as fast as he dared, all the while trying to reassure himself that Laurie was safe. She was going directly home and meeting Gregg there. But there had been something about her this morning that troubled him. Resignation. That was the word. Why?

As soon as he'd reached the car he'd tried to phone Sarah to warn her about the Hawkinses, but there was no answer at the condo. Every ten minutes he pressed the redial button.

He had just started north on Route 17 when the phone was answered. Gregg was in the condo. Sarah was out, he told Justin. He expected Laurie any minute.

"Don't let Laurie out of your sight," Justin commanded. "The Hawkinses were her abductors. I'm certain of it."

"Hawkins! *That son of a bitch!*"

Gregg's outrage sharpened Justin's awareness of the enormous suffering Laurie had endured. All these months Hawkins had been circling around her, terrorizing her, trying to drive her into madness. He pressed his foot on the pedal. The car shot forward.

He was turning off Route 17 at the Ridgewood Avenue exit when the car phone rang.

It was Gregg. "I'm with Brendon Moody. Sarah thinks Laurie may be with Hawkins in the old house. We're on the way to it."

"I was only there twice. Give me directions."

As Gregg spat them out, Justin remembered the way. Around the railroad station, past the drugstore, straight on Godwin, left on Lincoln . . .

He didn't dare speed as he passed Graydon Pool. It was crowded, and families with young children were crossing the street, heading toward it.

An image came to Justin of a fragile Laurie confronting the monster who had kidnapped her when she was a four-year-old child in a pink bathing suit.

115

LAURIE'S BUICK was in the driveway. Sarah rushed from her car up the porch steps. She rang the bell repeatedly, then twisted the knob. The door was unlocked. As she pushed it open and ran into the foyer, she heard a door slam somewhere on the second floor.

"Laurie," she called.

Carla Hawkins, her blond hair disheveled, tying a robe as she came down the stairs, said frantically, "Sarah, Laurie came in a few minutes ago carrying a knife. She's threatening to kill herself. Bobby is talking her out of it. You mustn't startle her. Stay here with me."

Sarah pushed her aside and bounded up the stairs. At the top she looked around wildly. Down the hall the door to Laurie's room was closed. Her feet barely touched the floor as she rushed to it, then stopped. From inside she could hear the rise and fall of a man's voice. With painstaking care she opened the door.

Laurie was standing in the corner, staring blankly at Bobby Hawkins. She was holding the blade of a knife against her heart. The tip had already penetrated her flesh, and a trickle of blood was staining her blouse.

Hawkins was wrapped in a floor-length white terry-cloth robe, his hair loose and full. "You must do only what the Lord wants of you," he was saying. "Remember what is expected of you."

He's trying to make her kill herself, Sarah thought. Laurie, in a trancelike state, was unaware of her. Sarah was afraid to make a sudden move toward her. "Laurie," she said softly. "Laurie, look at me." Laurie's hand pushed the blade a fraction deeper.

"All sins must be punished," Hawkins said, his voice a hypnotic singsong. "You must not sin again."

Sarah saw the look of finality that came over Laurie's face. "Laurie, don't," she screamed. "Laurie, *don't!*"

The voices were shrieking at her.

Lee was yelling, *Stop.*

Debbie was crying in terror.

Kate was shouting, *Wimp. Fool.*

Leona's voice was the loudest. *Get it over with!*

Someone else was crying. Sarah. Sarah, always so strong, always the caretaker, was coming toward her, her hands outstretched, tears streaking her face, begging, "Don't leave me. I love you."

The voices stilled. Laurie flung the knife across the room and stumbled forward to gather Sarah in her arms.

The knife was on the floor. His eyes glittering, his hair disheveled, the robe Opal had wrapped around him at the sound of the doorbell slipping from his shoulders, Bic bent down. His fingers grasped the handle of the knife.

Lee would never be his now. All the years of wanting her, fearing her memories were over. His ministry was over. She had been his temptation and his downfall. Her sister had kept him from her. Let them die together.

Laurie heard the hissing, swishing sound that had haunted her all these years, glimpsed the blade gleaming in the semidarkness, cutting the air in ever-widening circles, powered by the thick hairy arm.

"No," Laurie moaned. With a violent shove, she thrust Sarah away, out of the path of the knife.

Sarah, off balance, stumbled backwards and fell, her head smashing into the side of the rocker.

A terrible smile slashing his face, Bic advanced with measured step toward Laurie, the darting blade blocking her escape. Finally there was no place to go. Pressed against the wall, Laurie looked into the face of her executioner.

116

*B*RENDON MOODY floored the accelerator as he drove down Twin Oaks Road. "They're both here," he snapped as he saw the cars in the driveway. Gregg at his heels, he raced to the house. Why was the front door ajar?

There was an unnatural silence about the darkened rooms. "Check this floor," he ordered. "I'm going upstairs."

At the end of the hallway the door was open. Laurie's bedroom. He ran toward it. Some instinct made him draw his gun. He heard a moan as he reached the doorway and took in the nightmarish scene.

Sarah was lying on the floor, dazed, trying to struggle to her feet. Blood trickled from her forehead.

Carla Hawkins stood frozen a few feet from Sarah.

Laurie was backed into a corner of the room, her hands raised to her throat, staring at the wild-eyed figure approaching her, sweeping a knife in ever-widening arcs.

Bic Hawkins raised the knife high in the air, looked down into Laurie's face, inches from his own, and whispered, "Goodbye, Lee."

It was the instant Brendon Moody needed. His bullet found its target, the throat of Laurie's abductor.

Justin rushed into the house as Gregg was racing through the foyer to the staircase. "Upstairs," Gregg shouted. The shot sounded as they reached the landing.

She had always known it would happen this way. The knife entering her throat. Sticky warm blood splashing over her face and arms.

But now the knife was gone. The droplets of blood spattered over her were not her blood. It was Bic, not she, who had slumped and fallen. It was his eyes, not hers, staring up.

Laurie watched motionless as the gleaming, compelling eyes flickered and closed forever.

Justin and Gregg reached the doorway of the bedroom together. Carla Hawkins, kneeling beside the body, was pleading, "Come back, Bic. A miracle. You can perform miracles."

Brendon Moody, his hand at his side, still holding the gun, stood dispassionately observing them.

The three men watched as Sarah struggled to her feet. Laurie walked to her, her hands outstretched. They stood looking at each other for a long minute. Then in a firm voice Laurie said, "It's over, Sarah. It's really over."

117

TWO WEEKS LATER, Sarah and Justin stood at the security check in Newark Airport and watched Laurie walk down the corridor to the gate for United Airlines flight 19 to San Francisco.

"Being near Gregg, finishing college at UCSF is the best possible choice for her now," Justin assured Sarah as he noticed the worried expression that replaced her bright goodbye smile.

"I know it is. She can play a lot of golf, get her game back, get her degree. Be independent and still have Gregg there for her. They're so good together. She doesn't need me anymore, at least not in the same way."

At the bend in the corridor, Laurie turned, smiled and blew a kiss.

She's different, Sarah thought. Confident, sure of herself. I've never seen her look that way before.

She pressed her fingertips to her lips and returned it.

As Laurie's slender form disappeared around the corner, Sarah felt Justin's arm comfortingly around her shoulders.

"Save the rest of the kisses for me, luv."

Not sure what to read next?

Visit Pocket Books online at
www.simonsays.com

Reading suggestions for
you and your reading group
New release news
Author appearances
Online chats with your favorite writers
Special offers
Order books online
And much, much more!

POCKET BOOKS
A Division of Simon & Schuster
A CBS COMPANY

POCKET STAR BOOKS
A Division of Simon & Schuster
A CBS COMPANY

13456

WITHDRAWN

WITHDRAWN
No longer the property of the
Boston Public Library.
Sale of this material benefits the Library.